The Love Bug

~ A Christian Fiction Novel

Shakira R. Thompson

BELIEVER'S CHOICE
MEDIA

Printed in the United States of America

Titles are available at special discounts for bulk purchases by corporations, institutions, and other organizations. For more information, please contact the Specialty Markets Division at **Believer's Choice Media** at 407.864.7673

Believer's Choice Media
P.O. Box 2131
Yulee, FL 32041
www.shakirabelieves.com

The Love Bug
Edited by: Sonya Williams
Designed by: Gad Savage

Library of Congress Congress Control Number: TBA
ISBN: 978-0-9906725-2-4 (p); 978-0-9906725-3-1 (digital)

Scripture quotations are taken from the *Holy Bible*, King James and Common English Bible Versions.

The Love Bug is a work of fiction. All characters and places appearing in this work are fictitious. Any resemblance to real persons, living or dead, places, establishments, events, organizations, and/or locations is purely coincidental and a product of the author's mind. In no way shape or form do we accept any responsibility for persons attempting to date online. The content for online dating was strictly used for entertainment purposes only.

First Printing, 2014

*To my ignition starter,
my guiding star,
and my little fire cracker.*

———————————————

Shakira R. Thompson

PROLOGUE

"It's time," the smiling bachelor concluded. A new year, a new beginning. Taking gallant strides into "Boites a Bijoux," looking like he'd walked off the set of an "Ebony Man" magazine shoot, Lionel decided he was ready to propose.

A year had almost gone by and to him; that was long enough to know Marsha was The One to share his life with, to grow old together.

At Boites a Bijoux, French for jewelry boxes, you don't just go there to buy gifts, you go there for the experience, their brand has been established by not offering jewelry but emotional experiences. From the moment you walk into the strategically designed showroom with brilliantly shining lights from above and dazzling glass cases sparkling yet protecting, you are not a customer but a member of the family who wish to help you celebrate life through jewelry. So when the melodic chimes rang throughout the store alerting to Lionel's arrival, an associate from the Boites a Bijoux family was waiting for him.

"Welcome to Boites a Bijoux." Extending her hand for a warm handshake, the associate introduced herself, "I'm Maria Carne and I'm going to be your celebration specialist for the day. How may I be of service to you?"

Clearing his throat and smiling at the same time, "Nice to meet you Maria, I'm Lionel Webber and I'm here to pick out an engagement ring for my girlfriend."

Motioning for Lionel to follow her to an interview room, with a wide grin and eyes gleaming with excitement, Maria exchanged Lionel's introduction with a resolution, "I knew you had a reason to celebrate when you walked through those doors, you look like a man on a mission and I'm going to help you pick out a ring befitting your lady love."

Each person entering the store is escorted into an interview room for an initial consultation before going out onto the showroom floor. This way, the associates begin establishing long-lasting relationships with their customers as well as to gather a true understanding for the purpose of the gifts.

Maria shifted her casual conversation into more pointed questions, "So, what's her name, I want to hear all about her, like how did you all meet, do you know what type of ring she'd like...you know, all the good stuff."

Shuffling his posh chair closer to Maria's desk, Lionel was raring to go for a chance to speak about his girlfriend, his soon to be fiancé and wife, "Her name is Marsha Williams and she means the world to me, she is so beautiful, all I can truly say is, I'm a lucky guy." Thinking back to how they actually met, he smirked, "We met online actually."

Locked into Lionel's story, Maria in a softened voice filled with curiosity, leaned in closer, "Online, huh? How'd that happen? I'm afraid of online dating, too many crazies out there."

Sharing in the humor, Lionel continued, he understood Maria's concern but he had a different experience with Marsha, he was now about to ask for her hand in marriage. "I had been in San Antonio for about a year, after having moved my business here which didn't leave me much time to be social or even date but I wanted to. Unbeknownst to me, a buddy of mine created a profile for me on an online dating site. I didn't find out what was going on until I started getting emails from random women. I mentioned it to my buddy and he could barely contain himself. He finally admitted to his prank. He was communicating with the women he thought I might like and then he'd give them my actual email address. Being in the I.T. industry, I wasn't afraid of having a profile and I thought, hey, why not...I don't have anything to lose so I kept it up. While I did go out on a few interesting dates to say the least, I ended up meeting Marsha."

Needing to know more details, Maria probed further, "What type of business brought you here to San Antonio?"

By becoming more animated in answering the question, Maria perceived Lionel loved his job. "I'm a consultant, I consult on a variety of computer-related issues. I deal with vulnerabilities within computer systems. Unfortunately for San Antonio but fortunate for me, this city is a hotbed for cyber activity."

Maria interrupted, "See, I told you, a lot of crazies out there. So does she know you're going to propose and do you know what she may like in a ring?"

Happy to report to Maria, Lionel looked around as if what he was about to reveal was top-secret information, "She has no idea I'm ready to propose. I have been asking her certain questions here and there to see what she likes but not enough to clue her in, so I think I have a pretty good idea of what she wants. I think I'm ready to pick out a ring."

Maria concluded her fact-finding mission and led Lionel to the engagement section of the store where everyone in the area smiled at him because they knew what he was there for. He received a couple of pats on the back and several congratulatory high-fives.

After hours in the store, with Lionel negotiating back and forth with Maria, she found the ring Lionel would present to Marsha. They both knew it was perfect when Lionel had to hold back a tear, confirming what he felt in his heart, "Yes, this is it."

Selecting a flawless diamond would bring attention to Lionel's ability to choose right, the sparkling symbol would signal a significant achievement in his life.

Cupping the beautifully wrapped black box in his hand, he felt like he could conquer the world, he was ready to make Marsha his forever. He had found his good thing[1].

---

[1] **Proverbs 18:22**: "Whoso findeth a wife findeth a good thing, and obtaineth favour of the LORD."

CHAPTER 1

"Yes Lieutenant, I understand."

"Are you sure you understand because after this probationary period, if YOU don't close a case, I'll have to let you go."

"With all due respect sir, you and I both know some of these cases never get solved and some take years. I'm not sure why you are picking on me about not solving cases."

"It's as simple as this, we will continue to evaluate your progress every ninety days to see where you are and if I don't like what I see then....you're out. You're closure rate has been hovering around ten percent, wherein the department's rate is around forty-eight...you do the math. Now get out."

Erica's mind struggled to make sense of what was happening, in her mind, she wondered, *"Is this really happening to me? Probation? I haven't even had a chance to prove myself yet."*

Stewing away in the hot seat in her supervisor's office, Erica learned her work performance had been less than stellar since arriving to the Cyber Crimes division at the San Antonio Police Department. Her options, close a case or be terminated.

Having come highly recommended from her former captain, in Richmond, Erica Allen's reputation proceeded her, yet with such low numbers, those lofty expectations were following a rapid descent.

"Cheer up, Allen...it happens to the best of us." Rough handling and shuffling the papers on her desk knocked over a cup of the slightly burned coffee from the break room, Erica retorted, "Jesus. Maybe, but not to me. I can't seem to catch a break today."

Detective Marc Morris tried to console his partner, the detective known for not only her killer instincts but killer looks. Based on the way she appealed to human eyes, she was acutely in tuned with her natural ability to influence others which in most cases they didn't know they were being controlled. The spontaneity and vigor she lived with every day was enchanting to those in her presence, this caused her to take everyone by surprise as she walked a path of successful milestones in her career.

Morris stepped in and offered, "Hey, c'mon, let me buy you a cup of real coffee from the coffee truck out front, my treat. You look like you could use some fresh air."

Erica's cocoa flushed face was beginning to look like cracked eggshells dropped by mistake.

"I'll go as long as you don't try to patronize me; I don't need your sympathy Morris."

"Of course not, never that," Det. Morris winked.

The middle of the work day must have been an indication to everyone at the police station to grab coffee because the line to be serviced extended through the parking lot. The brisk breeze carrying throughout the January afternoon was the perfect occasion to be soothed by hot chocolates, herbal teas, and International branded coffees. The sweet and savory collection of scents from the truck heightened the anticipation of grabbing a warm cup to go.

Standing amongst their colleagues in line, Erica felt like everyone was staring at her because news of her job performance had already begun to spread. It never crossed her mind they were admiring the black and white, printed wrap dress that enveloped her body with precision, even with drops of coffee stains painted on it. Her presence was captivating and everyone around her recognized it. As sharp as she was, she doubted herself sometimes. The fashion-forward detective held her head down into her hand, shaking it from side to side.

Trying to offer the bright side of everything, Det. Morris picked up on her discontent, "Hey, it could always be worse, at least you have a few months; he could've fired you right then and there. There is no shortage of detectives trying to move up the ranks here, it goes to show he believes in you but he can't play favorites. Not even a recommendation from his fraternity brother can stop him from doing his job, you know what I mean?"

"I guess so, it's just...I don't know what is going on with me. I haven't found my groove here in San Antonio, but I need to find it and quick. I have got to get a 'W' in my column and close a case. 'Ole superstar here, you're track record for closing cases is highly impressive; I'm glad you're my partner but next to you, I look like a chump."

The two laughed as they took possession of the steamy, comforting drinks and sweet delectables from Charlie, a retired police officer who started the beloved coffee truck.

Almost sounding like a concerned big brother, Morris wanted to know, "So what's up with that guy you were dating?"

"Which one?"

Morris' face felt as hot as his coffee as he fanned the flames from both his face and cup, "Well excuse me, I remember those days but I can truly say, I don't miss them at all. I've been out of the game for over twenty years and I'm glad about it."

Pretending to gag on her pointy finger and holding her stomach for dramatic effect, "Please save me from the sappiness. No really, everyone can't be like you and Marjorie. I haven't found that thing y'all have and I don't know if I ever will. I'm very focused on my career right now. I don't know if there is room for anyone special which is why I date random guys. It makes it easy, I don't have to get serious or commit to anyone."

Staring at Erica with an amused look as if he had no words, Morris allowed her to continue on as he stood with his arms folded across his chest after chunking his cup into the trash like a basketball.

"I date multiple men so there is never enough time to get serious about any of them, there is always someone new in the rotation," she laughed as if to entertain herself.

"But Erica, what about...?"

Breaking up his question, she cautioned him, "Before you even go there, I said date, not sleep with. I don't get down like that. I just like having options. As soon as they start trying to get all serious, it's time to move on to the next one."

"I wasn't even thinking that, I was only going to ask, what about finding true love or committing to someone scares you?"

Putting up her hands up as if to defend herself in a boxing match, ready to duke it out, she pretended to deliver an upper cut to her partner's chin, "Who said I was scared, huh...huh?"

Deflecting the invisible punch, Morris bowed out, half-way joking, he said, "Alright tough girl, Miss Serial Dater, yeah, you're not scared. Hey, let's get back to work; you need to go solve some cases."

On the way back to the office, Erica tried to pretend her partner's words didn't carry any weight and were untrue but the truth of the matter was, the heaviness of his concerns for her finding love that would prove to be real, frightened her.

Chapter 2

"Yes mother, I know, you only remind me every time we talk."

Lionel's mother, Laureen chimed in, "Liney, you are the last of the children to get married, I just want to know what's going on with you and Marsha?"

Usually Lionel's ear would burn from his mother's pestering phone calls about getting married but not this time.

Exuding a calm disposition about the subject, Lionel offered a comforting guarantee, "Mother, you don't have to worry. I have everything under control; you will have a precious, new daughter-in-law in due time. Things are moving along quite nicely with Marsha."

In a moment of silence, Lionel changed the subject, "So, I heard you and dad met with an event planner about the party, how did it go?"

Lionel's parents were getting a jump start on planning their 50th wedding anniversary party that would be held at the end of that year. They wanted an extravagant affair, with family and friends to share and commemorate the blessed union. Having overcome colossal challenges throughout life including being an interracial couple, the Webbers wanted to celebrate their marriage in style.

The sanctity of marriage was highly revered within the Webber home, they'd built their life on a Christ-centered foundation. Due largely in part because the matriarch and patriarch withstood prejudices from others, the couple recognized early on they needed God in their lives. Through it all, the couple was determined to have a strong family unit. Dale Webber, a retired musician, instilled in his children that in life, you can't find anything better than a wife and he treated his wife as such.

Was their marriage perfect, no, not at all but even in the highs and lows, the family always stuck together. The Webber children, all eight of them, grew up in a tightly knit family and learned throughout their childhood experiences that love does indeed cover a multitude of faults. Each of the children grew up with a dream to have a marriage like their parents and extend the love within the family by branching off into their own respective families.

Lionel, a textbook middle child, was the last of his siblings to realize the most important dream in his life. Packaged squarely between three older brothers and three younger sisters, Lionel always tried to find his place in life, to be known for something. While he owned that space within the Webber clan he didn't own it alone, he shared it with his twin sister, Liona.

Unrelenting in her pursuit for a new daughter-in-law, Laureen, a former blues singer suggested, "We're going to be meeting the planner on a monthly basis until closer to the party, why don't you and Marsha come home one weekend and go with us? I'd love to see you both, I haven't seen you since the wedding and she wasn't able to make it."

Knowing a proposal was on the horizon, Lionel thought, *"That might not be a bad idea, Marsha and I could share the news with them together."*

For the moment, Lionel set his mother at ease, "Mother, I think that's a wonderful idea. If you can arrange it with the planner, next weekend would actually work out great. Just let me check with Marsha and I'll let you know. I have to go now. Tell dad I said hi, I love you, and I'll be in touch with you soon."

Hanging up with his mother, Lionel called the other important woman in his life.

"Hello there beautiful!"

"Hi Lionel, how's your day going?"

"Wonderful now that I'm talking to you, sunshine."

Marsha Miller of the famed Miller's Floral Design Company inherited her family's floral enterprise and was making a name for herself in the industry.

"Oh Lionel, you always know what to say to make a girl feel special."

Releasing an appreciative sigh, Lionel then spoke up, "Are we still on for tomorrow night?

"Yes."

"Great, well, I was going to mention it at dinner but I want us to go ahead and talk about it now. I spoke with mother earlier and she'd like for us to come for a visit in the next couple of weeks. Since next weekend is a long weekend, I was thinking that might work out well, will that work for you?"

The silence on the other end caused Lionel to ask, "Marsha, are you still there?"

Stumbling over her words, "Um, yes, I'm here, it's just, it seems like my staff is looking for me, the store is busy..." Looking for reasons to end the call and not answer Lionel's question, Marsha continued to create ways to escape. Pretending to answer someone, Marsha held her hand over the phone, "Yeah, I'm wrapping up a call now, I'll be right there."

Interrupting the charade, Lionel stepped in, "Hey baby, it sounds like you have to go. We can talk about this at dinner tomorrow night. Go ahead, do what you need to do, and I'll call you later."

A sinking sensation traveled through Marsha's body as she sat at her desk weighing the pros and cons and playing out the scenario in her mind. Left with the thoughts swirling in her head, she realized, *"Lionel is such a great guy but I'll have to tell him at dinner tomorrow night."*

CHAPTER 3

Laughter from round table conversations echoed off the brick walls in the restaurant, along with glasses clanking and corked bottles opening to the tunes of the live band performing at The Vines Wine Bar.

Weeks prior, Lionel made plans with the owners of the restaurant to secure the wine room, a secluded area reserved for private dining occasions such as birthdays, anniversaries, and engagements. He'd planned everything down to the finest of details.

Clothed in pure sophistication, from head to toe, Lionel arrived early to take in all of the elements of the night. Knowing his life was about to change, he wanted to experience every moment of the evening.

From the customized menu, the roaring fire in the fireplace, the luminaries, to the carefully selected tunes to be piped into their intimate setting, to the picturesque floral arrangements ordered from none other than Miller's Floral fragranced the room slightly, the setting could not be more perfect. On a scale of one to ten, the romantic ambiance scored one hundred.

Lionel toyed with the black box nestled in his pocket. The staff was waiting and ready to serve the future Mr. and Mrs. Webber. The only thing left to do was wait on Marsha to arrive.

Being led through the restaurant by the hostess, heads turned and smiled watching Marsha march towards the out-of-the-way dining room. Everyone knew it must've been a special occasion.

At that moment, checking the time against his Swiss, technographic wristwatch, Lionel stood to greet his love, "Wow, the lady in red...and as always, you're right on time."

Marsha looked gorgeous. The flower in her hair tucked in amongst a sea of loose spiral curls that caressed her bare chestnut shoulders had become a signature accessory after taking over the family business.

Embracing the contour of her body and drinking in her perfume scented skin, holding her a minute longer, Lionel whispered in her ear, "You are absolutely breath-taking."

Without any eye contact, Marsha pulled away saying, "Thank you," as Lionel quickly moved to pull out her chair.

Trying to settle herself and get comfortable, with a pasted on smile, and an attempt to lighten her mood, Marsha looked over at Lionel and said, "My, my, you look rather debonair tonight."

Watering his dry mouth with a glass of handpicked wine from the restaurant's cellar, Lionel responded flashing a wicked smile, "Don't I always?"

"*Oh my goodness, he is making this so hard,*" Marsha's mind raced. "*He looks good, he smells good; he is just...good.*"

Swept away by the ramblings in her mind, Marsha didn't hear the waiter announce, "Ma'am, tonight's menu has been carefully crafted by our very own Chef Dan and Mr. Webber. Which appetizer would you like to begin with?"

"Marsha, sweetheart, did you hear the waiter? What would you like as your appetizer?" Lionel asked pouring her a glass of wine.

Caught up in the midst of her troubled thoughts, Marsha quickly glanced down at the menu and ordered, "I'd like to begin with the jumbo lump crab cake please."

"I'll have the crab cake as well sir." Crab cakes, the couple's favorite.

Noticing Marsha's distracted disposition, Lionel took a hold of her hand and zeroed in on her, "Is everything alright Marsha, are you okay?"

Marsha sipped on the creaminess of the selected wine wherein she really wanted to gulp it down, she responded with a soft, "Yes, Lionel, I'm fine."

With her response, Lionel's smile grew a mile wide, "Well good because I have a couple of things I want to talk to you about. Tonight is going to be a special night and...."

Unable to continue on with the façade, Marsha broke her silence, "Lionel, before you go on, there is something I need to tell you."

Lionel's skin began to tingle, his muscles tightened as he drew his head back to listen. Instantly he knew something was not right.

"Lionel, you know I think you are an amazing guy, right? It pains me deeply to have to share this with you but I can't continue to go on lying anymore."

Lionel's heart began to race, "Lie about what Marsha?"

"You know that we met through an online site, right? Well, I meant to take down my profile after we started getting serious and I kept forgetting to do it."

The server was donning the doorway to bring out the appetizers but Lionel raised his hand to ward him off from approaching the table.

"So you forgot to take down your profile and what happened?"

Marsha struggled to find the right words, words that would crush Lionel.

"When I finally remembered to close it out, I went online but the system continued to send me matches. Things between us were going well but there was this one match that intrigued me and I thought I might see what it was about him that was attracting me to his profile. I know I shouldn't have but I did it anyway."

"And?"

The waiter tried to come to the table again but Lionel became more determined in his wave to ward off the server.

"I'm so sorry Lionel but I reached out to him and we've been seeing each other for the last three months and I think we are just perfect for one another...I think I'm in love."

Having mixed feelings about her confession because she hated what her words would do to Lionel but relieved to finally get out in the open how she felt about Dallas McCants.

Lionel excused himself from the table for a moment; he went to shut EVERYTHING down for the beautifully planned evening.

Upon his return to the table where Marsha sat nervously, Lionel took a moment to draw in a slow and steady breath to use a carefully controlled tone, "You mean to tell me that you've been seeing another guy for the last three months?"

Marsha immediately became aware of her surroundings, she noticed the inactivity of the servers, the music was no longer playing in the background, and the room was turning ice-cold.

Shifting in her seat, Marsha answered, "Yes, and I'm so sorry. I thought I could stop it but I can't. Lionel, I never meant to hurt you, this just happened. I do care for you Lionel but I need to see where this thing is going."

"You said he's a perfect match, what makes him so perfect for you?"

Careful not to show her true excitement about Dallas in front of Lionel, Marsha simply said, "He's just unlike anyone I've ever met before."

Every one of Marsha's words landed a one-two sucker punch combination straight into his gut. His washboard abs couldn't protect him from the agony of her unsavory conversation.

Lionel's voice hardened from Marsha's admission, the flickering candle light made Lionel's golden brown, wolf-like eyes, look glazed over, "I have no words for you. Right now, the words I'd planned to say are no longer appropriate and the words I want to say to you would be highly inappropriate."

In that moment, there was so much Lionel wanted to say but he honestly couldn't figure out the words to say. He searched for words that would deliver a "low blow" to Marsha to hurl insults upon her head but he couldn't. He couldn't identify the feelings whirling around through his mind, body, and soul. A whirlwind was going on inside and he didn't know how to stop it.

"Lionel, will you be okay?"

Lionel had become unresponsive towards Marsha. His blank, emotionless face concerned her. The light in Lionel's eyes had been extinguished; it was as if a shell of Lionel sat before Marsha. She had never seen Lionel like this and she was worried but she couldn't stay any longer, Dallas was waiting for her.

Marsha reached down to kiss Lionel on the cheek as she was about to leave. Lionel blocked her parting gesture of goodwill. She walked away with her hand sweeping across his broad shoulders.

Unbuttoning the crisp, powder blue shirt he wore under the stylish, velvet blazer, losing interest in his appearance, Lionel apologized to the staff at the restaurant for wasting their time on the failed proposal attempt.

The general manager came out to console Lionel as he handed him the invoice for the evening.

Lionel looked at the bill and thought had he seen this after the proposal, it would have been worth every penny, however; he now felt violated. She didn't even notice all he'd done for her.

He sat looking at the bottom line number, dredging up memories from the last three months with Marsha, trying to understand what led them to this night. A sense of betrayal rocked Lionel's mind to the very core as his thoughts became more and more fuzzy. *"What now? What's next? How do I move forward from here?"*

A collapse in his body posture signaled to himself that he now felt broken inside, all of the planning, all of the hard work, all of the excitement was all for nothing. It was over, she was gone.

Her words hung onto his heart. He sat the black box on the table and stared at it. He slowly unwrapped the box to uncover the radiant three and a half carat diamond set in a pave' diamond platinum setting. Lionel thought back to his time with Maria at Boites a Bijoux, he jumped to his feet, sending his chair flying across the room. It crashed on the wall with a bang masking the sound made from him throwing the ring box against the other wall, leaving the ring exposed on the ground.

He couldn't bring himself to go out into the main dining room, he wouldn't be able to face their stares; he wouldn't know how to react to their empathy knowing the engagement didn't take place in the private area. Lionel asked to exit the restaurant through the back entrance. His driver was waiting and the brake lights were already turning the corner as the manager came out to stop them with the ring.

CHAPTER 4

"Girl, I can't believe you let Lionel go for this guy, Dallas."

"I know, I feel rotten about it but, hmmm, this man. I hate to sound so cliché but he sets my soul on fire, honey."

"Cold-blooded I tell you, just cold-blooded."

Nicole Owens, Marsha's single and looking best friend was beside herself when she heard the news. "Marsha, are you sure you did the right thing? Lionel is such a good guy; he's super successful; you and I both know women would kill to go out with him. You know he was named one of San Antonio's most eligible bachelors and you let him go. Help me Lord, Jesus...what is wrong with this girl?"

"Nikki, Nikki, please don't make me feel worse than I already do. This thing with Dallas took me completely by surprise. I feel like there was a reason I never closed out my profile because if I had, I wouldn't have met him."

Not impressed by her best friend's explanation, Nicole yawned, "Uh-huh. I'm just saying, Marsha he goes to church, loves his mama, incredibly handsome....need I say more?"

Marsha wanted Nicole to understand, "Omigoodness, see Nikki, on paper, Lionel looked like the perfect match for me but Dallas feels like the perfect match. I can't explain it, it just feels right. I don't know girl, it was all quite unexpected but I feel like I owe it to myself to explore a relationship with him. I mean hey, Lionel hadn't put a ring on it so technically, I was still available."

Making jokes to liven up the conversation, Nicole started singing, Beyoncé's, *Put a Ring on It*, "All the single ladies, all the single ladies."

The two friends cackled together on the phone, "Nicole, you are crazy. Thanks for listening though. Hey, let me grab this, Dallas is beeping in. Oh hey, are you still coming over tomorrow night?"

"Yes ma'am, that is still the plan."

"Alright cool, see you tomorrow then."

While Marsha explained herself to her best friend, Lionel had to do some explaining of his own.

"So how did it go 'lil brother?"

Liona liked calling Lionel her little brother, she was born a whopping two minutes before him. Liona was the only person Lionel told about his plans to propose to Marsha. He had sworn her to secrecy. The mere fact they shared a womb together bound them together closer than any of the other siblings.

"I waited to call because I didn't know if you all celebrated late into the night last night."

Liona kept talking, she was so consumed with her conversation and the jokes she was making that it took her a moment to realize her twin brother had not said a word.

"Lionel, are you there, I thought you would be more excited this morning, what's going on?"

Lionel had not combed his honey dipped, truffle colored curls that morning and dragging his hands through his hair seemed to comfort him. He started speaking, stopped, and started again, "Ah, um – Marsha and I did not get engaged; I didn't even get a chance to propose."

Checking the phone to see if she'd missed what her brother said, Liona asked him to repeat himself.

Becoming disturbed, Lionel snapped, "You heard what I said... I'm sorry; I don't mean to get upset with you. I just can't believe I went through all of that for nothing."

Wanting to know all of the details, Lionel filled his sister in on the previous night's events.

"Oh, she must don't know who she's messing with. I'll kill that -."

Liona Webber was a model who had been discovered at the age of fifteen; she'd traveled the world and was well-known throughout the industry. When she decided to get married and start a family, she slowed down. However, she still dabbled in the industry somewhat through a local newspaper beauty and fashion column she wrote for.

Despite her poise and beauty, if anyone messed with her family she would leave all of that at the front door. Leaving home at such a young age and being exposed to various things made her tough.

"Calm down girl, it's alright....I'll be alright. You always ready to fight somebody. I don't need my sister going around killing my ex-girlfriend. I mean, I guess everything happens for a reason, this will work out the way it's supposed to. You can trust me on that."

Liona didn't quite know how to take her brother's words, he sounded cryptic but that was Lionel.

"Well, you know, I don't play when it comes to my family. Anyway, if you say you're alright then I'm alright. So, I hear you're supposed to be coming home soon."

Lionel let out a laugh, "Yeah, how funny is that, I was supposed to be bringing Marsha along so we could tell everyone the news...what a waste. Plus, I hadn't confirmed that with mother yet."

"Forget her, don't let that heifer stop you from coming home. Not only that, you know how she is, mother has already told everyone you're coming, it'll probably do you some good to be around family now anyway."

"You're probably right, I haven't been home in a while and it'll be nice to get away for a few days. I guess I'll see y'all next weekend then. Hey I'm sure you know it goes without saying..."

"I know Lionel, I won't say anything, it's not my story to tell."

CHAPTER 5

"*Am I really sitting next to one of San Antonio's most eligible bachelors?*" Erica screamed in her head.

Erica's conversation with herself continued, "*That picture didn't do him justice, he is really fine. I got bumped up to Business Class today and now I'm next to Lionel Webber, today is going to be a good day.*"

Taken in by his own thoughts, Lionel sat preparing himself for the trip home. He was not looking forward to answering his mother's questions about Marsha.

"*Marsha,*" heat flushed through his body as he thought about her. The thoughts were becoming overwhelming, Lionel leaned his body back into his seat and closed his eyes, "*She was supposed to be going home with me this weekend, she would have been seated here right next to me, but...*"

Lionel's thoughts were interrupted as the pilot's voice carried throughout the aircraft. As he opened his eyes, he noticed the woman seated next to him, in the seat where Marsha would have been. Repositioning his neck pillow, he wondered, "*When did she get here?*"

Pretending not to recognize him, Erica leaned back, "I guess we are about to take off, are you ready?" Adjusting her seat a little more, she continued, "Hey, I'm Erica by the way."

"Yes, I'm ready and nice to meet you, Miss Erica By-the-Way...I'm Lionel."

Lionel glanced at Erica to see what she thought of his attempt at being funny; Erica exchanged his glance with a grin of approval. Their glances lingered.

Could it be possible? Was destiny and reality now face to face?

Erica's approval seemed to provide Lionel with the permission he needed to keep talking to her.

Lionel felt the need to repeat his punch line, "Where are you headed Miss By-the-Way?"

Erica was happy to continue the conversation with Lionel, his corniness was intriguing, "I'm going to Chicago."

"For work or for play?"

"I'm going for work but in a city like Chicago, you can always get your play on, especially during a MLK Weekend. Are you going to Chicago as well?"

"No, not this time, I'm headed home for the weekend; my final destination will be in Florida."

Wanting to know more about this woman that now sat in Marsha's empty seat, Lionel probed more, "You say you're going for work, what sort of work do you do?"

For Lionel, Erica was now making what he thought was going to be a horrible flight an enjoyable one.

Adding nothing more, nothing less, Erica answered, "I'm a detective."

A feeling of wonder struck Lionel as Erica revealed her occupation, "Wow, you don't look like any of the detectives I've ever met."

Lionel's words crept up the back of Erica's neck and traveled across her face to her smiling cheeks, "Lionel, you are too kind. And what do you do?"

"Oh me? I'm a consultant, nothing too glamorous, but I love it."

The bells chimed to signal an announcement from the cockpit, "Good afternoon, the time now in Chicago is 12:55 and the current temperature is a brisk 29 degrees, please prepare for landing."

Lionel and Erica talked and laughed the entire flight, not realizing how fast the time had flown by.

"Here, let me help you with your bags." Lionel leaned across to assist a struggling Erica get her bag down, their eyes met on the way down and they both smiled.

"Thank you, it was very nice to meet you Lionel. I hope you enjoy your weekend."

Erica wanted to say more but didn't know what to say.

"It was my pleasure, detective, good luck in Chicago," Lionel smirked and walked off the plane.

Erica grabbed her bag and slowly walked off the plane, "*I really enjoyed his conversation but that joker didn't even try to get my number. Did he not think I was cute enough? That couldn't be it, I know I look cute today. Oh well, such is life, I'm in Chicago to follow up on this lead, work is my number one priority right now; I don't have time to get caught up in some guy, even if he is Lionel Webber.*"

Not looking forward to the three hour layover, Lionel went to the spa located in the airport to get a message. He needed to unwind and get his mind right before going home.

Laying on the massage table allowing the masseuse to work out the stubborn knots in his body, Lionel drifted into a deep state of relaxation where he let his mind wander. Surprisingly, his thoughts led him to the face he'd just left, Erica. There was something quite charming about her, her effervescent personality shown through during the two and a half hour flight. It hadn't crossed his mind until that very moment, *"Man, I must be crazy, why didn't I get her number?"*

CHAPTER 6

"Yeah, I see you. I'm walking out now."

Liona pulled up to the curb where Lionel jumped in her car, "Hey sis, it's good seeing you."

"Uncle Lionel, Uncle Lionel," Liona's three children were overjoyed to see their uncle. He always had gifts for his nieces and nephews.

"So, how was your flight?"

Lionel's answer started and ended with a smile, "It was good; I'm glad to be home."

"Hey, wait a minute, what has you all smiles like that; I see the dimples popping out, don't think I didn't notice."

Shrugging off his sister's suspicion, Lionel laughed at Liona, "Nah, it's nothing. I was smiling because I met this young lady on the way to Chicago and she was real cool."

"You're blushing, she must've made quite an impression on you. I don't care about cool, all I want to know is, is she cute and does she have child-bearing hips? You know how our family is."

Embarrassed at the fact he'd noticed both, Lionel spoke through his hands covering his face, "Yes and yes. I'm kind of tripping because I don't know what I was thinking; I didn't get her number or anything. I guess this whole thing with Marsha still has my mind. But, you know what, I work with some people that I'm hoping knows who she is, so hopefully I'll run into her again back in Texas."

"Yeah, about Marsha..."

Lionel's cell phone rang, "Hold that thought, I need to take this call."

"Hello there Lionel, this is Maria from Boites a Bijoux, how are you?"

"I'm doing well Maria, how's it going?"

"I'm calling you for two things, first, I wanted to follow up with you and say congratulations again on your engagement; did Marsha fall in love with the ring? I just know she did. And two, I wanted to let you know that a gorgeous wedding band came in yesterday that will go nicely with Marsha's engagement ring. When do you think you can come by and take a look?"

Lionel had not thought about the ring since that night, the restaurant mailed it to him and he hadn't opened the box. It sat in a pile of unopened mail.

"Maria, I'm sorry to report that Marsha and I did not get engaged, I didn't get a chance to propose. She never got to see the ring. With that being said, I won't have a need to find a band to complement the ring."

Liona was pretending not to listen at her brother's conversation.

"Lionel dear, I apologize the outcome wasn't what you planned, in my line of work, I see things like this happen all the time. At your convenience, bring the ring back in, we'll credit your account and if and when you decide to try this again, we'll be here to serve you."

Lionel tipped his head back into the head rest for a moment and closed his eyes, "Thanks Maria, your call means a lot."

Lionel ended his call as they drove up to the Webber family's waterfront home. Staring at the white marbled steps leading up to the front door, the stairway to heaven they all called it, seemed to calm Lionel, he was happy to home.

Liona took her time unloading the kids from the car as Lionel gathered his things and walked inside.

Dale Webber, a Canadian born musician found himself enthralled in the rhythm and blues music scene in the Motor City during the early sixties. He left everything to follow his passion for music.

At the time when a young, sultry singer rising through the ranks, Laureen Owens needed a backup drummer for her showcase in Michigan, Dale jumped at the chance.

Impressed by his love for music and work ethic, Laureen immediately spoke to her musical director to make Dale a permanent member of her band. While he played for Laureen, Dale continued to build his musical portfolio, he wrote, composed, and played for many on the circuit. He later became Laureen's musical director.

It wasn't long before Dale had Laureen's heart beating to the tune of his drum. Their combined love for music served as the foundation of their relationship and Dale knew he'd found his muse in Laureen. He felt like when Laureen sang on stage, she was singing a song only he could hear. Her milk chocolate skin never crossed the threshold of his mind, in fact, he often joked he was just another kind of chocolate...white chocolate.

Dale knew Laureen was a gift, he cherished her and in return she loved and admired him.[2] After a fulfilling career in music, the couple settled in a seaside town in the northern part of Florida.

---

[2] **Ephesians 5:33**: Nevertheless let every one of you in particular so love his wife even as himself; and the wife see that she reverence her husband.

Laureen couldn't wait for Lionel to walk inside, she met him out the door crying, "Oh, Liney baby....c'mon in son. I'm so sorry."

"Let the boy breathe Laureen, I'm sure Lionel doesn't want you making a fuss over him like that." Dale sighed heavily with exaggeration.

Lionel walked inside and saw all of his brothers and sisters waiting on him, looking like they didn't know what to say.

Liona finally made her way inside.

Turning to see Liona walk through the door, despite the painfully obvious answer, Lionel still asked his twin, "What happened to not my story to tell, huh?"

Liona pleaded, "I'm sorry Lionel, I was just so mad at Marsha after I talked to you. As soon as I hung up, Jr. called me and asked had I talked to you and I couldn't help it, it just came out. BUT I THOUGHT I TOLD HIM NOT TO SAY ANYTHING."

Tapping her foot, Liona's narrowing eyes blared into Dale Jr. as she tried to shift the blame onto him.

After Liona told Dale Jr, the news quickly made its way through the Webber down line:

- Dale Jr.
- Donald
- Dylan
- Laura
- Lynda
- Leontyne
- Mom and Dad

The news of Lionel and Marsha's break up brought everyone home for the weekend, they wanted to see him and make sure he was alright. Lionel did not want this break up to define him but his family was making it out to be that way. He'd had breakups before, what was the big deal? However, he'd never gotten to a point of proposing...that was the difference.

The house was filled with wall-to-wall Webbers and their families, from the oldest, Dale Jr. to the youngest, Leontyne.

Lionel was visibly upset from Liona's slip of the tongue but he understood how territorial she was about him and in a way he was glad everyone was there. It would spare him from having to tell the story a million times.

Dale Sr. pulled his wife close and stood amongst their brood declaring, "This is what we do, we're family; we come together when we need to. Your mother and I are happy to have everybody here and we're going to have a good time. It's Friday night and it's time to eat."

The family cheered, the mood instantly turned jubilant, Friday nights in the Webber house was always Seafood Night, a smorgasbord prepared by Laureen herself that rivaled any seafood restaurant on the market.

They would eat and then gather together in the music room and put on a show. Each of the children shared the musical genetic makeup from their parents. They all were musically talented.

The highly-spirited children ran in and out of the home enjoying themselves, the view of the children playing with the backdrop of the sun setting over the ocean's light blue waves was reassuring.

Around the table, Lionel looked at his family, thankful he was home; however, seeing all of his siblings paired off with their spouses reminded him he didn't have anyone, he was alone.

The loss of appetite he experienced was nothing compared to clouded vision he began to have as he thought of how Marsha betrayed him. All the lies she'd told over the last three months, the empty promises, the broken dates, he questioned their entire relationship.

For Lionel to make the decision to finally settle down, to choose a wife, to choose Marsha and then for her to leave him for someone else, was truly an injustice. What had he done to deserve such, he was loyal, he was kind, he had been nothing more than a gentleman to her.

Yet she found the need to overlook that fact and leave him to deal with her unfaithfulness.

CHAPTER 7

"Who is it?"

"Uh, hello. This is Nicole."

Wearing only a towel around his waist, Dallas opened the door to Marsha's high rise apartment.

"Oh hi Nicole, you are Marsha's friend, right?"

Trying not to admire, too much or too long, Nicole responded nervously, "Um, yes, I am...is she here?"

Dallas motioned for Nicole to come inside, "No, she isn't. She sent me a text saying she was going to be working late."

Stopping in the foyer, Nicole's face reddened, "I wish she would have let me know that before I drove all the way over here. Well, I guess I'll catch up with her later."

Dallas turned to her and smiled, "What's the rush? You did say you drove all the way over here, right? I ordered some food, it should be here any minute. I actually hurried out because I thought you were the food. Since I've heard so much about you, maybe we can use the time to get to know one another better. C'mon, hang out with me."

Nicole pinched her lips together, "*Is this cool for me to be hanging out with her man like this? I have to admit, my mind is cloudy looking at him in that towel. He's really making it hard for me to think straight.*"

"Hey, it was nice meeting you but I should probably go."

Dallas continued to coax, "Come on in here girl, I won't bite. Unless you want me to."

Nicole accepted Dallas' offer but with one condition, "I'll stay for a little bit, I am getting hungry but I'm going to need you to go put on some clothes or something."

In an overtly flirtatious manner, "I'll go with the or something. Normally, by now I'd be naked, I like walking around free but since you're here, I'll be nice and wear the towel."

Nicole's eyes bulged, "How are you going to be nice and wear the towel for me? You didn't know that was me at the door, would you have answered the door in your birthday suit for the delivery guy?"

Dallas smirked, "Maybe, maybe not. I guess it would all depend on how I'm feeling or shall I say, hanging."

Marsha had mentioned to her friend how much of a free spirit Dallas was and how he lived life doing what he wanted without it sometimes making sense. All along, she'd thought Marsha had to have been exaggerating but she was quickly learning the real deal about Dallas.

The food arrived. The two talked and laughed as they got acquainted over dinner and drinks.

"Oh Darling Nikki, do you remember that song? Do you mind if I call you Nikki?"

Nicole tried to hide her flustered face behind her hair, "Don't go there Dallas."

Dallas' conversation contained no filters, he spoke freely about topics that some might consider off-limits and caused Nicole to blush but his openness started rubbing off on her. He encouraged her to be free, kick back, and have a nice time. To aid in her freestyling, he'd smile and nod in encouragement as she spoke.

With multiple refills, the glasses of wine flowed throughout the evening along with conversations, the indoctrination was beginning to work, Nicole's inhibitions were becoming a thing of the past.

Establishing Nicole's direct eye contact, Dallas declared, "You are beautiful. Do you know that?"

Blushing in return, Nicole responded, "And I bet you say that to all of the girls."

"Only the ones sitting in front of me named Nikki."

The two began to submit to an unexpected compelling connection.

Not one time did Dallas ever think to change his attire but several times did he think he'd let the flap slip to divulge his secret and ample assets.

With the greatest intentions, Nicole struggled against noticing but it was too hard. Literally. The bulkiness he displayed made her wonder was he always like this or did she have anything to do with his manifestation.

Pushing away, Nicole said, "Oh Dallas, this has been nice but I think it's time for me to go home."

Dallas wondered aloud, "Who's waiting for you there? Are you going home alone?"

"Unfortunately yes."

Nicole made her way up from the sofa and stumbled over trying to catch her balance.

"Whoa, I think I might need to rethink leaving right now."

Dallas stood up with his directional sign pointed directly at Nicole, "I don't know why you'd want to leave right now anyway. I know I'm not the only one that feels this."

Dallas took Nicole's hand and gently grazed his muscular manliness.

Nicole breathed deeply, "You aren't the only one; I do feel that."

Dallas acted on his feelings and his lips were now connected to Nicole's.

Wherein she knew she should pull away, she couldn't. The temptation had become too much to overcome. Where Dallas should have been hands off, he and Nicole were completely hands on with one another

In between breaths, Nicole questioned, "Marsha is my best friend, how can this be happening?"

Dallas chose to consider the positives and dismiss the negatives, "I don't know but I'm glad it is, aren't you? I had to meet Marsha in order to meet you."

The mood-boosting escapades were over and Nicole immediately hurried to get dressed.

Dallas wanted to leave with her.

"No, what are you thinking? You can't leave with me. This should have never happened. Look, I need to go before Marsha gets home."

Dallas reached for Nicole, "How can you leave me after what we just shared? Don't go. From the moment you walked through that door, I knew something was there between us. I see this as a sign."

Nikki broke free from Dallas's grip, "It's a sign alright. A sign that I'm a horrible friend. I say, let's put this behind us and pretend that it never happened."

"Nikki, I've had a history of going with the flow when it comes to women, trying to find the woman who can truly fit with me, one understands and accepts me and I've finally found her, tonight...with you."

Nikki flicked her shoes on, shaking her head, "No, no, no this cannot be happening. Stop it, stop saying this. Listen, I've got to get out of here."

Dallas grabbed her again, kissing her fervently, melting her anxieties away.

"Listen to me, you go ahead and go home. I'll wait here until Marsha gets home and I'll tell her I'm going home tonight. Leave me your number and I'll come over so we can sort this out."

Nicole placed her hand on her forehead, "Dallas, this isn't a good idea. You need to follow through on whatever plans you and Marsha had for tonight."

"Nikki, my darling Nikki. I'm not taking no for an answer so you may as well give me the number or I'll just get it from Marsha."

Nicole let out a roar, "Alright fine."

Dallas kissed her again, stepping back and smiling he said, "That's my girl; I'll see you later."

CHAPTER 8

"An early morning run on the beach is just what I need...maybe it'll help clear my head." Lionel reasoned within himself about the sunrise exercise. Marsha's disloyalty was beginning to push some unfamiliar buttons in his mind, enough to concern Lionel with his state of mind.

Lionel, Dylan, and Leontyne were the lone rangers of the group, they all lived away from the homestead, living in different states. This weekend, they were all staying at the house.

Leontyne, the baby of the family, a newlywed opened the door where she saw her brother stretching, "Great minds think alike, mind if I join you?"

"Not at all baby girl."

"I'm a married woman now; you can stop calling me that you know."

"Matters not to me, you'll always be baby girl in my book."

Growing up in the Webber house, one could never find a dull moment. Dale Jr. was the baby of the family for the longest until every other child starting coming. It seemed like every time you turned around, Laureen was bringing home another baby. Dale Jr. didn't take kindly to being dethroned from receiving his parent's undivided attention. He turned his displeasure into being a tyrant of a big brother, always trying to tell the other children what to do.

Lionel had his three older brothers he looked up to and wanted to emulate and then came along his four sisters he felt like he needed to look out for and protect.

By Leontyne being the last born, everyone doted on her but because she was born prematurely, it was over the top. She was always the small one in the bunch and she hated it. Growing up, she demanded respect, yet, her brothers and sisters would just laugh and say, "Look at you, you are just too cute."

"I like those running shoes you have on there Lionel, are they custom?

"Look at you checking out my kicks. As a matter of fact, they are. I'm trying to break them in for this upcoming HBCU 5K I'm running in."

"Nice, that t-shirt looks cute on you too, it brings out your eyes, where did you get that from, I'd like to get one for Eddie?"

"Don't be trying to steal my running swag for your husband."

Leontyne smirked, "Whatever boy, let's go...and watch me leave you in my dust."

Gearing up to take off, Leontyne stopped, "Hey, wait, I just want to say, I hate what Marsha did to you and for the record, I never liked her in the first place. For some reason, I always felt like she didn't deserve you and to be honest Lionel, you didn't have the spark in your eyes when you looked at her. I can see these things you know."

Taking in his sister's words, Lionel stretched a bit longer, "Now all of a sudden I'm hearing how much you didn't like her."

"Lionel, it's not all of a sudden, I never liked her but mother told me to be nice, so I tried. Let's be real, you were only going to marry her because she was there. I know you didn't truly love her."

Stretching out the building tension in his body from having to hear about his ex, Lionel couldn't believe his ears, "What are you talking about girl. I could have married any girl before but I decided to choose Marsha."

"Because she was there. Lionel....before I got married, you and I were the only two left to be married off. Then when I got married, that left you. Marsha was the lady in your life and you decided to propose because you didn't like being the last one to get married. You didn't like how that made you look ...yeah, I said it, now deal with it."

There weren't enough stretches available to prepare him for what he'd just heard from his sister, was there any truth to what she was saying?

The youngest of the clan was not letting up, "Now that I think about it, that hussy probably lied about not coming to my wedding, wasn't she supposed to come and something all of a sudden came up please....give me a break. I love you Lionel and to Miss Marsha, I say good riddance. Okay, now that I've gotten that off my chest, we can run."

Back at the house, Laureen was up preparing a hearty feast for breakfast, everyone would be over to eat and hang out.

Since everyone was in town, Laureen invited the event planner over so they could discuss the plans instead of going to her office.

Like clockwork, the gang started arriving. Over breakfast, the family went over plans for the party with Simone Peterson, event planner extraordinaire.

In the midst of the anniversary party conversation, Simone changed lanes, "I want to say that I love everything this family represents. Thank you for inviting me into your home and I'm looking forward to this party. Hopefully, I'll get a chance to plan more Webber events like maybe Lionel's wedding? Where's Marsha?"

Looking around at all of the faces now looking into their plates, Simone cautiously continued, "Laureen told me her soon-to-be-daughter-in-law and son, Lionel were going to be here this weekend."

One by one, everyone got up and walked out of the dining room, the men went one way and the women went another, leaving Laureen and Dale Sr. with Simone who was seated with a blank stare, "Did I say something wrong? I'm so sorry. I don't think I've ever cleared out a room so fast in my life."

Laureen's downturned facial expressions signaled to Simone she had said something wrong, "Lionel and Marsha are no longer together."

Out on the verandah, watching the hide tide come in, Lionel and his three brothers sat and talked.

As the oldest, Dale Jr. always felt the need to steer the ship, "So, I've made plans for us fellas to go out tonight. There's a reggae band playing in town at this new spot and I thought we should go. Rachel is making plans with all of the girls for later so we should be good to go."

Dale Jr. and Rachel were high school sweethearts with a large family of their own, their union yielded six children.

Everyone nodded in agreement whereas Lionel didn't respond at all.

"We're leaving around nine, y'all going to be ready by then right? Lionel?"

Lionel felt like Jr. always had to be the savior of the group and he wasn't feeling like being saved by him, "I'll think about it, I have some work I need to catch up on and I may take advantage of the peace and quiet."

Dylan looked over at Lionel and offered a suggestion, "Why don't you go do your work now so we can go hang later? Let's go have some fun bro."

Donald jumped up rubbing his hands together, "I'll be ready at 8:30, I could use a night out, Michelle is driving me crazy."

Donald and Michelle had been married for twelve years and she was now pregnant with their first.

Michael echoed the same sentiment, "I know what you mean, I'm getting the same from Laura. This second baby is giving her, I mean us, the blues."

"I'm in," the brothers-in-law yelled in unison.

Dylan grabbed Lionel up into a head lock, choke hold like they did as children, "All of us are here and you came home to work? Oh, I forgot who I was talking to here, Mr. Fancy Pants Computer Guy."

Dylan enjoyed teasing Lionel but he loved him dearly, in fact, he admired him. "I'm just playing around man, go ahead and get your work done, so we can go hang, it won't be any fun without you."

Wrestling with his brother, Lionel conceded, "Alright, alright...I'll go."

Dale Jr. watched everyone, taking in their reactions, with a satisfied smile, "I guess it's settled then, tonight at nine."

Laureen yelled out to the men, "Lionel honey, I think your phone is ringing."

"Thanks Mother." Lionel grabbed the phone and stopped mid-stride, "*Why is she calling me?*"

Lionel had not spoken to her since the night at the restaurant. He hurried to his room.

Praying on the other end, Marsha was bargaining with God that Lionel would answer and then not hang up on her. Stumbling over words, Marsha greeted Lionel warmly hoping for a warm response.

"What do you want?"

"How have you been Lionel?"

"Couldn't be better, how about you and uh what's his name, Austin?"

"DALLAS is fine and so am I."

"Why are you calling me Marsha?"

Choosing her words carefully, Marsha began, "I hate to call you with this but I didn't know who else to call. I have a friend whose computer is acting crazy and they asked if I knew anyone that could fix it. They've taken it to those computer fix it guys in one of those big corporate electronic stores and even called in to the manufacturer but nothing is working. You are the only person I know who is a genius at working on computers so I thought I might check to see if you'd be willing to fix it?"

"What friend?"

"Uh Lionel, you don't know this person. I was hoping you'd do this on the strength of knowing me."

"On the strength of knowing you...I wish I didn't even know you. If I could I would use the delete button and erase you from my memory bank."

Marsha cleared her throat.

Lionel continued, "I'm going to go out on a limb here, please don't tell me you're calling for your new boyfriend?"

Marsha was stuck, she had no place to run, except towards the truth, "I...I...I knew it was a mistake to try and call, you used to be the guy willing to help anyone."

Doing a double take on the phone, Lionel couldn't believe his ears, "Are you seriously going to try and turn this on me?" Lionel's voice was shaky but firm. "I've had it with you. Marsha, do us both a favor, lose my number, go on with your perfect little match, Dallas, and live a happy life."

Marsha pleaded one last time, "I know you're angry Lionel but..."

Lionel thought better of it, his tone shifted, "You know what Marsha, you're right, I am that guy always willing to help; I'll do it. I'm going to email you some instructions that'll give me access to his system and we'll go from there. In the meantime, this changes nothing between us. I'm still done with you."

Lionel hung up. Touching his cheek, he become aware of the pain resulting from his clenched teeth and jaw bone.

Seated at his old desk, Lionel tried to slow his loud breaths and heaving chest. Opening his computer, he thought back over the call, *"What has this guy done to this chick, she actually had the nerve to call me to fix his computer."*

Once again, Lionel began to reminisce about their last night together. The humiliation he felt, Maria calling about another ring, the misfortune of not proposing, his family, the event planner, and now this, Marsha had gone too far. He need to do something, but what? He needed a release.

His irrational thoughts were speaking to him louder than the reasonable ones. All of his buttons were being pushed all at once. She had finally driven him to the point of no return. He closed the laptop and swirled around in the chair, adopting a pondering pose, *"Will it work? It has to. I'm so mad right* now; I feel like I'm going crazy. Will people understand why, will doing this make me feel better about this situation? No, it probably won't but it's going to be in the words of Marsha, perfect."

CHAPTER 9

"You look so good, girl. You are rocking that dress. And those shoes. And that bag. Girl, you have just got it going on." Erica piled on the compliments to her freshman year roommate, Lana Edwards while snapping her fingers.

"All complements of my wonderful husband, he loves to dress me."

"Well, I knew he had excellent taste when he married you."

"Oh Erica, that's so sweet of you to say."

Lana and Erica started out as roommates in college and continued on to be sisters. College had been an incredible journey for them, the two young women experienced a lot during their undergraduate years, impacting the lives of many students. They were both dual majors, Erica majored in both criminal justice and computer science and Lana majored in business administration and journalism.

"I was glad to hear you were coming to Chicago for work; I've missed you. Not to mention, it's been almost six months and I haven't met a lot of people yet since we've moved here."

During one of Lana and Kent's premarital counseling sessions, the pastor pointed out how back in the Old Testament when a man married, he took a year off to learn how to please his wife, to establish the foundation of the marriage.[3] Kent took it as a sign when he had to tell Lana his job was transferring him to Chicago.

"How's that year challenge been going?"

"Oh we've been cleaving honey," Lana and Erica slapped hands up in a high-five motion.

"So catch me up girl, what's been going on? Have you decided to stop dating like a mad woman and get serious about somebody?"

"Work, blah, dating life, blah, everything is blah right now. I came here to follow up on a lead but that was a big time bust. The good thing is when I called my boss to tell him, he didn't yell at me. Instead, he told me about this conference I'll be going to when I get back. All the movers and shakers in information security will be there. In my other job I never needed to keep up with trends and the industry because I was so good at my job but now I guess he feels like I need to be right in the middle of it. Shoot, I thought I was the mover and the shaker in all of information security. Teach me to think more highly of myself, huh? Nevertheless, it's in Houston, I haven't been there since I moved to Texas and I'm really excited. I'm hoping it'll be fun."

The roommates ordered a table full of food to keep them busy over the next several hours.

"Anyway, I went out with this guy the other night from church, it was like our second date and he invited me to go meet his parents for Sunday brunch. I stopped calling him that night."

"Erica, it was brunch. What was wrong with that?"

---

[3] **Deuteronomy 24:5**: When a man hath taken a new wife, he shall not go out to war, neither shall he be charged with any business: but he shall be free at home one year, and shall cheer up his wife which he hath taken.

"It wasn't the brunch I was worried about, it was the meeting the parents, if I'm not going to be around, why would I need to meet his parents? I'm now on the hunt for a new church."

Jabbing a fork full of lobster risotto in her mouth, Lana spoke between the bites, "Girl you are so crazy. Hey, I know why you are dating like you are but do you? This isn't like you, I know you. The Erica I know wants it all, the husband, the children, the career. There is no way you can tell me this dating marathon you're on is working for you."

The mood at the table changed, Erica could feel her pulse in her throat mix with her food as she swallowed bites of her appetizer.

Putting down her fork, she recalled, "He hurt me Lana and you know it, you were there. You literally had to drag me out of the black hole I'd dug for myself."

Erica met Patrick Henry at the police station in Virginia, he was leaving as she was walking in. Both engrossed in their own worlds, those worlds soon collided. Everything fell to the ground.

"Oh my God, excuse me sir. I'm so sorry for bumping into you."

"No, it was all my fault. Let me help you with that. Please forgive me. Today just hasn't been my day. Seems like I keep bumping into people today. I was in a car accident earlier. I'm down here to pick up a copy of the police report for my insurance and now I'm bumping into you. Hi, I'm Patrick."

"Hi Patrick, I'm Erica, nice to meet you. Hopefully, your day will get better." Erica gathered her things and turned to leave.

"My day would be a whole lot better if you'd let me make this up to you by taking you out sometime."

"Oh, I'm fine, you don't have to feel like you need to take me out for a simple little bump."

"Was it a simple bump or kismet? You don't want to see me beg do you? Now the betterment of my day rests squarely on your shoulders. I'd love to take you to dinner."

Erica laughed, "Kismet, who says kismet, you are something else."

That dinner date turned into a two year relationship where Erica and Patrick fell deeply in love. Erica dreamed of the day she and Patrick would marry and have children until the day she found out he was already married with children. He had been living a double life.

How could he do such a thing, what did he have to say for himself. He simply said, "Yes, I have a wife but I'm in love with you. If I'd only waited to meet you. I loved you the moment I saw you and I got caught up...I didn't know how to stop myself."

It didn't matter, Erica broke things off immediately.

The revelation changed Erica inside and out, some voluntary, some involuntary. The involuntary ones were the ones that scared her the most. She took a break from reality for a while. To go from having your heart beat for someone who means the world to you to now beat only for survival is tragic.

What was the right way to respond? There was a list of possibilities set before her. Would she slit his tires? Burst out his windows? Go to his wife and have a conversation? Embarrass him on his job? Blast him on social media? Would any of that make her feel better?

She did consider firing her service weapon, launching a burning bullet through his chest, tearing a hole next to his heart. Not to kill him but to provide him with a constant reminder of the hole she now had in her heart.

Instead she did nothing. She wanted to stop living but it was Lana who helped to snap her back into focus. Lana wouldn't allow Erica to waste away her life on a man, she fought for her friend.

With the realization that her shattered dreams with Patrick would never materialize she packed up and moved to San Antonio for a fresh start.

Lana flashbacked to the day she found Erica in the bed in her dark apartment, the thought of what Patrick had done made her want to vomit. "I told you to be careful of those guys with two first names, 'ole slime dog ho-heffa from...'"

Erica sprayed the table with her drink laughing at Lana, "Girl, I haven't heard that one in a long time, I remember your mom used to say that about her boyfriends."

Lana agreed, "Yeah, ma-dukes knows how to come up with some crazy sayings doesn't she?"

It had been about eighteen months since the break up and Lana thought she'd check the pulse of where Erica's mind was, "Do you think you're afraid to commit to someone because of Patrick?"

"You know, Lana I think it boils down to this. All my life, I've been known to do the right thing. I've succeeded in life by making smart decisions that have kept me safe. Well with the exception of...you know."

Both women let out a sigh.

Erica continued, "Other than that, I've made smart decisions. When I met Patrick, his pursuit for me was relentless and I loved it. I was crazy about him and he was crazy about me too. Unfortunately, I fell in love with the wrong guy. When you're in love and something like this happens, the struggle between right and wrong is hard to sustain. That wrong choice with him makes me question everything about myself. I'm a detective for crying out loud, I couldn't even detect my boyfriend was married? Crazy huh?"

Tears welled up behind her eyelids, she didn't stop them, they pooled in her lap.

Lana begged, "Please don't cry, if you cry then I'm going to start crying. I seem to now cry at the drop of a hat, not sure what's going on with me lately."

Erica confided in her best friend, "One of the things I miss the most is that he used to write songs for me that I would then sing. Now I don't sing anymore, he stole the song out of my heart. I go out because I'm lonely and I enjoy the fellowship, hoping to one day be able to find a tune again."

Lana lightly stroked Erica's forearm, offering her support. "Erica, you aren't alone, honey. Who among us hasn't had our heart broken? So you fell in love with the wrong guy. So what? I think it's time to finally let go of that and open yourself up to the chance of meeting the right guy. Those feelings you felt for Patrick were real but it's possible that him being the wrong guy left you clues for the right one. Erica, you need to know you are deserving. If a guy isn't willing to give you the relationship you deserve, then I say, hit the road Jack and don't you come back no more. I had to come to this realization myself. Let me ask you this, have you prayed about it at all?"

The plates had been cleared and the desserts were now arriving to the table.

"One thing I've learned my friend is that sometimes you have to die to one life to get the one you want. I left everything in my past, in the past, and you need to do the same. What we did doesn't define us, it's what we do going forward that will. I need for you to promise me over these yummy looking desserts that as of tonight, you are freeing yourself from your past and you'll stop hiding the true Erica. That's what you're doing with dating all these guys without any intentions of committing."

Erica's face burned with Lana's truth.

Lana remained steady in her observations, "Each date closes you off to the real dream you have. Stop doing that. Promise me you will open yourself up and let the world see how beautiful you are. Falling in love is easy. Staying in love is the real challenge. No matter who you end up with, you're going to have to work at it but it is possible to have a successful marriage. We try to do these things on our own but we shouldn't, not with such important life issues. Allowing the Lord to lead you to the right guy and then allowing Him to be the center of your marriage is the secret ingredient to a wonderful recipe for love. It happened just like that with me and Kent. It's early in our marriage but we are working it out as we trust God to grant us with His grace and provides us with directions for our lives."

Lana's words of encouragement soothed Erica's tormented soul.

Erica nodded and said, "I promise. You are absolutely correct. I actually hadn't been praying like I should but that is going to change. It's just, I'm not like you Lana; I wasn't born and raised in the church like you were. You seem to have it all together, even when we weren't doing the right thing back in college, you still seemed to be grounded in your faith. For me, I seem to get off track sometimes and stay off but I really want to change that."

Lana looked Erica squarely in her face, "Girl, I don't have anything together, my total reliance in life is upon God."

Pointing to herself over and over again, "See me, I'm a mess with and without Christ, I just choose to be a mess with Him because He can do a better job with me than I can. I learned a long time ago that no matter what, things may fail all around me but God is the strength of my heart. This thing is a daily walk, I'm not perfect by no stretch of the imagination but to God be the glory because He's my portion forever.[4]"

"I hear you on that, I know what God did for me back in the day so I need to stop tripping and trust Him completely. I do believe God has someone out there for me and I need to allow Him to do the matchmaking. You know what, I just realized that in spite of myself, He loves me with an everlasting love and things that concern me, concerns Him. I needed this Lana, thank you so much for always being there for me, through all my crazy ups and downs."

Wiping the corners of her eyes with her napkin, Erica gushed, "Oh my goodness, I'm so happy for you and Kent, you guys inspire me, the love you two have is a blessing to witness. Hey, I'm open and as of tonight, I'm freeing myself from it ALL. I'm leaving it all here on this table with all of these empty plates."

The two laughed, Erica and Lana locked forks in unity to Erica's pledge, "From now on, I'm ready to experience all that life will bring to me and I'm going to try and expand my heart and mind to be able to receive the right relationship."

Erica felt a sudden lightness and giddiness come over her. For the first time in a while, she felt excited about her new found freedom and the path she had just accepted.

---

[4] **Psalms 73:26**: "My flesh and my heart faileth: but God is the strength of my heart and my portion forever."

CHAPTER 10

"If you can play, you can surely get up and pray. This is the day that the Lord has made, we will rejoice and be glad in it. Rise, shine, and give God the glory. Let's go, it's time to get up and get ready for church."

Laureen walked through her house banging on the doors of her sleeping family. These declarations were well known in the Webber house.

Dale and Laureen taught their children, if you go out on Saturday night and party, you better be ready to get up and go to church the next morning. Just because they were all adults with their own families didn't exempt them from the rule. Plus, Laureen was beaming on the inside, she was happy all of her children and grandchildren would be going to church with her.

Slowly but surely everyone rolled themselves out of bed and filed down the stairs to make it to service. All of the men were the last ones to make it down. The girls had gone out too but they didn't stay out as late as the guys.

Laureen didn't let their dragging around bother her, she was pumped up and ready to praise the Lord. "Everyone else is going to meet us at the church, let's go, I don't want to be late."

On the way to the church, Lori, Dylan's wife, perked up the mood in the car by teasing her brother-in-law, "Lionel, I heard about all those ladies trying to get with you last night."

"Dylan, man, is this what life has become for you? Telling your wife everything, is this what you do now?"

Leontyne chimed in, "I heard about it too, I was just going to wait and bring it up at Sunday dinner. Whoop, whoop, my brother has it going on, I hear you were a regular hometown hero."

"You too Eddie? You guys are ridiculous." Everyone in the car laughed and joked around the rest of the way.

"So you guys had a good time then?" Dale Sr. smiled as he looked into the rear-view mirror, listening to the rowdy crowd.

Dylan snickered answering for everyone, "Yes, we did dad."

The parking lot was packed, luckily Liona and the others had already arrived and cornered off the section where the Webber's usually sat.

Laureen rushed up to the front of the church, she would be leading worship this Sunday. From time to time, she still loved to sing in front of an audience but she knew within herself, if she never sang before a crowd again, she could always sing praises to the King, the King of kings and Lord of lords.

That morning, the praise was jubilant and everyone was on their feet. Even at seventy-one years young, Laureen still knew how to get a crowd going, she had the congregation rocking.

The tempo slowed and Laureen led the assembly into worship, you could see tears flowing from people, hands stretched out and up towards the heavens, reaching for something, trying to connect to something very powerful.

From a young age, Lionel recognized he had a close connection with God even when he didn't understand it all. Being surrounded by his family, hearing his mother's soul stirring voice, in those moments of worship, he chose to forget his troubles and focus on what good may come of his life.

With raised hands and tears flowing, he ran through a range of emotions, regretful yet hopeful, ashamed, but assured, he was comforted by the love permeating the room. He decided to connect with it and surrender his all, receiving the generosity of grace available to him that morning. In that moment, all seemed to be forgiven and renewed.

The pastor greeted his flock as they welcomed him, he stood proudly behind the sacred desk with a resounding, "Good morning." He was ready, the atmosphere had been prepared for him to deliver his message. "We are celebrating MLK weekend today, we all know Dr. Martin Luther King Jr. is known for his historic, I have a dream speech. Today I want to deal with that a little and ask you a question. What have you been dreaming about? We're going to jump around to several scriptures today but one that I want to focus on is this, taken from Genesis 37:5. And it reads, Joseph dreamed a dream, and he told it to his brothers, and they hated him all the more."

Walking out to the edge of the stage, the pastor leaned over, taking a full glance of the entire group, and asking the question, "Who Is Hating On Your Dreams? I'm here to tell you today, don't let anyone stop you from realizing your dreams. Listen guys, don't let the dream die. Dreams do come true, you just need to wake up in order to follow them. High-five your neighbor and tell them, "I have a dream and I don't care who hates it."

The church erupted with spirited expressions, slapping hands, and hugging fellow parishioners, solidifying their decrees.

A slap to Lionel's back seemed to bring forth his long lost dreams, despite his split from Marsha, he still dreamed of a wife and a family, in a flash, he justified his irresponsible responses to his injustices caused by Marsha and declared, "I'm not going to let my dreams die, it's time for me to wake up."

CHAPTER 11

"Thank you for calling Match Up America, how can I help you?"

"Uh yeah, I'm a member on your site and some strange things are happening in my account."

"Strange like what sir?"

"I went to click on a banner ad and now love songs are playing through my speakers and I can't get it to stop."

"Sir, let me place you on hold for a moment."

"Good morning, thank you for calling Match Up America, how can I help you today?"

"I'm calling to cancel my membership to this crazy site."

"I'm sorry to hear that ma'am, may I ask why?"

"Over the weekend, I received an email from your site, thinking it was the weekly video blast about singles events going on in my area and when I clicked on it, this crazy message came up with circus music in the background with a clown dancing around laughing saying I'm a fool for love."

"We've never had anything like this happen before ma'am, this is all very strange. I do apologize for your inconvenience. I'm going to submit a trouble ticket to our IT department."

"I am highly offended, I came to your site because I don't have time to go and date the traditional way, not to be made a fool of. I will be closing out my profile and moving my membership elsewhere."

"Good afternoon, thank you for calling Match Up America, how can I help you?"

"Some match up service y'all are. I'm calling to cancel my subscription."

"I'm sorry to hear that sir, what happened?"

"I normally receive personalized matches from you all and last week I received a new set of matches. There was one lady I really liked and I reached out to her. We emailed each other a couple of times and then we decided to meet. Based on her profile, the computer suggested she and I would have a very high probability of having a successful match, darn near perfect."

"That's how our system is set up sir. We have proprietary software that sends out those matches."

"Well I think y'all need to get your money back on that software. I got to my date and I'm like, well I'll be a monkey's uncle, the woman I thought I meeting was not there. I thought I had been catfished, you know like that show on MTV, but that wasn't the case. She didn't purposely try to deceive me, somehow, her profile and picture got mixed up."

"I'm sorry sir. Let me submit a trouble ticket for you sir."

"No need, cancel my membership please."

For the next two weeks, calls like these came from all over America into the online dating website. Members were cancelling at an alarming rate, fast enough to get the attention of the site's owner, Harold Johnson.

"What am I paying an entire staff of tech people for if they can't figure out what is going on with the site? I need someone to figure out what's going on with my system, these little bugs in the site are costing me members, literally. If I'm losing members, I'm losing money. I hate bugs, computer bugs, love bugs, any kind of bugs, I hate them all."

Leonard Baker, the Chief Information Officer at Match Up America informed his boss on the latest from the attack. "I understand, for the last couple of weeks we've been diligently trying to determine the source of the problem, there are just so many tickets coming in. We are so overwhelmed, we haven't been able to figure out how this happened. I've been trying to keep you informed and keep the site going. As I look over everything, I think it's pretty safe to say our system was hacked."

"If you and your guys can't figure this out, then you need to find someone who can and fast. My company is under a cyber- attack; I can't believe someone is trying to destroy me. I'm going to put a call into the San Antonio Police Department and see if they can get someone out here to start an investigation.

Harold Johnson, the man behind the scenes of one of the largest online dating sites in the country and abroad was not your typical entrepreneur.

Going through life he never really excelled at anything, orphaned at a young age, not knowing his parents and being tossed from various foster homes, he seemed to wander through life. However, he always lived with an abiding thought he'd do something remarkable.

Miraculously he managed to graduate from high school but he didn't have many options available to him, he hadn't thought about college and it never occurred to him to go into the military.

He did however put his faith in a one dollar lottery ticket on the night of his graduation that yielded him millions. Harold became the sole winner of one of the largest jackpots in the history of Texas which also made him the youngest ever lottery winner. Winning the lottery was like a blessing and a curse for Harold. He learned early on that people wanted him for what he could buy them, not because they wanted a real friendship or relationship with him. The irony in that was he truly believed the money didn't mean anything to him if he couldn't share with others.

The women, oh the women, yes he could pay for the companionship and buy their affections but he didn't want that. The majority of the women he came across didn't seem to find him attractive enough. Harold wasn't unattractive but his plump, average build would put you more in the mind of pound cake as opposed to eye candy.

After years of blowing obscene amounts of money. He decided he wanted to do something smart and worthwhile with his fortunes. As a result, he turned his current love life problems into a business. Harold figured, if he couldn't be happy in love then he wanted to be able to provide people with an opportunity to find love across America, hence the launch of www.matchupamerica.com. His business venture would mean something to people, the matches, the relationships, the marriages, all would bring happiness to people. Something Harold had not been able to find. Despite having over five anonymous profiles of himself on his own site, he hadn't gotten many hits in over ten years.

With an increased desire to investigate after her trip to Chicago, Erica was glad to be tagged as the lead detective for the website case.

"Mr. Johnson, I'm Detective Erica Allen from the cybercrimes division with the San Antonio Police Department, and I will be leading the investigation into what happened to your site."

"Detective Allen, it's very nice to meet you. You and your department will have full cooperation from my staff in your investigation. I'd like to call in our head IT guy, Leonard in here, if you don't mind."

Erica proceeded to inform Leonard and Harold of how she planned to initiate her investigation, "Leonard, if you don't mind, I would like to request access to your computer servers, external hard drives, network logs, and website data logs. I would like to go back as far as the last three to six month if possible."

Impressed by Erica's professionalism and demeanor, Leonard responded, "I'd be happy to get that information and access for you, however, it could take a while. Our data retention policy is such that anything over three months is stored offsite. Anything onsite, I can gather but it'll need to be organized to a point where I can hand it over to you."

Harold didn't like what he was hearing, he didn't even know a data retention policy existed. He realized in that moment why he paid Leonard the salary he did. He usually didn't busy himself with the day to day dealings of the company but he'd been called in due to the breach. "How long is a while Leonard?"

If I made it a top priority, which I will, I can get what's onsite to Det. Allen within a week, and then put a rush on the archived files, will that work for you two?"

Harold slammed the table, "Leonard, I don't want to waste a lot of time on this, I want you to make sure that you put a rush on everything and whatever Det. Allen needs, you get it for her. Am I clear on that?"

"Yes, next week will be fine Leonard. I actually have a conference to attend this weekend, so when I get back you should have everything ready for me, correct?"

Leonard nodded, "Yes ma'am, we really need to find out the source and put a stop to this, it has stumped everyone and it's affecting everything. Let's set up a follow up meeting for next Monday morning, shall we?"

"Sure thing, don't worry, I'm committed to doing everything within my power to catch whoever did this. Gentlemen, it was nice to meet you; I'll see you next week."

CHAPTER 12

"I'm so excited about going to Houston this weekend and especially on the department's dime. This will be my first time going to Houston since moving to Texas."

Erica could hardly contain herself in the seat next to her partner, Det. Morris. Riding with them were two other colleagues from the station, Detectives Corey and Brown.

Ever since Chicago, Erica seemed to be enjoying her new lease on life, she slowed down the dating and was concentrating more on work and her spiritual well-being.

Det. Morris parked the car, "We're here. Let's get checked in."

The group would be attending the annual InfoSecCon, a convergence of information security professionals ranging from various fields including, former hackers, academia, business, law enforcement, and governmental agencies. Leaders from all sectors dealing with the issues of information security were all descending upon Houston.

The convention hotel was buzzing with convention goers from all over the world. Several conventions and meetings were taking place at the same time as the InfoSecCon.

Flipping through the program booklet for the conference, Erica couldn't believe her eyes, "No way, you have got to be kidding me."

Det. Corey looked over to see what was going on, "What's wrong Allen?"

"Nothing really, I just can't believe the speaker for the opening night of the conference is Dr. Lionel Webber. I sat next to him on my flight to Chicago a few weeks back."

The most eligible bachelor article was apparently a playful write up because his professional bio was quite impressive. Lionel graduated from high school at the age of sixteen. He'd attended well-known, prestigious schools, including an HBCU for undergraduate school.

Erica had also attended a Historically Black College. Lionel had enough degrees and certifications to wallpaper a room. Erica thought back to the flight, *"He never mentioned any of this. He's intelligent and fine, oh, he will get my number this time. I'll make sure of that."*

Det. Brown, the only other female detective in the department flipped through the booklet to see Lionel, "Oh yes honey, I'm very familiar with him; I'm looking forward to hearing him speak....maybe even get a chance to meet him. I'm a big fan of his tech blog. If I had sat by him on that plane, I guarantee I would have been coming here with him instead of you guys."

Ignoring Detective Brown's comment, Erica announced, "Well, according to our Lieutenant, I need continuing education credits for my ethical hacker certification so looks like I'll be going to his address tonight. I'm going to go check into my room and get ready for Dr. Webber's session."

Prepped for professionalism mixed with a hint of sensuality, Erica wore a sleek, sapphire colored sheath paired with a classic, black jacket that looked tailored made for her silhouette. For an added bonus to showcase her style, she turned up the sleeves and the collar. The black and gold shoes and accessories brought the entire outfit together seamlessly.

Lionel walked onto the stage looking sharp like the first day of school, he was greeted with warm applause.

Graciously accepting, he began, "It is indeed an honor to have been chosen to be the opening speaker for this weekend's conference."

He got all of his pleasantries out of the way and then opened with a joke, "I think some of the staff was misinformed here at the hotel. I asked one of the ladies where I could find the fitness center and she looked at me and said, "I'm sorry sir but everything is protected this weekend, we were told to secure all of our information; I'm sorry but I can't tell you anything."

Those gathered for the opening session were amused by Lionel's wit and rewarded him with their closely held chuckles. It was a tough crowd but Lionel waded through it like a champion.

"Let's face it, we are here this weekend because in our line of work, everything isn't always what it seems. Nothing is safe. We all know that applications are being made and released at an alarming rate. As more and more people, businesses, governments, and institutions continue to rely and depend upon the Internet, the more we all become targets for criminal cyber activity."

Across the room, heads nodded in agreement with Lionel, this was indeed a bothersome problem. It would be up to professionals such as themselves to stop such attacks and stay ahead of the game hackers seemed to enjoy playing with people's information. Erica was taking in every word Lionel spoke.

"I've come to notice majority of the applications that are brought to market have been thrown together without any real consideration for security risks and vulnerabilities. The only way a person can take over a system is there has to have been a door left open for them to walk through."

Lionel could feel the winds of change, the group was lightening up, the tightness in the room was gone. He went in for the close.

"There are a variety of tools out there to help close those gaps and keep the bad guys out. However, I'd like to announce, I'm in the last phase of testing for my latest product. I've researched the flaws with some of the tools currently on the market, corrected them and in the process, created an advanced web-based application that will scan websites for vulnerabilities."

The end of Lionel's speech landed him a standing ovation. He'd done it. The convention loved him.

Surrounded by a sea of well-wishers and admirers, Lionel was busy talking and shaking hands when Erica managed to make her way to where he stood.

"May I have your autograph please sir?"

Overwhelmed by those trying to get face-to-face time with him, Lionel lost track of everything going on around him until he heard her voice.

Turning around for confirmation, "Tell me, should I make this out to Miss By-the-Way?"

Without thinking, Lionel grabbed up Erica in a familiar hug. Both of them were taken by surprise from his gesture but interestingly they rested in it. The airplane ride seemed to have bonded them more than they realized. The raised hairs on Erica's neck and Lionel's strong heartbeat signaled to them they should break the embrace.

"You can make it out to Erica, I'm officially introducing myself to you. I'm Erica. Erica Allen and it is indeed my pleasure meeting you." Brushing a hair from his shoulder, she asked, "Hey, I almost forgot, how was Florida?"

"Well in that case, I'm Lionel. Lionel Webber and trust me the pleasure is all mine. Florida was um, let's just say interesting. What about Chicago for you, how was your trip?"

"Chicago was interesting as well. And you're not just Lionel, you are 'The Dr. Lionel Webber' who just headlined tonight's opening ceremonies and did an amazing job, if I might add."

A growing group of people were waiting to speak with Lionel including Det. Brown but they had become invisible to him as he stood getting reacquainted with Erica.

"Yeah, yeah, yeah. I do have those designations before and after my name but I don't let those titles define me. Right, detective? Plus, it's starting to get harder to do these days but I try to keep my personal and professional life very separate."

Before she could respond, the conference organizers were coming to gather Lionel for the ticketed reception about to take place. One that Erica didn't have a ticket for, she hadn't planned on going. She and the other detectives had planned to go see the sights in Houston.

"Do you have plans for the evening, were you planning to attend the reception? I would love for you to go as my guest so we could keep talking...if you don't mind."

Erica quickly responded shaking her head, "Nothing that can't wait; I would love to go to the reception with you."

Erica figured her friends would understand. They wouldn't want her to turn down Dr. Webber himself, now would they?

Locking her arm with his, Lionel asked, "Shall we?" Lionel and Erica followed the organizer into the grand ballroom where a grand reception was taking place. Polished wood floors, gourmet food stations, open bars, strategic lighting, amazing music, the organizers had done a great job.

Conference guests were filing into the ballroom, mingling, and networking. Old friends and new friends were interacting with one another and Lionel and Erica were doing the same.

She liked how she looked on his arm, walking through the crowds and people wondering who was the woman with Dr. Webber. Lionel enjoyed having Erica on his arm, as they made their way to his table, he liked how people looked at them trying to figure out who she was.

Lionel whispered in her ear, "You have the whole room trying to figure out who you are. I hope this doesn't ruin your weekend here."

The opening night speaker was generally looked upon as the person to watch in the industry, if the speaker did well, their career would be catapulted into a rock-star status among the InfoSec crowd and most often, rock stars have groupies. Tonight, Lionel was no different but they'd have to wait, he was captivated by Erica.

Returning a whisper to his ear, "I'll take my chances." Erica knew after the killer performance Lionel delivered in front of the standing room only crowd, there wasn't a single woman attending the conference who wouldn't want to be in her shoes.

Included in that number was Det. Brown, "How is Erica just going to stand us up like that? I thought we all were supposed to be going out tonight. She's not answering her phone. Wasn't she the one all excited about coming to see what Houston was all about?"

Det. Morris defended his partner, "I'm sure all is well with Allen, we all can still go out and catch up with her later."

The band playing at the reception was earning their pay, they were playing it up for the room, keeping the energy up for the party. Lionel noticed Erica was dancing in her seat as he sat down from talking to a former business associate. "I see you over here seat dancing, care to dance?"

The two danced until their feet were tired. "You are tearing it up on this dance floor girl."

Erica could not think back far enough to remember the last time she'd felt free enough to dance. It felt good to be footloose and fancy free.

Erica's freedom on the dance floor was appealing to Lionel, he caught himself smiling at her for no reason other than for her being herself. He wondered what was the cost behind her openness, was she born like that or had life made her that way? Whichever, he found it attractive.

The duo spent the entire evening together, learning different things about the other. The reception was winding down but they were still wound up, they were still enjoying each other's company. Neither one wanted to end the night but Lionel knew the proper thing to do was call it.

"The reception will be ending soon, I guess we should call it a night, huh? I'm participating on the breakfast panel in the morning, are you attending?"

Another event Erica had not planned to attend but was quickly trying to figure out a way to get a ticket. Lionel noticed the wheels turning in her head.

"Since you've accompanied me here tonight, it would only be right for you to join me in the morning for the panel discussion. It seems like you have become my date for the weekend. Are you alright with that?"

Erica felt as if her insides were vibrating, she was enjoying the communal energy being shared with Lionel, "Yes, Dr. Webber, I would love to join you for the panel in the morning. You think I'll learn something from you?"

Lionel leaned in close and smiled, "I have plenty to teach if you're ready to learn Detective."

Glancing away for a moment, Erica's thoughts carried her away briefly, *"Is he really interested in me or is he just being nice? Is this his slick way of saying he wants to continue getting to know me? Am I in a dream? How did I end up standing here in front of Dr. Lionel Webber?"*

"Oh, I'll be the judge of that. You'd better bring your 'A' game in the morning. I'll be taking notes and watching to see if you'll make a good teacher or not."

"Sounds like a challenge to me and boy do I love a good challenge. So, I'll meet you in the morning in front of the meeting room. Do you mind if I have your number in the event something happens. That way I can call you if any of the plans change."

The two were standing close but not touching as nervous laughter proceeded Erica's answer, "Sure, here is my card and yes; I'll see you in the morning."

On the outside, she was composed, on the inside, she was jumping up and down, *"This guy is smooth as silk, he's trying to play it off like he might need to call me in case something happens, yeah right. I don't care how he did it, I'm just glad he did it this time and got my number...whoo hooo."*

Going in for a hug good night, Lionel reeled in Erica like a fish on a hook, "Until tomorrow."

Lionel's touch was sincere, Erica didn't want to let go but she did, and replied, "Until tomorrow."

CHAPTER 13

"Morris, did you hear from Allen last night?"

"Only by text message late last night. She apologized for not going out and said she'd had a change of plans and probably wouldn't be able to hang out today either. She said she would call me later today."

Detectives Brown, Corey, and Morris were already seated and conversing when Erica walked into the meeting room with Lionel. Morris and Brown watched Erica be seated at an upfront table near the stage where the panelists would be seated. Lionel pulled out Erica's chair and smiled at her as he took his place on the stage with the other platform guests.

Unkind thoughts about Erica began to fill Det. Brown's head, *"Who does she think she is? How did she get to be a guest of his? She wasn't even planning to come to this meeting? She's always catching a break. She's not that good at her job anyway, she should've been gone. My closure rate is much higher than hers. She don't even look right to be walking in with him, what is she even wearing anyway?"*

Det. Brown crossed her arms over her chest, turning her mouth downward, "I guess now we see the reason for the change of plans."

Det. Morris was elated to see his partner, overlooking Brown's comments, he said, "Wow, you go Allen, walking in with the big dogs....great outfit choice, she looks amazing."

The servers began serving breakfast as the panel discussion was underway, the topic: "**Why Do Hackers Hack? A Glimpse Inside the Mind of a Hacker**." Serving as a panelist along with Lionel was Jason Walsh, a former hacker who was most known for hacking into a well-known bank's infrastructure and compromising millions of customers along with other well-known companies. He struck a deal and decided to convert into an ethical hacker for law enforcement to profile and understand hackers.

At times the discussion was quite lively and animated while other times it was dull and dry. The tone seemed to shift when Lionel chimed in on the conversation, "We are here trying to figure out why people hack. I would ask the question, why do people do any of the things they do whether good or bad? There's always a reason behind why people do the things they do. Sometimes people do things just to see if they can do it, some really do have malicious intent, some people want to leave a legacy or be known for something, some people do things driven by passion, betrayal, or hurt. In order to figure why a person may hack into a system, we should first try to understand and uncover the real reason for the act. We might actually learn something."

Lionel finished his comments and drank from his glass of water, putting down his glass, he searched for Erica, she was already looking at him and they shared a brief glance. They both shared an enchanting smile.

A hush fell over the room as they soaked in Lionel's words, they seemed profound amidst the roller coaster discussions. Erica listened intently every time Lionel spoke and this time after he spoke she wondered, *"He seems to be speaking from experience almost, like this seems personal to him. I can relate to where he's coming from, there is always a reason. I'm a living witness. What an intriguing man; I guess he can teach me a thing or two."*

Another panelist, Dr. Lydia Gardner, a professor of information technology and former mentor to Lionel, asked the question, "I would have to agree Dr. Webber and based on your assessment, I'm curious to know from you, do you ever think hacking is justified?"

Drinking another sip of water, Lionel thought carefully, before he spoke, "Dr. Gardner, as with anything, there are always exceptions to every rule. I think the problem is that we always look at the bad act of hacking but never the root of it to learn more from it. Growing up in a house with eight children, I learned early in life that justice has the opportunity to take on many different forms. Although, if you were to ask my twin sister, she'd tell you the only justice worth having, is getting even."

The crowd laughed at Lionel's joke about his sister.

Erica was shocked, *"He has seven other siblings and he's a twin, could he be any more interesting?"* Growing up it was only her and her younger sister. She couldn't even imagine what it would be like to grow up with that many children.

The panel discussion continued on until the moderator announced they had gone over their allotted time for the event. "This session has been fantastic but our time is up and there are other sessions and trainings going on that some of our participants would like to attend. Thank you to all of our panelists and their contributions. Thanks to each of you and enjoy the rest of your day."

Gathering his things to leave, Lionel was approached by a few of the members from the panel, inviting him to a late lunch. Erica sat waiting, not sure what to do next. She looked up and noticed Lionel motioning for her to come up and join him on the stage.

Before walking out of the room, Det. Brown looked back and saw Erica walk up to the stage where Lionel stood waiting for her. He gently grabbed her by the waist, pulling her close and introduced her to his colleagues. He figured introducing Erica would be a good reason to back out of their lunch invitation.

Det. Corey called out for Det. Brown, "Hey Brown, what's the hold up, let's go to the next session. I'm sure we'll catch up with Allen later."

A small group now encircled Lionel and Erica, Dr. Gardener suggested, "Oh Dr. Webber, bring her along with us, the more the merrier, we're just going right across the street. Come on let's go."

"It looks like you're stuck with me again. Do you mind, Det. Allen?"

"Not at all Dr. Webber."

Over lunch the delegates from the conference were charmed by Erica's conversation. She told stories from her days on the force back in Virginia. She had to work patrol for two years before becoming a detective, the hardest two years of her life. She seemed to shine from within their social circle at the lunch table. Lionel sat back and enjoyed watching her steal the show, he carefully observed how everyone was taken in by her. Erica was a hit, she was a natural. He watched her through the eyes of his table mates, in their eyes, she made him look good.

Jason Walsh, the reformed hacker slid Lionel a note that read: **"Dude, you struck gold, you better not let her go or I'll be there to scoop her up."**

Lionel tried to maintain his composure after reading the note, he tried to keep his true emotions from bubbling to the top; he knew Jason was right. Erica was definitely a gem and he was happy to be in her presence. His only problem, *"Was it too soon to start a new relationship after Marsha? Should I not overthink it and see how things progress? Things have unfolded naturally over the weekend, it seems like we keep being thrown together for a reason. You win some, you lose some, I lost out with Marsha but I feel like I'm winning with Erica. What's a man to do?"*

"Please excuse me for a moment," Erica got up and excused herself to the ladies room. Shortly following behind her came Dr. Lydia Gardner. At the sink, Dr. Gardner interjected, "I've enjoyed your company and conversation today, Det. Allen. You have been a delight, my dear."

Drying her hands, Erica said, "It's Erica, please, call me Erica."

"Well, Erica. Since you insist, let me get right to the point. I've known Dr. Webber for a long time. The last I knew he was dating Marsha and they were doing well. Nevertheless, I don't know where you came from or what your plans are where my Lionel is concerned but he means the world to me and my family and I don't want to see him hurt. He could have any woman he wants and he knows it but he's careful about who he chooses to spend his time with. So if you don't mean him any good, move out of the way for the next woman who will...dear heart."

The words coming from Dr. Gardner's mouth was not matching up with the smile on her face. Erica was slightly confused and didn't quite know how to respond. Dr. Gardner was like an overprotective fairy godmother mixed with a touch of Mary Poppins goodness.

Overwhelmed by Dr. Gardner's candor, Erica tried her best to come up with an appropriate response, "Whoa, wait a minute...I assure you Dr. Gardner, I don't mean Dr. Webber any harm. He and I met on a flight a few weeks ago and I never expected to meet him here and we've gotten reacquainted since yesterday and it has been nice. So far, I think he's a wonderful man."

Still drying her hands, Erica wondered, *"Overbearing much? I said call me Erica and this lady went in on me. Why am I telling her all of this, it's none of her business but in a way I feel like I better or she might get me or something...hold on...who is this Marsha chic?"*

Dr. Gardner took notice of herself in the mirror, making sure her coiffed hair was in place but also keeping her eyes directly on Erica.

Introducing a revelation, Dr. Gardner said, "I saw you with him last night and then again this morning. I invited you to lunch with us today so I could see you in action for myself. I like what I've seen and I especially like the look in Lionel's eyes when he looks at you. Whatever you're doing, don't stop because it's working."

Erica was beginning to feel more at ease, taking in the advice from the silver haired beauty. Her response to the older woman, "I'm not really doing anything other than being myself."

Stepping closer to Erica, Dr. Gardner shared some information, "Well then that's perfect dear. Be you and let him see that. In fact, we all see it. There is something most people here don't know, Lionel is my godson; his parents and I are old friends. His mother and I used to sing together way back in the day. We try to keep our personal and professional relationships separately but I thought you should know why I have such a vested interest in who my Lionel is taking up time with. We can't just have any 'ole body trying to come up in our family, I check out all contenders for Lionel's heart whether he knows it or not."

Dr. Gardner continued as she opened the door, "I think we should probably head back before they come looking for us. Right dear?"

Erica nodded, "Yes ma'am," she got the hint, *"Don't breathe a word to anyone about our little conference in the ladies room or I'll have to cut you."*

Lionel stood to welcome the two back to the table, "I was about to come check on you two. Everything okay?"

Patting Lionel on the shoulder, reassuring him, Erica sat down with a smile, looking over at Dr. Gardner, "Everything is just fine."

"Good. Hey listen, I don't know if you have plans for this evening, I know I've taken up a lot of your weekend. I have a college buddy who works for the Houston Flyers and he's gotten me tickets to the game tonight, courtside suite box tickets...would you be interested in going?"

Erica happened to look up and noticed Dr. Gardner looking at them, she nodded in approval for Erica to go along with Lionel to the game.

Shaking her head and laughing on the inside, "Heck yeah I want to go. Who would want to miss out on a chance to be courtside of a professional basketball game, I'm all in for that."

Jason perked up, "Suite box? Who said something about suite tickets, I want to go to the game tonight. How many tickets you got man?"

Lionel looked around the table, "I'll call my buddy and see what he can do. They may not be suite tickets but I'll see if he can round up a couple more tickets. Anyone else want to go?"

Lionel got a few takers on the offer. "Okay then, I'll check with him and let you guys know what the deal is shortly. It should be fun."

Lionel and Erica walked back across the street to the hotel, "It's all settled then, he's sending over a car later that'll take us over to the game. Let's plan to meet up in the lobby around 6:15, is that alright with you?"

"Yes sir doctor," Erica signing off like a soldier at attention.

Lionel held Erica's hand in his, "Until then pretty lady."

Erica reciprocated his gesture and squeezed his hand, "Until then."

CHAPTER 14

"Lionel, hey, can you hear me? It's us, shoot, did I do it right, are we all here? I can never get this three-way thing to work right."

"Yes, Laura I can hear you, who else is on the phone?"

"Hey Lionel, it's me, Lynda."

"Laura, you did it right. Hey y'all, what are you two doing?"

"Not a whole lot, Lynda and I wanted to call you because we both realized we didn't get a chance to talk with you much when we were all home the other week. We know you are in Houston at a conference so we won't keep you but we just wanted to check on you and see how you are doing."

"How did you know about me being in Houston?"

Lynda spoke up and revealed the source, "You know good and well Dylan told us. Since he's been home from Iraq recuperating he's making sure he knows what everyone is doing and where everyone is. Plus Lydia called mother and told her she was going to see you in Houston at the conference."

"Yeah, she's here; I had lunch with her today along with some other people."

In the Webber house, the boys looked out for their sisters but the sisters didn't play around when it came to their brothers, they all were very protective of each other. If something happened to one, it was as if it happened to all of them, even as adults. Which meant, they were all hurt by what Marsha had done to their brother.

Clearing her throat to make room for the matter at hand, Laura went for it, "Lionel, I just want you to know that you dodged a bullet with Marsha. She just wasn't right for you. Now that the word is out about you two, I have a friend at church that I'd like to introduce you to, she's a very nice girl and pretty too, you think you'd like to meet her?"

Lynda let out a theatrical groan, "Laura, there you go, always trying to play matchmaker. I can answer for him, N-O. He is not interested in meeting your friend."

Lionel was enjoying the playful banter between his younger sisters. He was grateful to have them call and check in on him and offer their support. The love of his family grounded him.

"Lionel, listen to me, don't listen to Laura. We all know you are the last one in the family to get married and you actually want to be married but you don't have to settle for someone who seems right just for the sake of getting married. One thing Laura did say was true, Marsha wasn't it."

"You know, all y'all are a trip, how is it now that it's over between us, everybody now saying she wasn't it. I got you two here now saying it and Leontyne said it when I was home. Y'all already know Liona was ready to fight the girl. You girls are something else, I should've heard this long before now."

Laura confessed to the conference call, "Truth is, I never liked her but mother told me to be nice. To be honest with you, I've never liked any of your girlfriends Lionel."

Lionel and Lynda cracked up on the phone listening to their sister's admission. "Leontyne told me the same thing about Mother, telling her to be nice to Marsha...that is hilarious."

Lynda shared with her siblings, "I just didn't get a warm and fuzzy from her when I met her but you seemed happy and that's what I tried to focus on. I only want what's best for you and what makes you happy."

Laura sneered at her sister's comment, "Well aren't you just the sweetest sister?"

Lynda shot back, "Oh hush Laura, and yes, I am the best sister. Lionel, if I can say anything to you that can help is to let God do it. When He does it, He does all things well. You know how we were raised. Mother always taught us to consult God about important things in our lives and Bubba, this is important. The bible says, He that finds a wife finds a good thing and obtains favor from the Lord. You need His help to find her Lionel."

When the children were smaller, they couldn't say brother, it would come out as Bubba and so often times, they would refer to their brothers as Bubba, even still to this day.

Lionel felt the need to assure his sisters, "I'm doing well you two. I tried to handle my break up with Marsha the best way I could. In some ways I think I did a good job and definitely in other areas I didn't do such a good job. Nevertheless, I released it all at church that Sunday we all were home and I'm over it now. I actually put God back in the driver's seat that day. I'm good, in fact, I'm great."

Both sister's chimed in, "Hallelujah, that's wonderful news."

Lynda started to cry, "Lionel, you just don't know how much I've been praying for you. Everything is going to work out, I see this thing with Marsha, like you should let it work towards your benefit not your detriment."

Lionel responded, "Don't cry sis. I think I may have already met someone but it's too early to tell so I'm taking my time to see if it will go anywhere."

The shrieks from his sisters made Lionel pull the phone from his ear, "Who is she, what's her name, where did you meet her?"

"I'm not telling y'all nothing, it'll be all over the news before I get back to town. If it goes anywhere y'all will be the first to know. Hey, I actually need to get ready, I'm getting ready to go out with some friends. I'm glad y'all called me though."

Laura had to try, "Is your new girlfriend in that group of friends you're going out with tonight?"

"Laura, I never said anything about a girlfriend. See how you are already starting rumors?" But to answer your question, yes, she will be there."

"Oh my goodness Laura, I can literally hear our brother blushing over the phone, I think he really likes this girl."

"I think you're right Lynda. What do you think he's going to wear girl, I know he's going to knock 'em dead. My brother is always looking fly."

"Uh ladies, I hate to interrupt as y'all talk about me like I'm not here but I'm about to hang up on you two. I love you both and I'll talk you with soon."

"We love you too Lionel and have fun tonight. Call us when you get back to San Antonio."

"Will do, bye."

CHAPTER 15

"So, I thought we were supposed to be painting the town of Houston red Allen, what has happened to you this weekend?"

"Morris, I know and I apologize. The craziest thing has happened. All I can say is that I met a guy named Lionel on a flight a few weeks back not having any idea that he was indeed the Dr. Webber who is here this weekend. The little I knew about him was from that most eligible bachelor article I saw in the beauty salon that all the women were fawning over. I recognized him on the flight from the article and we talked the entire flight but that was it. Suffice it to say, when I saw him here I was completely blown away. I went to speak to him after the opening session and we've been literally thrown together at these events all weekend."

Happy to hear the report from his partner, Det. Morris continued on, "So what do you make of it? Are you having a good time with him?"

"I'm not sure what to make of it, I've learned a lot about him over the last couple of days, he's quite an interesting person. I think so far, he's a wonderful man and yes, I'm enjoying my time with him; I'm having a blast. That's part of why I called you."

"What do you mean?"

"I know you guys were going to show me around Houston and I've been a no show since we've gotten here but I'm going to be going out with Dr. Webber and some of his friends to the basketball game tonight so I won't be able to hang out tonight either."

"Basketball game huh, Houston Flyers?"

"Yes and courtside suite seats too. I'm looking forward to it."

"Well Allen, that sounds great, I'm happy to hear you are enjoying yourself. Now depending upon how well things go with Dr. Webber are you telling me now on this day, on this phone, that you would be willing to stop all of your serial dating shenanigans? You know I worry about you with that, right?"

"Morris, depending upon how things go, I'm telling you this day, right now on this phone, that I would stop all of my shenanigans to go out with Dr. Webber."

"Wow, Allen I think we might be on to something here. I'm writing this down on my calendar. He seems to be a nice guy, I've enjoyed hearing him over the last two days."

"I know, he's great isn't he? He's such an amazing person and I'd like to get to know more. I like how I feel around him, he makes me smile."

"I will tell you though as happy as I am for you, there is one person who won't be happy to hear this news."

"And who might you be talking about Big Brother Morris?"

"Det. Brown doesn't appear to be happy about your connection with Dr. Webber. This weekend, I've watched her whole demeanor change when she's spotted you two and she's very upset you haven't been around to hang out with us."

"Well, I don't have time for her. She'll be alright. She really shouldn't concern herself with what's going on with me. I thought she had a man anyway?"

"I don't know anything about that but I'm just letting you know since you haven't been around and we do have a near three hour ride back home tomorrow."

"I appreciate it man, I can always count on you to have my back. What time are we leaving in the morning?"

"I need to leave early because I'd like to make it to my son's basketball game tomorrow afternoon. So probably around nine."

"Okay Morris, I'll be ready. I'll see you guys in the morning."

"Allen....have fun tonight. You deserve it."

CHAPTER 16

"Det. Allen huh? I told you earlier but you should hear it this time, you better be glad you got to her first man because I would have scooped her up the first minute I saw her, she's gorgeous."

Jason and Lionel were talking in the lobby as they waited for the remainder of their group to arrive to leave for the game.

"How long have you two been together because at last year's conference you were talking about someone named Marsha, I think."

Tugging at his corduroy jacket that coordinated well with his Houston Flyers t-shirt and faded indigo jeans, annoyed at even the mention of her name, he declared, "That was last year and this is another year, brother...Det. Allen and I are friends."

"So you won't mind if I try and holler then? You sure have been keeping her close to not have nothing going on between you two."

With a snort of dismissive laughter, Lionel stated his claim, "Try it and see what happens; I don't think you want to do that my man."

Jason knew something was going on, Lionel's words were not matching up to his actions. You could clearly see the connection they shared. He felt Lionel was being coy with him. When Erica walked into the lobby to greet them, Lionel's defensive disposition changed. There was an overall brightening of the entire lobby as Erica made her way towards the gentlemen, more specifically, to Lionel.

"Gentleman."

Lionel stood to greet Erica with a hug, "You look beautiful, as usual. We are waiting on a few more to come down and we'll be ready to go. The driver is already here to pick us up."

Checking his watch, Lionel decided to check on the others, "I'm going to go call and check on Arnold and his wife and Thomas and Gretchen. Will you two excuse me for a moment?"

Jason took advantage of the alone time with Erica, "So Det. Allen, how have you been enjoying the conference?"

Watching Lionel walk to the front desk, Erica was still thinking about how cute Lionel looked and how good he smelled when he stood to hug her. She was not interested in any small talk with Jason. Pretending to dig in her clutch, she looked up briefly and said, "It's been great, I'm having a great time and I'm looking forward to this evening. Thanks."

She was looking forward to having another opportunity to spend with Lionel.

Jason carried a twinkle of mischief in his eyes, he could tell something was going on between Erica and Lionel but if Lionel wouldn't admit it, he felt he'd push hard enough to make him. He thought he'd test the waters again, "So do you think I can buy you a drink while we wait?"

Erica shifted her weight in the cushy lobby chairs, "I don't drink and the only offers I'm accepting tonight will be from Dr. Webber."

Checking her makeup in her compact, she snapped it closed as she looked at Jason. His wide-eyed look from her response dissolved into laughter as Lionel walked back up to them with the rest of their party. Jason thought to himself, "*I knew it, she's just as smitten with Lionel as he is with her.*"

Lionel stood at the van assisting the women and at Erica's turn, he carefully helped her up saying, "Precious cargo here guys."

The other women swooned over his comment and the embarrassment from his kind words caused Erica to lose her footing as she stepped onto the van. Her heel got stuck and didn't follow her ascension into the van. She fell back into Lionel's arms, he was right there to catch her. Her ear was right by his mouth, "I got you...as I said, precious cargo, I'm not going to let anything happen to you."

As Lionel took his seat next to Erica, she disconnected for a moment, struggling with the thought, "*This can't be happening, I can't believe I almost fell. Darn heels, I knew these were too high for a basketball game. In front of his friends. Could this be any worse? I'm so embarrassed.*"

Lionel reached over and grabbed Erica's hand and squeezed it for a second, as a gesture of reassurance, to make her feel comfortable again. He could tell by her body language she was struggling, maybe a little embarrassed even and he didn't want a little slip to keep her from having a good time.

The squeeze of the hand seemed to change her mindset, she thought, "*While it was a little embarrassing, at the same time it was amazing. He was right there to catch me. I felt like I was in a movie or something.*" Thinking back on what he said when she landed in his arms, the words radiated through her body with a warming effect. The coldness she felt from the embarrassing slip was being melted away by Lionel's attentiveness.

The van pulled up into the VIP parking garage where Lionel's friend was awaiting their arrival. Corey Johnson and Lionel met during their sophomore year after dating twin sisters. Even though the relationships with the sisters was short lived, Corey and Lionel remained close friends throughout the years. Lionel was Corey's best man and was now getting ready to be the godfather to Corey's soon to be firstborn child, a son.

Corey was able to secure a suite for Lionel and his friends, after meeting everyone he escorted them to their courtside suite.

Upon entering the suite, Corey asked for Erica and Lionel to join him at the table in the middle of the room. "Erica, it is so nice to meet you, when I spoke with Lionel earlier and he told me you would be joining him this evening, he mentioned this was your first time ever to H-town."

"Yes, it is and I'm so happy I came here, much different than what I was expecting."

"Well, my wife is on bed rest so she couldn't be here tonight but we put together a welcome gift basket for you with some various things reflecting the things we love about Houston. We hope you like it and I hope you have a great time tonight at the game. I know my man here wants you to have a good time."

Doing a double take at the enormous gift basket, Erica was overwhelmed by the couple's ample consideration. "This can't be all for me?" Her hand graced her chest as she tried to digest their kindness towards her.

"I'm jealous, you guys didn't do this for me the first time I came to Houston."

"Man please, you know we set it out for you all the time. Quit playing."

Erica walked over to Corey, repeating thanks and appreciation, and gave him a hug of gratitude, "Please tell your wife, I love it and how grateful I am for this. Really, you guys didn't have to do this."

"I most certainly will tell her, I actually need to go finish up some work and then head home to her. It was an absolute pleasure meeting you, I'm certain this won't be the last time."

Corey exchanged a look of endorsement with Lionel and then he turned to leave them.

"Oh, hey guys, if you need anything tonight, there is concierge service waiting to assist you. You're food and drinks should be arriving soon. Enjoy the game."

Lionel was all smiles, the night was already turning out great and now Thomas was calling everyone over to the player tunnel windows. The group stood and cheered at the window looking out as the Houston Flyers team made their way out onto the court.

The servers arrived and everyone tackled their first round of food and drinks for the night. Tip-off was to start in the next twenty minutes.

"Hey there, are you having a good time?" Juliet, the wife of one of the conference participants asked Erica off to the side while refreshing her drink.

Nodding before actually answering, Erica tried to control how much of a great time she was indeed having. She wondered about why Juliet was choosing to talk to her. She was curious if this lady was going to be another Dr. Gardner like earlier or was she really just trying to be the homey. "I'm actually having a nice time tonight, how about you?"

Juliet expressed with delight, "I'm having a great time, I've never been to a professional basketball game before and for my first time to see it like this is great."

Erica agreed, "I know what you mean, this is really nice."

"Hey, I hope I'm not being too much all in your business but I just wanted to offer you a little female solidarity and encouragement, you know us ladies have to stick close so we can support our men. I travel with my husband to all of his conferences and we see Lionel all of the time. I don't know if it's you or the success from this year's conference, but I've never seen him this happy...even when he was with Marsha."

For a brief moment, Erica's neck bent forward, *"Is she crazy? I just met the man and she's already trying to recruit me to the tech nerd wives club? What is up with these women that keep telling me about this Marsha chick? I would never bring up the reject to the prospect....but I think I do need to find out why I keep hearing about this Marsha person."*

Tugging at her earlobe and looking at Juliet, "Well in the spirit of female solidarity, who is Marsha and why did you feel the need to mention her to me?"

Standing solidly, ready to spill the beans about Marsha, Juliet moved in closer to Erica, "Girl –", hearing their names being called, Juliet held up one finger, "Hold that thought, the game is starting."

Feeling let down somewhat from not hearing about the infamous Marsha, Erica put on a smile for an unsuspecting Lionel.

Lionel grabbed Erica by the hand, "C'mon, let's go and have some fun."

CHAPTER 17

"Happy Birthday Samantha, oh my....on this day thirty-five years ago, I gave birth to a beautiful baby girl. A baby girl who has grown up into a beautiful woman, a women that I'm proud to call my daughter. Happy birthday baby, how has your day been so far?"

"Thank you mama. My day has been something else to say the least."

"How so, did your kids do something special for you?"

"Yes, my kids did something, one of my room moms put together a party and they all pitched in for a gift. It was nice. But some of my so called coworkers are just plain evil....evil I tell you. Apparently some people who had nothing better to do thought they'd try and embarrass me on my birthday."

"What happened baby?"

"When I came back to my room from getting the kids from lunch, my office was filled with all sorts of party decorations, balloons, streamers, signs, you name it."

"Well that doesn't sound embarrassing Samantha."

"Wait. I haven't gotten to the good part. The signs were posted on the walls and they read: Happy Birthday to the 40 Year Old Virgin, The 40 Year Old Virgin; It's Your Birthday. I walked over to my desk where they had a cake with a tag attached, Better Than Sex Cake."

Samantha's voice began to give way.

Filling her mother in to the obnoxious details, she said, "The kids were all excited to see the balloons and the streamers, they thought we were having another party. I think I blanked out for a minute because I couldn't believe what I was seeing. I rushed in the office to turn off the lights so they wouldn't be able to read the signs. I sagged up against one of the walls for a second to collect myself before going back out to the children. They were ready to party some more while my heart felt like it was shrinking."

Samantha's mother, Ernestine experienced a slow build from a low cackle to a full-fledge belly laugh.

Slamming her hand down on the table, Samantha yelled, "Mama, I can't believe you are laughing at what I just told you. I just told you that some people on my job tried to humiliate me, no, I take that back, they were actually quite successful in humiliating me by trying to make me older than I am and make fun of something that I truly hold near and dear to me."

"I'm laughing because that's what the Lord does honey. Fret not yourself because of evil doers, the word says when these people make plans and schemes against good people, the Lord laughs, He considers them a joke because He knows their time is short lived. Earlier this morning I came across a devotion that blessed me so and I'm starting to think I read it today to be able to share with you. I'm not going to preach to you on your birthday so when you get a chance, I want you to read over Psalms 37 and meditate on it for a little bit."

"I'll look at it but mama, I have to say that what they did hurt me...on my birthday, I can't believe that. The truth of the matter is, I am still a virgin but it's because I want to be but real talk....I'm tired of waiting mama."

Through the phone Ernestine could feel her daughter's strains of desperation.

Samantha continued, "I'm so sick and tired of hearing people say, "You're so pretty, why aren't you married...like that has something to do with it. I don't think people really give thought to what they say sometimes. Like, I hate hearing every mother's day, when am I going to be able to wish you a Happy Mother's day...again, like I have anything to do with it."

Ernestine offered up a deep sigh followed up with thoughtful expressions, "Samantha, you know what the bible says about waiting[5]. Listen here, when you and your brothers and sister were younger, I shared with you all about covenants and how the shedding of blood was symbolic for entering into covenant relationships, it had a profound impact on you. You were sixteen at the time and with tears in your eyes, you came to us and said when you got married you wanted to be able to have your husband cut covenant with you through the shedding of your blood on your wedding night. Now you are a beautiful woman, you could have gone out and gone back on your commitment, you've had plenty of opportunities but I think this thing really means something to you. Listen honey, you can't base your life choices from the comments of others."

Samantha's body temperature slowly began to rise, in a way she knew her mother was right but it didn't take away the feelings she was presently experiencing.

"Samantha, don't let a joke from a few good for nothing teachers get you off track. Now don't get me wrong, I'd love to go down there and ring their little scrawny behind necks but I'm not going to do that. We are going to see who has the last laugh. You are one of the best teachers the entire school district has ever seen. You go way above and beyond the call

---

[5] **Isaiah 40:31**: "But they that wait upon the LORD shall renew their strength; they shall mount up with wings as eagles; they shall run, and not be weary; and they shall walk, and not faint."

of duty as it relates to your students. You don't see your job as teaching but nurturing and investing, you are sowing seeds of change in the lives of these young people and baby trust me, your labor is not in vain. Your students always have the highest marks and you are constantly being recognized for all of your hard work. That is the real reason you got that nice surprise in your office today. Unfortunately, our best sometimes brings out the worse in others and it shouldn't be like that but it is...you've lived long enough to see that."

"Yeah, I guess you have a point there, I never really thought about it like that. But mama, hear me out though; I think I'm like the only adult virgin left on earth. Plus, do you know how many weddings I've not only been in but have gone to in the last several months? If I'm not going to weddings, I'm being invited to baby showers, and birthday parties for other people's children."

The sobs got louder and louder with each occasion she mentioned.

In anguish, Samantha inquired, "I really want to know when is it going to be my turn mama? I'm tired of waiting, I'm ready mama; I really am. I'm trying to do the right thing and people are around here making fun of me for it."

"Samantha Grace Richards, let me ask you something. How long would you be willing to wait for the blessing? That's all I have for you right now. I know it hasn't been easy but what sacrifice is? How long girl? I'm telling you, make sure you go ahead and read that chapter. Samantha choose to trust the Lord and I guarantee, He will see you through this. Or you can go out and do it your way and then see what you get, you decide."

Ernestine felt the words coming from her mouth welling up in her belly as they came out with a forced twinge filled with love and encouragement. She'd lived long enough to see women like her daughter who were not willing to wait end up in worse situations.

"I'm not a betting woman but if I were, I'd put money on the women that didn't wait on God and went out and got husbands not ordained by Him, wish they had waited. Likewise, for the women that did wait, I'm willing to bet they are grateful they did. Honey, I'm telling you, there is a reward in the waiting. You think you are ready for marriage but let me tell you, you don't even know how it's spelled. Did you know marriage is actually spelled W-O-R-K?"

Samantha belted out a chuckle through her tears, "Mama, c'mon on now."

Staying steadfast on her convictions, Ernestine continued, "I'm serious honey, no matter who you end up with or the circumstances around it, whether you are a virgin or a veteran, you are going to have to put in some serious work in order to have a successful marriage. So it would seem to me that you should want to make sure that you've chosen the right person to share the work of marriage with. God knows honey, He sees all and knows all and I know without a shadow of a doubt He has someone crafted just for you."

"Okay mama, you don't have to call me by my whole name and you don't have to go off on me like that. I'm going to read it, in fact, I'll read it before I meet up with you all for my birthday dinner tonight. I have one other thing I'm going to do before I get ready too."

"Oh yeah and what is that Samantha, you don't want to be late and have everyone waiting, I mean I know you are the guest of honor and all but I'm sure everyone will be ready to celebrate with you."

"How about one of the other things on my desk was a one month subscription to an online dating website. I'm so sure they were trying to be funny but guess what, I'm going to take them up on their offer and create a profile and see what happens. After my last break up, I did think about giving online dating a try."

It had been six months since Samantha and Nolan had broken up, they were in the process of making decisions about marriage and one day out of the blue, he decided he wasn't ready to settle down. He said he felt a call to serve on the mission field for a while.

While Samantha didn't quite believe Nolan, she decided she was in no position to discredit someone's calling.

"Well Samantha, I think that's a good idea. That's how young people are meeting up and dating these days, you never know who you might meet. You know the bible says he that findeth a wife, not she that findeth, I guess you are going to use technology to increase your chances of being found, huh? I guess in this case, nothing beats a failure but a try."

Giggling at her mother's new found appreciation for choosing to meet people online Samantha responded, I guess you're right, the only thing that beats a failure is a try and mama, oh and to answer your question, for the right blessing, I'd be willing to hold out forever."

Ernestine closed her eyes with her hand to her chest as she listened to her daughter, "I'll see you later tonight Samantha and know this, when you're willing to wait forever, you won't have to wait very long. I love you."

CHAPTER 18

Harold muttered under his breath as he also tried to figure out what was going on, "Wait, hold up, this can't be happening, I have another match?"

Another match had come through from his profiles on his dating website.

In all of the years of the site's existence, he barely received any bites on his profiles but this was the tenth one this week. For the last few weeks, he'd been talking to women and even daring to meet a few for dinner.

Strangest thing, those he'd chosen to meet up with were not the women he thought he was going to meet.

The security breach on his site was the cause for the mix ups. The last date was a complete disaster, they were actually having a good time after the confusion was cleared up but in the middle of dinner, the woman's husband showed up.

Harold began to think the single life was his destiny, any hopes of finding true love seemed to be a waste of his time.

He'd convinced himself to believe that he'd rather work and make more money, that having a family wasn't all that important, or was it?

Not only did he not grow up with his parents, he never even knew them.

Growing up without them, in unstable environments, Harold dreamed of having his own family one day, a beautiful wife, a bunch of kids, and a dog all in a house they would call their own, the typical American dream.

Winning the money didn't help him achieve that goal because it clouded the judgments of most of the women. Most of them only wanted to be with him because of it and Harold could always tell. He'd developed a sixth sense around women and their intentions.

It wasn't hard to become consumed with work and withdrawn from the dating scene, however, his recent reintroduction to dating made him hopeful that maybe this time he might find someone.

However, he still had the problem with the security breach, either keep getting mixed up matches or correct the problem and stop getting matches all together.

Picking up the phone, he dialed Leonard, "Hey, I know Det. Allen is coming to meet us next week about the investigation to the site but I think I'd like to get an opinion from an actual security professional. Find me the best consultant in the city and patch me through to a call with whoever you find. I'd like to include them in that Monday morning meeting as well."

Leonard obliged, "You got it Harold; I'll get back with you shortly."

Shortly after hanging up with Leonard, Harold received a notification. He'd been alerted to another potential match up.

Harold looked at the latest match he'd received, "*Hmm, should I try to pursue this match since I know it's probably all screwed up or just leave well enough alone? SRich35 huh? Who are you really Ms. SRich35?*"

Starting and stopping with uncertainty as to what to do next, Harold experienced an array of opposing emotions. With no one else in the room, he started a conversation with himself as to see whether or not he should respond.

Harold started out by saying, "Something is telling me I should respond but I don't know because my site is all jacked up right now. This is the first time in years that I've had so much activity on my profile, do I really want to mess that up, even if it is all wrong?"

Voicing more and more of his conflict as he paced the floor, "This is a tough decision, I've enjoyed the attention and talking to these women, even if half of them are crazy. Who am I kidding, I'm crazy. What if I'm not who she thinks I am, then what? Another disaster. Do I really want the drama or the rejection? If they fix the problem, the matches will go away but if they don't fix it, I will continue to lose members on the site."

Unable to wait to hear back from Leonard, Harold called him again. "Hey, uh Leonard, have you found anyone yet, I really need to know if you've found that consultant?"

Picking up on his boss' anxiety, Leonard tried to calm his employer down, "Hey there, I was actually about to call you. I found a guy who comes highly recommended, his name is Dr. Lionel Webber. He's supposedly the best in the business, my contacts assured me you won't be disappointed. I had to call in a few favors to track down a number for him. You know, it is the weekend and from what I understand he's at a conference out of town. But I did get his cell number. Let's try and call him and see if we can set up that meeting."

"Good work Leonard, before you call him, hang on a second, I need to do something real quick."

Harold paused for a moment to send his newest match a message, **"Good evening, it seems that you and I have**

been matched up. Please respond if you're interested
in talking further."

He couldn't take the chance, the feeling wouldn't leave
him alone; he needed to reach out to her, even if the site had
made another mistake.

"Okay Leonard, I'm ready now, make the call."

CHAPTER 19

"What a great half-time show. Erica, can I get you something while I'm up?"

"No thanks Lionel, I'm fine for now."

As soon as Lionel left, Erica hopped up and made a b-line towards Juliet, only Juliet didn't see her coming and she walked out of the suite hand in hand with her husband. *"Dang it, Juliet...where are you going, you and I need to finish our conversation."*

"Hey Erica, would you like to sit on the floor during the second half of the game or stay inside the suite?" Lionel stood smiling as he waited for Erica to respond, hoping she'd want to go.

"I'd love to, the suite is nice but I'd like to partake in some floor time as well, I want to take in the whole experience, you know what I mean."

"I agree, shall we?"

Locking arms, Erica smirked, "We shall."

Within minutes of them being seated and getting settled, the unexpected happened. The kiss-cam came on and by chance or happenstance, who did it stop on....Erica and Lionel.

Caught up in each other's conversation, they hadn't even noticed, they guy next to Lionel tapped him on the arm and pointed to the jumbo-tron.

The two looked up and were immediately embarrassed, yet excited, is this how the first kiss would happen? Being the gentlemen he is, Lionel asked was she alright with it and the grin on her face answered for her. This happened all within seconds, Lionel reached in and grabbed Erica's face, with her eyes closed and both hearts racing, Lionel reached in and kissed her softly on her forehead.

The entire audience clapped and cheered at his gesture. It was quite an endearing sight between two people.

"*Forehead, really?*" Erica didn't see it as such but she tried to play it off well, yet Lionel could see her disappointment.

Leaning in close to her ear, his warm breath seemed to revive her spirit and breathe breath back into her, "When we share our first kiss, I don't want it to be in front of a basketball crowd for a quick second and a gimmick. This would have been memorable but I want our first kiss to be magical."

Despite being seated, Erica felt as if her knees buckled from under her. At that very moment, the heavens opened up and struck. She felt the elusive bolt in her stomach her mother always talked about. Her mother believed and instilled in Erica and her sister when they found 'The One' the sign would be like a bolt of lightning hitting them in the pits of their stomach.

She'd never felt it before until that very moment with Lionel. The longer she sat in that moment and the feeling, the more freaked out she became. She couldn't sit there another minute, she excused herself from the court; "I'll be right back, Lionel."

Charging towards the ladies room, Erica nervously dialed her mother, "Mommy, mommy please pick up, pick up, pick up the phone."

"Hey honey, what's going on?"

Pacing back and forth down the hallway, Erica stopped when she heard the comforting voice of her mother.

"Oh mommy, you are never going to believe this. It's happened....Or at least I think it has."

Helen's mind began to race as she searched for a possible answer to what her daughter was referring to, she couldn't pinpoint the tremble in Erica's voice, "Uh, honey...what do you mean, what's happened?"

Erica was holed up in a corner, with her back against the wall, with teary eyes, she whispered, "The sign mommy, the one you always told us about, it just happened to me and I'm freaking out about it...I think I may be in love. It's just so crazy because it's all happening so fast but I just felt the bolt of lightning hit my stomach like you described to us."

Helen squealed, hooted and hollered, "Who, what, when, where, how honey, tell me everything, I need details."

Erica filled her mother in all of the events surrounding around the whirlwind named Lionel. "Mommy, this man is nothing short of amazing, he –."

Interrupting her daughter, "Honey, did you say that you left this amazing man on the floor at the basketball game all by himself?"

"Yes ma'am, why?"

In a true motherly expression, Helen sat straight up and pointed her finger as if Erica was right in front of her while making a pointed suggestion, "Girl, you better listen to me...you better get your behind back to that man right now. If everything you are telling me is correct, trust me when I tell you, women are always circling, they circle like sharks. If you feel like he might be it, you better go stay close to your man. You and I can talk later, now go on girl."

Erica belted out a laugh deep from within her belly, "Alright, alright, you've talked me sane again; I guess I just needed to talk to my mama. I'll call you when I get back home tomorrow; I love you mommy."

As Erica walked back to Lionel on the floor, she stopped in step at the scene before her, *"Dang, mommy wasn't lying, who is this woman sitting in my seat?"*

Catching sight of Erica, Lionel motioned for her to come over. "Erica, there is someone here who wants to meet you."

Squinting her eyes, Erica asked, "Someone wants to meet me?"

"Yes, good evening Ms. Allen, my name is Alexis Byrne and I'm the in-house publicist for the Houston Flyers and I have some exciting information for you. Please, do you mind if we go back to your suite to discuss?"

Inside the suite, Alexis explained, "During the kiss-cam, the two of you were captured on there with Lionel kissing you on the forehead. Apparently someone caught it on video and has now uploaded it to all of their social media accounts with the following hash tags, **#foreheadkiss, #HoustonFlyers, #BBallLove**. The video and the hash tags are currently trending across all networks, in all of the franchise history, nothing like this has ever happened. People want to know more about the couple in the video. I wouldn't be worth my salary if I didn't see this as an opportunity to endear our fans with more of the Houston Flyers, and especially a Houston Flyers love story.

Holding her palms up to stop Alexis from dumping on more in an effort to catch up while Lionel sat grinning, Alexis stopped to ask, "Are you okay Ms. Allen?"

Erica sat down exclaiming, "I'm really trying to understand all of what you are saying, this is totally unbelievable to me. It feels as if I'm living in a dream and I keep thinking I'm going to wake up at any moment."

Alexis stretched her arms out wide, echoing Erica's dialogue, "Ms. Allen, I couldn't have said it better myself, you have summed up the situation quite perfectly; you guys are like a real-life fairy tale."

Checking her tablet with the latest stats of the video, "Hey guys, this video has 'gone viral' written all over it. Now this has all come about within the last hour so I haven't had time to really put together a proposal but off the top I'm thinking of putting together a campaign where we feature the two of you as a couple for the remaining part of the regular season. Hopefully with our two new good luck charms, we will make it to the playoffs and then we'd look to do more segments with you. So what do you guys think, please tell me you're on board."

Grabbing Erica's hand and remaining steady and cool, Lionel looked at Alexis saying, "Whatever Erica is comfortable with, I'm fine with."

Erica looked at both Lionel and Alexis and then said, "Alexis, do you mind if Lionel and I have a moment alone?"

"Sure thing, I'll grab a drink."

Trying to keep her composure, Erica turned to Lionel, "This is crazy, huh?"

"I guess it all depends on how you define crazy. I actually think it's great. Nothing like this has ever happened to me in my life and it's happening with you. To be honest, I love the idea but I'm only going to go along with what you are most comfortable with."

The talk with her mother began to bounce off the walls of her brain, *"He's right, this has been the best weekend in my entire life and right now I don't care if it is a dream, I'm going to live in this for as long as I can."*

As Erica stood thinking Alexis approached them, "So, do we have a deal or not, are we ready to make history? With what's going on here, we have an opportunity to take social media by storm and keep the Houston Flyers name out there. I think it's brilliant, good move with the forehead kiss Lionel."

Squeezing Lionel's hand ever so tightly, Erica responded, "Let's do it."

"Great, I'll be in touch with you two concerning details, I understand you're leaving tomorrow but I'll set up a video conference for next week. Sound good?"

They both replied, "Sounds good to us." Erica and Lionel shook hands with Alexis and she rushed off through the doors of the suite.

CHAPTER 20

"Happy birthday to you, happy birthday to you, happy birthday dear Samantha, happy birthday to you." The small group of family and friends serenaded Samantha as she entered into the private dining area reserved for her birthday dinner.

One by one they all stood to greet and hug her. She knew everyone with the exception of one guest, Joshua Ewing. "Happy birthday Samantha, I'm friends with your brother and he invited me here tonight."

Samantha's brother, Caleb walked by and whispered in Samantha's ear, "You can thank me later sis."

Joshua Ewing, a beacon of light in the State of Texas regarding juvenile delinquents and the answer to many single mother's prayers. A social entrepreneur by profession but big brother to many personally. Seeing his young cousins getting caught up with the wrong crowds and getting into trouble due to the lack of fathers in their homes, he founded the Ewing Leadership Academy. The mission, to provide a comprehensive program for misguided young men to receive a high quality education and support in areas of leadership, spirituality, public service, athletics, and discipline.

Joshua's organization goes into the juvenile court systems and petitions judges across the state of Texas on behalf of first-time offenders in exchange of punishments to have the teens remanded to him and his court-diversion program. In only his fourth year of service to the young men, the Academy is already boasting a 100% college placement rate.

As everyone returned to their seats, Samantha was escorted to the head of the table and the seat next to her was where Joshua had his belongings, "You don't mind if I sit next to the birthday girl do you?"

To Samantha, time seemed to be slowing down, she couldn't believe such a fine looking man was seated next to her on her birthday especially after the stunt her coworkers pulled earlier.

"No, not all, please let's sit down." Responding with pleasant chivalry, Joshua took her coat and pulled out her chair.

During the entire dinner, the table was filled with chatter and laughter, the room was festive and appropriate for a birthday celebration.

Joshua and Samantha talked the entire time, getting to know one another better. Laughing at one of Joshua's jokes, Samantha threw her head back and as she looked back up, she saw her mother motioning for her to come to her seat.

"Excuse me for a moment, will you Joshua?"

On the walk down to her parents, Samantha could feel Joshua's eyes fixated on her.

"Yes, mother dear, I see I've been summoned."

"When we talked earlier, I thought I told you not to be late to your own birthday dinner. I promise girl, you were born prematurely but since then, you've been late to everything else in your life."

Samantha leaned in forward towards her mother and spoke in a soft yet excitable tone, "I know mama but I did go ahead and set up a profile on that dating site and guess what,

I've already gotten so many hits, I'm actually scheduled to have coffee with a guy tomorrow after work."

Ernestine hesitated for a second, "From the looks of it, you might not need to have that profile much longer considering the young man seated next to you."

With a good-natured push and getting the giggles with her mother, "I know right mama, this is turning out to be a great birthday after all. Who knew? I'll definitely have to thank Caleb for bringing Joshua here tonight, he seems to be a great person."

"Hey, you mentioned you'd received several suitors, what made you decide to have coffee with this one guy tomorrow? I hope you're being careful."

"Well, you know I'm very new to this and so I'm really having to trust my gut, my spirit, you know what I mean? When I came across his message, it was very generic, not all flashy like some I'd come across in just a short period of time. You'd be surprised at how some of the guys, who claim to be Christians, seem to find a way to turn the conversations sexual. Can you believe that? Oh and trust me, I'm being very careful, I haven't shared any of my contact information and we're meeting in a public place."

Ernestine verbalized her shock, "Are you serious, you young people, I tell you."

"Anyway mama, this guy...his name is Harold and from a few email conversations, he seems to be quite genuine, so we shall see. I'll call you after our little coffee date and fill you in."

"Did you read that chapter before you came?"

Samantha's eyes sparkled as she got up to return to her seat, "Can't you tell?"

With Joshua standing to greet Samantha back to her seat, she noticed how well the skinny charcoal grey and white striped tie rested upon his towering and chiseled torso.

"Did you have a nice chat with your mother?"

"I sure did, are you having a good time tonight?"

Joshua added, "If I didn't know any better, I'd think you two were talking about me; and to answer your question about tonight, the best."

Blushing and being playful at the same time, Samantha responded, "What would have ever given you that idea?"

The pleasant teasing was interrupted as the servers came into the room with a delightful display of a birthday cake adorned with brilliantly-lit candles that sparkled in the room's lighting. Another round of Happy Birthday was sang and everyone enjoyed their dessert.

Near the end of the evening, Joshua took a chance and asked, "Hey, Samantha. I, uh have enjoyed your company and conversation tonight and would like to know if you'd join me for dinner tomorrow evening?"

Samantha smoothed out her cream and gold sheath dress as she thought back on her previous commitment with Harold but certainly not wanting to miss an opportunity to go out with Joshua. She tossed around the idea, "*I'm meeting Harold after work, late afternoon, so I can go meet him and still have time to meet Joshua for dinner...yes, that's what I'll do. A girl needs options, right?*"

"Joshua, I would love to join you for dinner tomorrow night."

CHAPTER 21

"Oh my goodness, can you believe the sun is starting to rise?"

Lionel and Erica had been in the lobby all night after returning from the basketball game. They weren't ready to stop riding the wave they had been on, it had been a wonderful evening.

Lionel checked the time, "I was planning on hitting the road around nine this morning, and since you've kept me up all night, I think it's only fair you ride back with me to keep me awake on the road."

Erica made a sweeping motion where she threw her head back and placed her hand over her chest, "Oh, I kept you up all night?"

Lionel smiled as he scooted in closer to her, "Yes, you did ma'am. I don't see how anyone would even want to sleep when they have an opportunity to be in your presence."

Erica rolled her eyes, "Oh please give me a break; you're laying it on a little thick aren't you?"

Lionel placed his hand on Erica's neck and cupped it, "What I'd like to do is give you a kiss."

Lionel's kiss touched Erica deep within, deep enough to unlock feelings she didn't think she'd ever feel after Patrick. She sensed the magic he referenced at the game.

Lionel peeled back and said softly, "Was that thick enough for you?"

With her eyes still closed and her lips still puckered, Erica replied, "Oh yes and I think I'll take you up on that ride."

"Now that's what I'm talking about. How about we go get changed and ready to check out. Do you think you'll be ready by nine?"

Erica stretched and yawned, "Yes, I might even try and catch me a little nap."

Lionel stood and reached out for Erica's hand to help her up.

"I guess I need to let Morris know I'm going to ride with you, I haven't seen those guys since we got here on Friday."

"I'm sure they will be alright, let's go on up and I'll see you in a couple of hours."

As Lionel and Erica were parting ways, she ran into Det. Brown who was on her way to the fitness center.

Erica stopped her and asked, "Oh hey girl, how's it going?"

Det. Brown wasn't all that excited to see her colleague, "Good morning stranger, funny seeing you down here. I came down here to get a work out in before we leave this morning."

Erica raised her finger, "Oh yes, about that. I'm not riding back with you guys. Just let Morris know I'll see him in the morning at that meeting, he and I are starting a case tomorrow."

"What case?"

"It's a case we've been assigned dealing with a security breach, I've already met with the company but we have a meeting with them in the morning."

Det. Brown drank from her bottled water, "I'll tell him but I need to point out that you were the one all excited about coming here and hanging out and you have been M.I.A. the entire weekend and now you aren't even riding back with us."

Erica gushed, "I know right. I'm sorry I didn't hang with y'all and I'm sorry that I'm not riding back but when duty calls, you have to answer right?"

Det. Brown scoffed, "What duty are you talking about?"

With sheer delight, Erica answered, "Girlfriend duties honey. My new boyfriend wants me to ride back with him which is why I'm not riding back with you all. In fact, I actually need to get going so I can get myself together. I'll see you girl, y'all be safe on the road; I'll see you in the morning."

Det. Brown watched Erica walk towards the elevator as she drank another sip from her bottle, "Your new boyfriend, huh?"

CHAPTER 22

"It's a shame what happened to Morris huh Allen?"

Erica looked at Det. Brown and rolled her eyes saying, "I just don't get why someone would try to hurt him and especially while he was at his son's basketball game."

During Morris' son's basketball game, he walked out to his car to grab his headphones so he could hear what the sports radio station was broadcasting about his son.

Before he could make it back inside, two masked men drove up and cornered him off. They jumped out of the car, attacked Morris, and left him on the side of the road, bruised and bleeding, crying out for help.

Inside, his son was playing his best game yet.

Not missing a beat, Det. Brown asked, "So, what time do you want to leave for that meeting?"

"I'd like to leave in about an hour, I've emailed you the case file so you can get up to speed before we go."

With Morris' violent assault, he would be out for a few days, leaving Erica without a partner. Det. Brown was now assigned to Erica during Morris' time off.

"I'm going to go down to the next floor to see if those guys have any leads on who may have done this Morris, I'll be back before it is time for us to leave."

"Alright Allen, take your time, I'll be here carefully reviewing this file."

Det. Brown glossed over the file, not with particular interest but enough the get the basics. Closing the file she looked up to see a floral delivery guy on their floor carrying a lovely bouquet of flowers.

"Good morning, I'm looking for Det. Allen, I have a delivery for her."

Det. Brown stood up, "If these flowers are for her then I'm Detective Allen."

Det. Brown reached in her desk drawer and tipped the delivery guy and sent him on his way.

Instead of placing the flowers on Erica's desk, she put them on her own and commenced to reading the card that read:

Beautiful flowers to a beautiful woman to whom I had a beautiful weekend. Looking forward to many more.
- Lionel

Brown smirked as she thought, "*Sorry Erica, you won't be getting these beauties today, they look better on my desk than yours anyway.*"

In no time, Det. Brown tore up the card and tossed it in the waste basket at her desk.

Erica walked back towards her desk, "Hey lady, you think you're about ready to go?"

Sitting with a Cheshire cat grin on her face, Det. Brown responded, "Yes, I'm ready to go but before we leave come look at what my boyfriend sent me."

Erica admired the lavish display of flowers, "This guy knows how to treat a lady; you better hold onto him girl."

Det. Brown agreed, "I couldn't agree with you more Allen, I'm going to do my best. Let's go."

The two women exited the building and drove to Johnson Enterprises.

CHAPTER 23

"Dr. Webber, you have no idea how happy we are you decided to consult with us. We feel privileged to have you on board. We're just waiting on two more to join us before we get started."

"Harold, it's my pleasure to be here. Ian and I have an unlimited amount of favor cards and if he's calling me for one then I know it's important. He told me you guys were in a bind and needed help so I'm here."

"I'm sorry I had to call you while you were at that conference, speaking of that, how was it? Weren't you one of the speakers?"

As Lionel was answering, he didn't see the two women walk into the conference room as his back was facing the door.

"The conference was awesome, I had a blast. It was the best weekend I've had in a very long time."

Leonard stood to greet the ladies, Harold and Lionel followed suit.

Leonard went to make the introductions when Lionel interrupted by saying, "There is no need to make introductions, I already know these two."

Lionel tried to play off seeing Erica and she did likewise.

Lionel speculated, *"If she's the detective on this case, I wonder how is this going to impact our relationship?"*

Erica wondered, *"Am I now involved in a workplace romance? Should we disclose to them that Lionel and I are dating? This just got weird."*

Det. Brown thought, *"I've just hit the jackpot. This should be real good."*

Leonard started out the meeting by handing over the items he'd promised Erica he'd have for her by the next meeting.

As he passed out the information, he asked, "Dr. Webber, this breach is hurting us, our customers are losing confidence in us. This didn't seem to be a concern of ours until it happened, are other companies finding this to be true?"

Lionel approached the subject with ease, "Unfortunately for others but fortunate for me, cyber security threats and cybercrimes are on a rapid incline. I'm of the mindset this trend should not be ignored."

Everyone at the table listened intently to Lionel speak.

Lionel directed his attention to Leonard, "Leonard, let me ask you this, when I took a brief look at your system, I didn't notice an IDS, do you have one?"

In an uncertain tone, both Leonard and Harold asked, "What is that?"

Before Lionel could respond, Erica answered the question instead, "IDS is short for an Intrusion Detection System, long story short, it monitors the network looking for suspicious activity, it signifies a hack or an attempted intrusion."

Lionel smiled and nodded, he was impressed, "Det. Allen is correct. If it detected anything it would send alerts or in some instances lock down the system until further investigation was done."

Leonard accepted responsibility, "I'm the I.T. director and I wasn't aware of such a thing."

Lionel assured him, "No need to blame yourself, this is a problem for corporations worldwide, you aren't the only one. The good news is, I'm here to help you close any vulnerabilities that would make you more susceptible to other attacks."

Harold followed up behind Leonard, "Detectives, do you have what you need to continue on with the investigation?"

Lionel interjected, "The drives they have include server logs, network logs, data collected from the website logs, source codes, date and time stamps, and IP addresses of all site users."

Erica held up the portable, external hard drive, "As soon as I get back to the office, my partner and I will get started sifting through all of this information."

Harold gave a two-fingered salute, "I'm confident with this team we've assembled, we'll get to the bottom of this."

The meeting was adjourned and the attendees broke off into separate groups to chit chat. Lionel made a beeline over to Erica.

"Missed me that much huh?"

"And how much is that?"

"So much that you got yourself assigned to a case I'm consulting on?"

"In your dreams Webber; I was on this case long before you."

Lionel moved closer into Erica's personal space and whispered, "I'm just messing around with you but you were in my dreams last night."

Erica's cheeks burned from blushing but she maintained her composure, "So, does this change anything with us? What is the protocol here, should we disclose the nature of our relationship?"

Lionel spoke evenly, "It doesn't change anything for me, in fact, I think it'll be great working with you, helping you to catch the bad guys. Harold and I are becoming fast friends, I'll talk to him and give him the heads up. If he has a problem with it, I'll just quit...simple as that."

Det. Brown walked over without an invitation and joined their conversation, "Dr. Webber, I thoroughly enjoyed your presentation at the conference and I look forward to working very closely with you on this case."

Erica stood and watched her partner in utter amazement, she was bold. Erica realized in that moment, working with her as her partner was going to be an adventure.

Lionel cleared his throat, "Thanks detective, I believe this is probably going to be one of the most interesting cases I've ever worked on."

Det. Brown tried to conclude the meeting by saying, "So Dr. Webber, we have our work cut out for us, I think it's time for Det. Allen and I to leave now."

With a nice-nasty smile, Erica replied, "I'm right behind, you can go ahead to the car if you need to Det. Brown. I'm going to finish up here and say good-bye to Harold and Leonard."

Lionel inquired, "Hey, I thought your partner was a guy?"

"Long story, I'll have to fill you in later."

"Sounds good, meet me for dinner later?"

"I'd love to, just so long as you wear that shirt. You're looking rather handsome in it."

"If that's the case, I need to either buy me a case of these or buy more laundry detergent because I'm never wearing another shirt."

The two laughed and smiled as Harold and Leonard

walked over, "Sounds like too much fun is happening over here, is this what I'm paying you for Lionel?"

"No, not at all but I believe in every great achievement at some point they broke down and had a little bit of fun, right?"

"Harold, my friend, you don't have anything to worry about, Det. Allen and I make an excellent team."

CHAPTER 24

"I can't tell if this rumbling in my stomach is nerves or that chili I had for lunch earlier."

Harold sat at the coffee shop waiting on Samantha. Expecting the worse but hoping for the best, Harold did not want to have another disappointing date but he couldn't help but think Samantha was probably another mix up and not an actual match up.

Turning to leave thinking he'd make a run for it before Samantha arrived, he walked right into her.

"Excuse me, I'm so sorry. Are you alright?"

"Yes, I'm fine. You look like you're headed out for an important mission."

Harold laughed, "Nah, I was just um –."

Samantha cut him off, "Hey, I'm sorry but do you mind sitting down with me? I'm a little nervous and I need to talk out my jitters. I'm supposed to be meeting a guy here for coffee and I'm a little nervous."

Samantha leaned into Harold and whispered behind her hand, "Online dating, crazy, huh?"

Samantha looked around at everyone, "I apologize; I tend to talk a whole lot when I'm nervous. I hope I'm not keeping you from something."

Harold pulled out a chair for Samantha and carried on the conversation hoping this was the woman he was to be meeting.

Since the initial alert, they'd exchanged a few emails and they'd moved beyond the screen names into using their real names, he was just waiting for the right moment to find out this woman's name.

Crossing his fingers, Harold wanted this woman to be Samantha. He figured, if he'd put on the charm when she realized who he was, she'd want to continue talking.

"Can I get you something, coffee, tea, or whatever you'd like?"

"My nerves are getting the best of me, I definitely don't need any coffee. I think I will have some tea though."

Samantha was so nervous she wasn't aware she'd brought a complete stranger into her world, sitting, talking, and sharing tea.

"Oh my goodness, this has been so nice of you. Do you always rescue crazy women in coffee shops waiting to meet men off of the Internet?"

Harold laughed, "I'd have to say this is the first."

"I'm Samantha. And you are?"

He was right. It was her. Here was his big moment. He prayed all of his goodwill was going to pay off.

"It is indeed my pleasure to meet you Ms. Samantha, SRich35. I'm Harold, IAm007."

In the second it took for Samantha to make the connection they both started to panic.

In her mind, she lost it, "*I'm such an idiot, I've been going on and on about my online dating and lo and behold the man is right across from me.*"

He couldn't help but let his thoughts take him away down an unknown path, "*Ah man, see. She looks disappointed, I knew this was a mistake.*"

Not knowing how to clear the awkward moment, Samantha decided to meet it head on and make a joke out of it.

"So Harold I feel like I know you already, now when we get married, we won't have to say we met online but that we bumped into each other at a coffee shop."

Harold displayed a wide grin and exchanged witty commentary with his new coffee shop mate.

The atmosphere in the store was quite relaxed and laid back, allowing for Harold and Samantha to be the same. No pretenses or facades, just good 'ole conversation, in the hopes of getting to know one another.

"What type of work do you do Harold?"

Harold always had a base line answer for people he was first meeting, "I'm in business for myself."

"Oh really, what type of business?"

"Mainly websites. That kind of stuff...you know. What about you?"

"Oh me, I'm an elementary school teacher. I love children and I love teaching."

Samantha glowed as she talked about reasons for being an educator. It was clear to Harold, teaching for her was more than a career but a calling.

Harold was fascinated by Samantha, in his wildest dreams he could only dream that a woman like her would be just as interested in him.

During their time together, Harold had forgotten about the box he'd brought for her, he'd dropped it on the floor when they bumped into one another.

The lady next to them picked it up and asked if it belonged to either of them.

Harold grabbed the box and placed it in front of Samantha, "Just that fast I forgot I had this, but here you go, this is for you."

"You bought me a present?"

"Well, according to your profile it stated that yesterday was your birthday so I thought I'd get you a present."

Samantha took her time to open the beautifully wrapped gift box that housed an exquisite bracelet that dangled with a lady bug charm on it.

On Samantha's profile, one of the tidbits she'd posted about herself was that she loved lady bugs.

"Oh my goodness Harold, this is gorgeous. This is too much, you are too much. I can't believe you paid that much attention."

"Please, enjoy it. I figured, if by chance I never see you again, at least you'll always have something to remember me by."

Their afternoon coffee meeting grew into an evening chatting session.

Noticing the clock on the wall, Samantha jumped to her feet, "Oh wow, would you look at the time? What is it they say, time flies when you're having fun? Where has the time gone? Harold, I'm going to have to leave now; I have another obligation."

Harold hated to see her leave but he was grateful for the time they shared. Samantha was a breath of fresh air.

"Samantha, I completely understand, I should actually be going too."

Samantha carefully gathered her things, "Harold, thanks again for everything. I had a nice time, I'll be in touch, okay."

She was leaving wearing the bracelet, it fit her wrist like it was made especially for her.

Harold stood to help her up, he wanted to care for her like the flower she was, "Yes, this was nice. We'll talk soon. Have a nice night."

Harold sat for a while thinking over the last three hours with Samantha. The time with her was unlike any of the other mix ups he'd experienced recently.

Before Harold decided to leave, he walked up to the cashier and paid for a round of drinks for everyone in the store, making a bold pronouncement, "The next round is on me, I think I just met the future Mrs. Harold Johnson."

Happy to receive the free treats and goodies, everyone cheered and congratulated Harold, wishing him all the luck in his new pursuit.

CHAPTER 25

"Good evening Samantha, you're looking lovely as ever tonight."

Joshua reached in and gave Samantha a light hug with a soft kiss to her check.

"Thank you Joshua. Sorry I'm late, I had an earlier meeting that ran later than I thought."

"Who said anything about being late, now that you're here, I think you're right on time. The hostess is waiting for us over here, are you ready?"

Joshua and Samantha followed their hostess inside of the restaurant to their table.

Samantha and Joshua's first date was taking place at the newest restaurant in town, it was trendy yet elegant.

Joshua looked dashing as he was always well put together, he wore a certain panache about himself.

Samantha was pleased with what she saw in front of her. She was actually tripping at the fact she'd been on two dates in one day. This was a first but she was now hoping it wasn't the last.

"What a beautiful bracelet you're wearing."

Samantha beamed with pride, she'd already fallen in love with the bracelet, "Isn't it? It was a birthday gift and I love it."

Joshua leaned forward and admired the bracelet for a bit longer, sitting back in his chair, "Beautiful bracelet for a beautiful lady."

Samantha tossed her head back and rubbed her exposed neck, "I guess what they say is true, flattery will get you everywhere."

"Speaking of your birthday, did you have a good day?"

Samantha broke her eye contact with Joshua, "Well, it was an interesting day, it had some peaks and valleys but I'm grateful to God that it ended on a peak."

"Yes, the peak of the evening for me was getting a chance to meet you. I almost didn't come but your brother insisted, he stripped away every excuse I had not to come but I'm so glad I did."

Joshua took Samantha's hand and kissed it, looking straight into her eyes.

Samantha responded with a shy smile.

As the two continued to enjoy their small talk they were briefly interrupted by Mayor Zephon Webster and his wife.

"Well hello there Joshua, so nice to see you out and about tonight."

Joshua stood to greet the power couple and to introduce Samantha.

"How very nice to meet you Ms. Richards, I hope my boy here Joshua is showing you a nice time tonight."

Extending her hand for a handshake, Samantha replied kindly, "He is, and it's nice to meet you both as well."

The mayor's wife caught a glimpse of Samantha's bracelet, it picked up the lights from the restaurant perfectly.

"Ladybugs are my favorite, your bracelet is so pretty, you have such a dainty wrist; you wear it well."

Joshua spoke up, "I just told her the same thing."

Mayor Webster and his wife didn't tarry they finished their pleasantries and went off to their own table.

Over dinner Joshua engaged Samantha in a conversation about their professions, he knew from her brother, Caleb that she was a passionate educator.

Finding common ground, Joshua said, "So, from what I understand, you and I have similar interests when it comes to helping the youth of today."

"Yes, I am so impressed by what you've been able to accomplish in such a short period of time. That goes to show that all these children want is for someone to care."

"Samantha, you are so right, when they feel no one does, they start believing, why bother? We have to give them a reason to believe in themselves because when they don't they become bothersome to society and everyone around them."

"Joshua, you're doing a great work, balancing out justice with compassion and I pray that God grants you a spirit of wisdom and revelation knowledge. I pray that you may receive insight and that you are strengthened and anchored in love as you continue on."

Joshua tapped a loose fist against his heart, "I appreciate you saying that. It means a lot. It's nice to be able to talk to someone who understands."

"I do understand, I see what I do as more than being a teacher, I know I'm changing lives."

When talking about education and children, it didn't take much to get Samantha started, "I aspire to have my own school one day. While I love to teach, I hate the politics of education. For years, I've been researching and observing, waiting on the right opportunity to step out. I want to be able to give parents an option to provide their children with a Christian education without having to pay private school prices. I'm really sick and tired of these corporate-funded curriculums disguised in negative agendas. So, until I get there, if there's anything I can do to help, please let me know."

"I hear you, being a private institution, I kind of get to keep control of how I want things to be done at my school. Don't stop doing what you are doing, your time will come."

The hour was drawing nigh, they'd had a wonderful time of fellowship.

"Joshua, it's getting late and I have a long day scheduled for tomorrow. As much as hate to do it, I think it's time for me to go."

"Samantha, I hope you've enjoyed yourself tonight because I sure have and if it's alright with you, I'd like to see you again."

Samantha was enjoying being able to be in the driver's seat of her new social life.

On her way to meet Joshua, Harold called to check on her and to reiterate how much fun he'd had and they'd scheduled another meet up.

"I'd like that Joshua, let me check out my schedule and I'll get back with you. Is that alright with you?"

"That's fine with me and I look forward to seeing you again, real soon."

They exchanged hugs and Samantha said, "Oh and to answer your question, I did have a nice time tonight."

Joshua clicked his heels, "That's nice to know and hopefully this is the start of many more nights together."

CHAPTER 26

"Allen...Brown, in my office."

The two women jumped up from their desks, being called into the Lieutenant's office was equivalent to being called into the principal's office when you were a kid.

No one liked that.

"I have an update for you two. Morris will be back to work next week but since Brown has already been working the case with you, I want you two to remain on this case together."

Erica lowered her head.

"You have a problem with that Allen?"

"No sir, I don't. I just miss my partner. I still don't get why two, seemingly random men with no affiliation to him would want to jump him for no reason. They didn't steal anything from him, they just roughed him up. It doesn't make sense to me."

Det. Brown spoke up, "Sometimes, these things don't make sense. Why do people do any of the things they do? You're trying to make sense out of something that was senseless."

Lieutenant Conroy broke up the speculation session, "I've given you two an update, now I need one from you. What's going on with this dating website case? It's been a week now, please tell me you have something."

Erica stood up and asked, "Do you mind coming into the war room for a minute?"

Erica led them into the hub where all of their investigations took place. Inside the room, wall to wall big screen monitors mounted the walls, computer stations covered the room, each system running red hat enterprise Linux, a known platform for hackers.

"When we met with the company last week, we established with them and their consultant how things were going to be run. We determined we're going to be leading the charge as the computer incident response team and their consultant would advise and work in tandem with us."

"Okay, that's pretty standard Allen, I know all about protocol. I want to know what's going on with the investigation."

Det. Brown snickered under her breath.

"I apologize, I'm getting to that sir. The company provided me with an external hard drive comprising of the normal things we look for and I started trying to go through the information as soon as we arrived. Unfortunately, when I started running the data, the drive was completely empty. Some kind of way, the drive had been wiped clean."

Carefully trying to control his voice and tone, the Lieutenant asked, "What do you mean wiped clean? What was the chain of custody here, where is the evidence log?"

"I'm certain Det. Brown followed the proper procedures for logging the drive as evidence, sir. I've been in contact with the company trying to see if we can get the information again."

"Do you know how amateur that sounds, you having to go back to them? They asked for our best. Allen, you already know what your situation is and you two encounter a situation like this. So now what?"

Erica went into frantic planning mode, "I know this may look bad sir but the company completely understood, I didn't present it in a way of incompetence. Hopefully, they'll be able to get the information to us again. In the meantime, I started putting together a list from our database of known hackers and I've begun interviewing them. I'm scanning the underground forums looking to see if anyone is taking credit for the breach."

Det. Brown spouted off, "Why didn't I know anything about this?"

"Hey, I have a case to solve. I didn't have time to tell you then so I'm telling you now."

Lieutenant Conroy walked over to Erica and placed his hand on her shoulder, "I want you to work every angle you can but tell me, what is your gut telling you about this case?"

Erica sat down and began to review her notes, "Deep down inside, I feel that while this was a brute force attack, the person who infiltrated that system was trying to make a personal statement. You know these days, hackers aren't hacking to just steal, there is a whole new breed of hackers, hacktivists if you will, having social agendas. Whoever hacked this site figured out the company's weak spots and found a way to exploit them."

Conroy thought on what Erica was saying, "Whoever did this is very skilled but we need to figure out the motives behind why someone would want to hack a dating website and mix it all up with these crazy matches."

Erica agreed, "I've been thinking along those lines too sir."

"Listen to me girls, the owner, Harold Johnson knows a lot of top people here in the city, he's quite the philanthropic one which also means, he has a way of getting what he wants, when he wants it, and he wants this case solved. So I need for you two to do everything you can to solve it. I don't want to regret having put you on this case, it is very high profile with a lot of eyeballs on it."

Det. Brown nodded, "I understand sir; I plan to do everything I can for this case. Thank you for putting me on it."

The war room briefing was over and everyone went back to work.

"I'll be back Brown; I'm about to go and take a little break. You need anything?"

Det. Brown responded, "No, I'm good, take your time."

Erica's timing was off by five minutes.

Wouldn't you know it, on the floor was the same delivery guy from the week before from Miller's.

Walking right up to Det. Brown, the guy remembered and said, "Hey there Erica, I have another delivery for you."

Pretending to play the role, Det. Brown acted so surprise, "Flowers, for me...again. This guy, I think he might be a keeper."

She reached in her drawer and tipped the delivery guy again just as she had previously.

She stood up to admire the bountiful bouquet and to help herself to the card that read:

I never knew one could be so happy, until I met you and I'm enjoying every minute of it. You've entered my life and made it so beautiful.

~ Lionel

Det. Brown tore up the card again thinking, "*I can't believe he is crushing on her like this. She's no better than me. I should be the one getting flowers from him not her. Everybody always thinks she's so wonderful....I don't. I don't see what all the hype is about.*"

Erica walked back to her desk with an added pep in her step.

"What are you so happy about Allen?"

"The guys investigating Morris' attack called me down because they thought I'd be interested in going with them to talk to one of their C.I.s."

Det. Brown pinched the skin at her throat, "Interesting. Did you find out anything?"

"No, but we are going back later. This person seems to have a solid lead. I'll be so happy when we find out whoever did this. I want whoever did this Morris to pay. He's a good man who does his job and takes care of his family."

Erica clapped her hands and rubbed them together, "We'll get them, I'm sure of it."

Noticing the flowers on Brown's desk, "Flowers again, huh? You must be doing something right."

"Yeah girl, aren't they beautiful? I actually told the delivery guy that I think he might be a keeper."

Trying to rub her partner's face in her make-believe romance, Det. Brown never once considered what might happen if Erica ever found out about the flowers. It didn't cross her mind that Lionel might get suspicious. It didn't dawn on her because she was too busy gloating.

Erica looked up from her desk and said, "Good for you Brown, it's nice to see you so happy, you deserve it and everything coming to you."

CHAPTER 27

"Hey Michelle, can you come in here for a minute, I need to ask you something."

Lionel's assistant, Michelle walked in his office, "What is it Lionel?"

Lionel sat on the corner of his desk, "Hey, I need to know something. Have you ordered the flowers I asked you to over the last two weeks?"

Without hesitation, Michelle answered, "Yes, I have. Just like you asked me to."

"Can I ask where you are ordering them from?"

Michelle answered slowly, "Millers. You still have an account there so I ordered the flowers through them. Lionel, I'm so sorry, I should have known better."

Lionel laughed, "It's all good Michelle, I'm not tripping over that really. I mean, I want Erica to have the best and it just so happens that Millers is the best in town. It is crazy though that I'm getting flowers for my new girlfriend from my ex."

Lionel and Michelle shared a laugh.

"If what you're saying is true then, I'm not sure what's going on. Two deliveries have been made and Erica hasn't said anything about receiving the flowers. I've been trying to figure out whether or not I should say something to her."

"Do you think she'd get them but not say thank you or acknowledge the gesture?"

Lionel got up and grabbed an energy drink from the minibar in his office.

"No, not at all. She's not like that. I'm pretty sure she would have said something by now."

Michelle switched her position in the office chair, "You don't think Marsha has something to do with this do you?"

Lionel laughed out loud, "I don't see why she'd have anything to do with this, I mean, it shouldn't matter to her one bit who I'm sending flowers to. She made it very clear to me that she didn't want me anymore. Talking about how she owed it to herself to see what was up with her and Dallas."

Michelle tried to choose her words carefully, "Um Lionel, are you sure you've moved on? I don't mean any disrespect but you talk about her like this is still fresh."

Lionel laughed harder, "Michelle, trust me; I'm completely over Marsha. I have been blessed with a wonderful girl who I am enjoying getting to know. I'll even go a step further and let in you on a little secret."

Michelle sat up and listened closely.

"I think Erica might be 'The One'. Before, you even go there, yes I was going to propose to Marsha but that was because I was ready to settle down and she was the woman in my life. Listen, when a man is ready to get married, typically he goes for whoever is in the slot at the time. Sometimes, men don't always wait on that special one."

Michelle paused for a minute, "Tell me more because I've been trying to figure out this knucklehead I've been dating for a few months now."

"I tell you what. Bring him by the office and let me meet him, I'll be able to tell you in less than five minutes if you are wasting your time."

"Alright, that sounds like a plan. I'll be setting that up real soon."

"Back to Erica though, I think she's the one Michelle. I'll know for sure if she and I can make it through this case without it destroying us."

"You sound like there might be some doubts about the case."

"Well, you just never know about these work/life relationships. I don't want what happened with that dating site to ruin what we might be working towards. You know what I mean?"

Michelle didn't really know what Lionel meant but she went along with her boss like she did. Over the years, she'd learned how to do that with Lionel.

"I'm just saying Lionel, I mean, you are one of San Antonio's most eligible bachelors and you got dumped. I know how that must have hurt. I just don't want you to still be caught up over her."

Lionel's laugh this time contained somewhat of a yell, "How many times do I need to tell you that I'm not still hung up on Marsha."

Holding her ears, protecting them from Lionel, Michelle said, "Okay...okay, I hear you loud and clear."

"I appreciate the concern but I'm fine. Listen, break ups happen to the best of us. Now, I'll admit, I didn't handle it well in the beginning but I picked myself up, I kept myself busy with work and that helped me. I took some time to figure out what I really wanted in my life partner and I realized Marsha was nowhere close to that. In the meantime, life introduced me to an amazing woman that I can't seem to stop thinking about. I am enjoying every minute that I have with her."

Michelle placed her hand over her heart, "Sounds like a man in love. I have to say, you do seem much happier these days."

Michelle had been with Lionel from the very beginning, from the first day he decided to start his own consulting firm. She'd seen him at his best and also at his worst.

A slow smile crept across Lionel's face, "Maybe you're right."

"So do you want me to do anything about the flowers?"

"Hold off on that for a minute, I'll keep you posted on that."

"Alright, I'm going to get back to work."

Lionel sat down behind his desk, "Yes, I need to do the same. I need to make some final touches to the dating site case. I'd like to be able to move into the implementation phase real soon."

Michelle looked back at Lionel before she walked out of his office.

"Michelle, thanks for the talk and I promise I'm fine. In fact, I've never been better."

CHAPTER 28

"Hey there pretty lady, I'm checking to see how long before you get here."

"I should be there in about ten minutes."

"Alright, guess what? I'll be counting down the minutes 'til you get here."

Erica and Lionel had planned to get together at his office to discuss the Match Up America case. She was interested in working every angle and sometimes that didn't include involving her newly assigned partner.

Erica knocked on Lionel's office and entered in looking incredibly stunning. Lionel was overpowered by her presence.

"Well, aren't you a sight for sore eyes?"

Lionel stood to greet his lady love.

"Just when I think you can't possibly get any more beautiful, you always have a way to prove me wrong. How's my girl this evening?"

Erica greeted Lionel with a warm kiss and a full bodied hug, "Lionel, you are too kind. I'm doing well, how about you?"

Popping open the top of an energy drink, Lionel responded, "Much better now that you are here. Can I get you something to drink?"

Erica waved her hand, "No thanks, I'm okay right now."

Lionel downed his drink and tossed it in the wastebasket next to his desk that was full of empty drink cans.

Noticing the contents in the trash can, Erica asked, "Do you really need that much energy? I hope your cleaning crew forgot to take out the trash and that is several day's worth."

Lionel grinned, "You would be happy to know that since you've come into my life, energy levels have been through the roof; you seem to energize me."

Erica could feel her belly knot up, Lionel always knew the right words to say to her. He was turning out to be a true Prince Charming.

"So babe, I'm almost ready for the implementation phase, I should be ready to go over there tomorrow and patch them up. The way I see it, once I clear up their weak spots, it will be nearly impossible for anyone to be able to penetrate them again."

"You think you're that good huh? You closing up their vulnerabilities doesn't help me solve my case though."

Lionel came from behind his desk and sat next to Erica.

"I don't mean to brag but I am just that good. I take my job very seriously. Most people wouldn't understand this but I feel like what I do is artistic. There is definitely an art form to understanding the intricacies of cyber security. Throughout my career, I'd like to think I've made some masterpieces, some abstract and some very dark."

Erica crossed her legs, "Explain, I don't understand what you mean by that."

Lionel scooted his chair closer and turned her chair to face his, "Haven't you ever gone to the dark side?"

Erica threw her hands up, "What's up with all the mystery talk? Can you talk plainly to me sir?"

Lionel laughed with Erica, "I mean, you're in I.T., and at the basic level, you can't tell me most people in information technology hasn't had the thought to cross their mind about hacking into something after finishing up an intro to hacking or ethical hacking class."

Lionel continued talking about his college days, "Hey, speaking of college, I'm running in the HBCU 5K this weekend and I would love to have my good luck charm waiting for me at the finish line. We could even get some pictures and send to Alexis for the Houston Flyers. What do you think?

Erica thought accompanying Lionel to the run would be great but she couldn't help but giggle at his hypothesis, *"Lionel might be on to something. Hmmm, if he only knew."*

During Erica's college years, she and Lana ended up on the dark side Lionel referenced.

The two roommates made the decision to pledge a sorority one semester and at some point, trying to pledge, work, go to school, and entertain a social life, their grades began to suffer.

Lana knew upfront that if her grades failed, she would not be able to continue with her hopes of joining the organization. Erica and some of the other girls were in the same position.

What was a girl to do?

They did what they thought was best.

Armed with Erica's newly acquired information technology skills, they hacked into the University's registrar grading system and changed their grades before they were mailed to their respective homes.

Over the Christmas holidays, the two pledgees stressed out whether their plan would work.

Not only did the plan work but no one suspected any foul play. Everyone's parents were pleased with the semester grades and their grade point averages were protected.

Upon returning for the next semester, Erica and Lana did indeed pledge but they were now being hit up to change grades for other people.

With Erica's computer science background and Lana's mind for business, their misconduct turned into a booming enterprise.

They were smart about their deception. Everything was done completely underground. No one knew exactly who was responsible for changing the grades, the word on the street was simply that there was someone on campus who could.

Staying under the radar, the two cronies were making money hand over fist. Lana and Erica had strict controls in place to keep their identities concealed. Until one Sunday afternoon.

Their sorority celebrated and ended their chapter's anniversary weekend with a church service. The sermon, taken from Acts 5:1-11, *"The Great Cover-Up"* touched Lana's heart in a deep and personal way.

Upon hearing how the couple, Ananias and Sapphire tried to cover up what they'd done and lied about it thinking no one would know and then subsequently dying from the deceitfulness, Lana made her way to the alter to distance herself from their elaborate grading scheme.

When Lana got up, Erica immediately knew her reasons for going and she joined her.

The pastor talked about how Barnabas didn't have anything to hide when he sold his possessions, he was being a true disciple of Christ, whereas Ananias and Sapphire tried to hide what they'd done in selling their goods which made them master deceivers. They thought they were lying to a man when in all actuality they were lying to the Holy Spirit.

Lana and Erica decided that day they no longer wanted to be deceivers but disciples. They left it all at the altar that day. Their business went belly-up, they were instantly out of commission, they closed up shop.

The next day, Erica doubled up on her major and included criminal justice so that she could now use her talents to stop cyber security fraud instead of contributing to it.

In that moment Erica, not ready to disclose that part of her life tried to change the subject, wondering what dark exploits Lionel had ever participated in.

For now, that would have to wait.

Tuning back in to the conversation, Erica added, "All this talk about the dark side, I think if I don't get something to eat soon, you may see mine."

Lionel reached in and kissed Erica's cheek, "Well, we don't want to have that happen now do we? I had Michelle make us a reservation for dinner before you got here so this should be right on time for you, huh?"

"Yes, can we go now or do we need to wait? What time is the reservation for?"

Packing up his things and shutting down his office, "We can go now sweetheart. Even if we're a little early, hopefully, they'll go ahead and seat us. I can't have my girl going all dark on me. I'm going to make sure you eat and eat real good tonight."

Erica packed away her things and followed Lionel towards the door saying, "Oh my, you're just too good to me."

Lionel turned out the lights and said, "Everyday, all day baby."

CHAPTER 29

"So missy, tell me why haven't I heard from you in the last few days?"

Samantha giggled in the phone to her mother.

Pretending to be in trouble, Samantha answered, "Because I've been having the time of my life."

"What do you mean by that?"

"Mama, oh my goodness, even though I'm single, I've been enjoying myself getting my mingle on."

Ernestine shook her head, "Oh lord; I'm scared to even ask."

Samantha laughed harder than before.

"No need to be afraid mama. I've been blessed to meet two wonderful men in one week and I'm enjoying getting to know more about each of them."

"So then tell me about them. I want to hear what's so wonderful about these two guys."

"Well, you met or at least saw Joshua the other night, right?"

Ernestine acknowledged, "I didn't get a chance to actually meet him but I did see him."

"Well, need I say anymore? You saw how fine that man is and he's smart too. We both share a passion for educating young people and helping them be the best they can be."

Ernestine interjected, "But does he love the Lord?"

Samantha turned her head and closed her eyes, "I haven't gotten that far with him yet mama."

Ernestine huffed in the phone, "Well what are you waiting on? Christmas?"

"Mama."

"Samantha."

Samantha knew her mother was right to be asking.

"Honey, the last time we spoke you said you were ready to get married. Now, to me that means you are in a position where you should be interviewing potential husbands not just dating for the sake of dating. See, you young people have lost the art of courting. When you meet someone, you should be seeing if their goals match up to yours, seeing if you could see yourself building a life with that person and seeing if they will be able to lead you and your future family in the ways of the Lord."

"Mama, you're right. It's just been nice getting to know Harold and Joshua. I hadn't allowed myself to go out much since you know, since Nolan."

"Well sweetheart, Nolan made his choices and while you may not have liked his choice, he proved he was not God's choice blessing for you. So, what's the deal with this Harold guy?"

Samantha snickered somewhat, "You know what, he's definitely not the typical guy that I might be attracted to looks wise but he is such a nice guy. I can't seem to put my finger on it but there's something about him that I like. I can't wait to show you the beautiful bracelet he got me for my birthday."

"A bracelet? For your birthday?"

"Yes, I got it the day after, when we first met. Then, the day after we met I had a bouquet of flowers delivered to my school from Miller's that were gorgeous."

"Okay, that sounds nice and all but I'll ask you once again, does he love the Lord?"

"Geesh woman, you don't stop do you? It's funny you ask that about him though. During a conversation, I mentioned how important my relationship with Christ is to me and he said he had already picked up on that and wanted to know more. We are actually going to go to bible study this evening."

"Oh Samantha, that sounds wonderful. Now as your mother you know I'm going to put in my two cents whether you want to hear them or not. It's praying time young lady. Your father and I made a promise to you that we would be your partners in finding a mate. We want to be here for you honey. We need to be praying for the Lord to reveal to you the hearts of these two men, whether you are to entertain them any longer because time is winding up and we don't have time to play games. If these two don't mean you no good then you need to know that before too much time goes by."

Samantha took a deep breath, "I hear you mama and I appreciate you guys looking out for me."

"Trust me honey, God's going to do it, if you can remain, you'll be able to gain."

"But Mama, I think I like both of them."

"Again I say, its praying time girl."

"I love you mama. I'm going to get ready to go so I can meet Harold up at the church."

"Oh yeah that's right, I wasn't going tonight but maybe I will so I can bump into you two."

Samantha lowered her head, "Oh boy, here we go."

Ernestine laughed, "No need to be scared; I promise I won't embarrass you. I do want to get a good look at the fella and see if anything comes up. You know the bible tells us to try all spirits to see if they are of God."

"I feel like I better warn poor Harold, he has no idea what he's getting ready to encounter when he meets Ernestine Richards."

"If Harold is on the up and up, he'll have nothing to worry about and even if he isn't he still won't have anything to worry about because I'll pray his butt right on out of here."

"Mama, you're crazy but I love it. I'll see you shortly."

CHAPTER 30

"Hey girl, I hate that we've been playing phone tag for the last two weeks. I hate I missed you the other night and I've been so busy at work but maybe we can get together for dinner this weekend. Call me back when you can."

Nicole rolled over Dallas and went into her bathroom to listen to the message from her best friend of twenty years.

After listening to the message, Nicole stared at her bare body in the mirror, *"How have I become that girl? The one who sleeps with her best friend's boyfriend? The side chick? I can't even stand to look at myself."*

Calling from the bedroom, "Baby, what's taking you so long in the bathroom. Your spot in the bed is getting cold and I'm ready to warm it back up again."

"Oh Dallas, don't you ever tire?"

"Not when I'm with you. My sweet, darling Nikki isn't so sweet and she drives me so crazy. I'm falling for you fast and I just can't help myself. You have turned my world upside down girl."

Dallas and Nicole had been secretly seeing each other since the night they'd met at Marsha's. They were infectious around each other. It was unexplainable. They both knew what they were doing was wrong with their unthinkable betrayal but the magnetism they shared was uncontrollable.

They'd tried. Nicole struggled with the history she shared with Marsha up against the future she was envisioning with Dallas.

"How long do you think we can keep this up Dallas?"

"Baby, everything is going to work itself out. Marsha has been so busy at work, she hasn't even noticed me not being around."

"Sometimes I just feel so awful about all of this. I never meant for any of this to happen, I was only supposed to be dropping off some souvenirs from my trip to Brazil to my best friend and instead I got picked up by her boyfriend."

Dallas pulled Nicole back into the bed under the covers, "Isn't that the beauty of all of this? It was unexpected and sometimes the things we can't explain end up being the best things that ever happened to us and Nikki, look at me, you are the best thing that has ever happened to me."

Nicole pulled away.

"How can this be the best thing when my best friend in this whole entire world is going to be hurt by this Dallas?"

Dallas sat up, "Yes, Marsha will be upset but just like anything else in life, she will get over it. I guess the question I have for you is, can you get over it? Would you rather end this now to preserve her feelings or be with me?"

Dallas followed a trail of kisses down Nicole's arm where he embedded one last kiss on her hand.

Nicole screeched from her belly, "Oh this is so not fair. How am I to choose? I can't choose. Dallas, this is the worst."

"No, Nikki, this is actually the best. You and I were meant for each other. I mean, I'm not sure how much loyalty means to Marsha anyway. She dumped her boyfriend to go out with me only after we had been seeing each other for a short while and she had been with him for months. She will understand that these things happen."

"But not with her best friend Dallas and I think that's the part you seem to keep forgetting."

Growing impatient, Dallas tilted his head back and looked up at the ceiling, "I'm not forgetting anything, I'd like to remember how you and I have fallen in love. Yes, it's a tough situation but what I think you are forgetting is that had it not been for Marsha, I would have never met you. To me, unfortunately, Marsha happens to be a casualty of love and war."

Dallas got up and walked out of the room in his full glory, in a way, he wanted to show Nicole that he could walk away.

Nicole perceived his subtle attempt.

Dropping her head in her hands, *"I don't want him to leave me, I just pray Marsha understands."*

CHAPTER 31

"I've been making a small fortune on the double gratuity from Lionel's orders and it looks like I'll be making one today."

Marsha overheard her delivery guys talking and walked over to question Louis, one of her delivery guys, "Um, Louis did I just hear you say something about Lionel...my Lionel?"

When the boss shows up everyone straightens up and while Louis tried to tighten up his demeanor he couldn't help but think, "*Uh, Miss Marsha, I don't think he's your Lionel anymore.*"

Nevertheless, he tried his best to answer, "Well, what I meant was that Lionel always includes ample gratuity with his orders and since I've been making deliveries to the police station, I've been getting a nice tip from there as well...us guys call that double grat."

Marsha walked over to the orders that were scheduled to go out that day. She found Lionel's order to Erica. Reading the card, she also checked the archived orders to see how long he'd been sending her flowers.

"Louis, are you getting ready to make this delivery?"

"Yes ma'am, I was waiting for one last order before I left."

"Well come and get me when you leave. I'm going on this delivery with you today."

Stumbling over his words, "But ma'am, you never go on deliveries. Are you sure, trust me, it's not that glamourous."

Marsha answered in a polished and professional manner, "As an entrepreneur, I need to periodically be involved with every level of the business, including spending time with my delivery guys. So as I said, come and get me before you leave. Okay Louis?"

Louis could see the other guys trying to hold back their laughter and thinking of all the jokes they could think of about the boss riding along with him.

"Yes ma'am. It shouldn't be too much longer."

Fifteen minutes later...

In trying to keep up the concerned employer pretense, Marsha asked, "So Louis, how long have you been with us now?"

Proud to answer, Louis responded, "Going on two years now."

Louis was a rehabilitated convicted felon, in an attempt to give back to the community, Marsha's family enrolled the shop into a network that provided jobs for those seeking to reenter society with a renewed sense of responsibility and Louis was doing just that.

"Well, let me be the first to tell you that I'm proud of you and the work you are doing for Millers. I know that my dad is smiling down on you, he would be so proud of you."

Pulling into the precinct's parking lot, Louis beamed with pride, "Thank you ma'am; that means a lot coming from you. We're here."

Inside, Marsha was intent on seeing the woman Lionel had been sending flowers to now for weeks. She followed closely behind Louis.

Expecting another great tip, Louis gladly led the way.

Traveling the same path he'd done previously, Louis walked right up to Det. Brown's desk.

"Hello again, looks like I have another delivery for you."

Det. Brown stood to receive the flowers, it had become a routine for her now, "This guy, I tell you. He never ceases to amaze me."

Marsha took in every inch of Det. Brown logging every detail about her from the way her hair was coiffed to the pointy pumps covering her feet. Sizing up the other woman, she thought, "*She doesn't look like Lionel's type? I don't know what's so special about her?*"

Det. Brown took notice to Marsha's presence, "I see you have someone with you today, are you training someone new?"

Marsha smirked, "Hardly; I'm the owner. Marsha Miller, nice to meet you Ms. Erica. I actually happen to know the guy who sent you those flowers. Tell him I said hi."

Det. Brown played it off well, knowing she would never be able to deliver that message, she still said, "Very nice to meet you, I'll be sure and let him know what you said."

The only reason she was there to intercept the flowers again was because Lionel and Erica were out on a lunch date.

As usual, Det. Brown slipped Louis another tip, continuing on his double grat streak with this particular order.

"Thanks again, enjoy your flowers."

On the way back to the delivery van unbeknownst to the other, as Erica walked into the building, Louis and Marsha walked out.

Back at her desk, Erica paid attention, "Flowers again, I see."

"Yeah girl, my man loves me."

Erica sat down to her desk smiling, thinking on the beautiful lunch she'd just had with Lionel. She was falling for him and it was showing in everything she did.

Det. Brown perked up even more, "Hey Allen, whatever happened with that informant you were supposed to be meeting up with about Morris' case?"

Erica dropped her head, "Do you know that joker never showed up and now he's nowhere to be found. Right now it's looking like a lead that led us nowhere."

Det. Brown shook her head, "That's too bad. Well keep me posted. I think I'm going to take my lunch now. I'll be back."

"Alright, enjoy. Lord knows I enjoyed mine. This man has completely swept me off my feet and I don't plan on my feet touching ground any time soon."

Det. Brown felt a twitch in her right cheek, "That's nice to hear, I can tell there is something going on with you these days. I just hope with your head all in the clouds it doesn't interfere with you work performance."

Giving her partner a bit of side eye action, "Oh trust me honey, no interference here, in fact, I feel like I'm doing better than ever which means everybody better watch out."

Det. Brown shrugged her shoulders, "If you say so, I'm just looking out for you as my partner. Sometimes, we see things others can't."

Erica nodded her head, "You are indeed correct but I assure you my eyes are wide open to everything going on around me but good looking out for a sister."

"It's the least I could do Allen. I'm going to lunch now. For real this time."

CHAPTER 32

"How is it that with every other gift, I give to Erica she seems so grateful but she hasn't said a word about the weekly floral arrangements I've been sending her?"

"So she still hasn't said anything about them?"

Lionel stood from his desk and looked at the panoramic view from his office window.

"No, she hasn't and that just isn't like her Michelle. I feel weird by asking her, did you get my flowers today when she hasn't said anything. I'm just not sure what to make of it."

Michelle broached the awkward subject, "You know I didn't ever change florists, you don't think Marsha has anything to do with this?"

Lionel popped open one of his favorite energy drinks, "You know, even though my mind tried to go there, I really didn't want to go there with her. I mean, what does she care who I send flowers to?"

"Michelle turned to face Lionel, "Hey, she maybe dating someone else but believe me, this is Marsha we are talking about here, her ego makes her care. She probably thinks you're supposed to be sitting around waiting for her to come back and not enjoy your life."

Lionel shook his head and laughed, "Was she really that bad? I think it is hilarious how now after the fact, you plus all of my sisters have all of these opinions about her but didn't say anything while we were dating."

"I mean, c'mon Lionel. It's not easy telling someone who appears to be happy that the person they are with isn't a good fit. Be honest, would you have listened had we said anything?"

Lionel thought for a second and laughed, "Nah, probably not. It's all good though because I have found the right fit with Erica. Listen to me, when a man sees what he wants, it doesn't take him forever to figure out if he wants to be with that woman. He will do whatever he needs to take her off the market."

Michelle's interest was piqued, "So what are you saying Lionel?"

Lionel turned to his trusted assistant, "I don't know when but I think it's time to go back to Boites a Bijoux."

Michelle squealed for joy, "Oh Lionel that's wonderful news and I'm so happy for you. I can see you are a changed man. Erica is a lucky woman."

In a brief moment of quiet reflection, "No Michelle, I'm the lucky one."

"Do you have a time frame in mind Lionel? Do I need to plan anything or help you do anything? Oh my goodness, I'm so excited. Have you told your family yet?"

"Not really. Of course, I'd like to do it sooner rather than later to show her how serious I am but it's only been a couple of months so I don't know how that'll go over. No, I haven't told the family yet, they know about her but that's about it. All I need to do is tell one and you know them, it'll spread like wildfire. Based on how my botched engagement went with Marsha, I think I'm going to keep this one close to the vest."

Michelle stood up and commanded Lionel's attention, "Hey, no you listen to me, when it's right, it's right. Marsha was all wrong, forget about her and focus on Erica. My grandparents were introduced on a blind date on their first date. Seven days later they were married and they've been together for sixty-five years already."

"Wow, now that is a blessing."

"I feel the same way, every time I see them. Those two renew my faith in love and that it is out there for me and it looks like it has found you. Finally. Mr. Most Eligible Bachelor."

"I will gladly give up that title for Erica. As a matter of fact, Michelle, I think you just gave me an idea. I think if all goes well with this basketball thing, I'll propose at one of their games. Let's give the fans what they want, right? A basketball championship and more of Lierica's love story."

Turning the conversation back to where it started, "I think that's a great idea but Lionel, what are you going to do about this flower situation, something is obviously going on and it's been going on for a while."

Lionel grabbed his keys, "Come on, forward the calls to the answering service, let's take a ride."

CHAPTER 33

Nowadays whenever Marsha's number came across, Nicole seemed to experience a small panic attack, *"Should I answer or shouldn't I? Does she know or doesn't she? I can't keep going through this. Let me see what she wants."*

"Nikki."

"Hey girl, what's up?"

Nicole could hear the steam emitting from her friend, *"Oh no, she knows."*

"Girl, you will never guess what just happened."

Trying to remain calm, "Well, if I'll never guess, why don't you go ahead and tell me."

"I'm so mad right now, I could scream."

"Well scream then."

Marsha took her best friend's advice and screamed out into the atmosphere. The release was empowering.

"I actually feel a little better now."

"What happened?"

"Okay so, I'm in my office and I get a call that someone is here to see me. Nothing to do but when I turn the corner I see none other than Lionel and Michelle. At first I was like what are they doing here?"

"Was this your first time seeing him since the, you know, the breakup?"

"Yes, and even though I'm still fuming; I hate to admit it, but Lionel was looking so good. I've talked to him since then because he helped me out with a computer situation but yes, that was my first time actually seeing him."

Nicole threw in a judgmental remark, "I told you I thought you were crazy for messing that up. But that's neither here nor there. So tell, why were they there?"

"Lionel came in here all accusatory about me not delivering flowers to his new girlfriend, thinking I was doing something to the orders because I was jealous."

"No he did not, are you serious? Wait, he has a girlfriend? Um, how are you feeling about that?"

"I'm dead serious and yes, he has a girlfriend and I could care less, especially after what I saw today or shall I say who I saw today."

"What do you mean by that?"

"Well, the funny part in all of this is that this morning, I overheard one of my drivers talking about him and from there I realized he was still using us for flowers. If I'm honest and since you are my girl, I can be that with you, I was curious to see who the new lady in his life is, so I went on the delivery."

"Wait, what...you went on a delivery? That's not curiosity that's just plain nosey. You wanted to scope out the new girl."

"When I tell you that she ain't nothing to write home to mama about, I mean that."

"You sound like a hater to me."

"No, I mean don't get me wrong, she look alright but she looks nothing like me or even his type for that matter."

"Is it possible that after what you did to him he might be trying to steer clear of your type?"

Marsha's tone of anger was being replaced with sounds of laughter, "You might have a point there."

"So, he accused you of being jealous and then what?"

"Oh, I had the pleasure of getting him right together. Instead of showing out in front of my customers, I pulled him into my office and I went off."

"Oh Lord, I can only imagine what you said."

"Yeah, it wasn't pretty. Of course, I had to let him know that I'm happy with Dallas and who he dates is of no concern to me. I'm running a business and I'm not interested in getting a bad reputation for not delivering flowers because he thinks I'm trying to keep some stupid flowers from his new girlfriend."

At the mention of Dallas' name, Nicole grew still and quiet.

"Hello, Nikki...are you still here?"

"Yeah girl, I'm here. Well knowing Lionel, I know he wasn't happy to hear that. Speaking of Dallas, how are things between you two?"

"Actually, I used to be able to say things to Lionel that I knew would get to him but this time, he seemed completely unphased by me."

"Oh wow, you think that's because of the new girlfriend? Or is he really different now?"

"He's definitely different and in a way that I'm going to hate admitting again but his different was actually attractive to me and to answer your question about Dallas, I haven't seen much of him lately. Between my schedule and his, we've been on different pages."

Nicole decided to tread lightly because she needed to know, "Do I hear that you might be in interested in going back to Lionel and if so, what does that mean for you and Dallas?"

"At this very moment, I'm not sure what any of it means. They just left and I called you as soon as they hit the door. What I do know is this, Dallas and I are supposed to be going to the 5K run this weekend and I know Lionel will be there because he and I signed up together. So I'm sure that'll be interesting. You're still planning on going, right?"

"I'm not sure; I'll have to see. I haven't been feeling the best lately, but I'll let you know."

Dallas was beeping in.

"Marsha, it sounds like you've calmed down some and I need to take this call but I'll call and check on you later."

"As always, you know how to talk me down from the ledge. I don't know where I'd be without you in my life. I know one thing, you definitely keep me sane. I feel better now and I'll talk with you later."

"No matter what Marsha, I need you to know that I love you girl."

"Go ahead and take your call, I know that, and I love you too."

CHAPTER 34

"Good morning gorgeous, I'm so glad you could join me."

"Hey there Joshua, well you know me, I do what I can for the kids. While I'm not running, I have made a financial contribution and I'll be here waiting for you at the finish line cheering you on."

"My own personal cheerleader, I like the sounds of that. Do you own the outfit too?"

Blushing a bit, Samantha replied, "No sir, I do not."

The annual HBCU annual 5K Walk/Run was all the buzz, this year's theme, *"We Run It"* had thousands of participants arriving early in anticipation of getting their bibs and warming up for the race.

Lionel and Erica arrived together and at the last minute she decided to participate and run in the 3.1 mile fundraiser.

Neither Dallas nor Nicole showed up to the race, leaving Marsha to run alone. She thought about leaving but in the same thought, realized there was a chance she might run into Lionel.

Hob-nobbing under the sponsor's tent, Harold was in great spirits as he couldn't help think about how much his life had changed in such a short period of time.

His association with Samantha had led him to the greatest decision of his life, at the bible study they attended, he invited Jesus to live in his heart. In all of his years, he was beginning to finally feel like there was purpose to be fulfilled in his life.

He was now seeing life through a completely new set of eyes and he was loving every minute of it.

Thinking he would have loved having Samantha there with him, he wasn't ready to reveal to her that the size of his bank account was as large as the State of Texas. Therefore, events like these would be off limits for the time being. But hopefully not for long.

Johnson Enterprises had been a faithful sponsor of the run from the beginning. While Harold himself never went to college, he believed that those who wanted to go should have the opportunity. He was quite charitable in areas related to education.

His brightened countenance was not going unnoticed by the other sponsors that knew him. Many of them commented on the apparent change within him, wanting to know what was the cause or possibly, who was the cause.

In response, Harold proudly proclaimed, "I'm brand new, baby. You're looking at the new and improved Harold."

At church, Harold learned that if by accepting Jesus, he was new creature and he took that message to heart. The day after his confession, he went out and decided to undergo a complete makeover to match his internal makeover. He joined a gym and started working out. To most, he was almost unrecognizable.

Anna Patterson, owner of one of the largest real estate firms in the area was one who was especially taking special interest into Harold.

Over the years, there had been harmless flirtation between the two but Anna never seemed interested enough in Harold to take it beyond flirting.

"Well hello there stranger. You're looking well and prosperous."

"Good morning Anna. You say that like I haven't always."

Caught off guard by Harold's response, Anna answered, "Listen at you Harold, I like it and by the way, to me, you always look well and prosperous."

Distinguished alumni from across the country were in attendance, it was like a combined Homecoming of sorts.

The announcement was made for everyone to make their way to the starting line, the race Marshal would fire the shot within five minutes.

While Harold continued to circulate and mingle around the tent, Anna kept finding her way back in his face.

Before heading off to the starting line, Joshua leaned in for a good luck kiss from Samantha and she returned his gesture with a kiss on the cheek, "Good luck...see you at the finish line."

Lionel and Erica were already there and were busy figuring out what their wager was going to be for the one who finished the race first.

"Hey babe, if I win, you buy me lunch and if you win, I'll buy you lunch. The way I see it, even if I lose to you, I'll still be a winner because I'll get to have lunch with my favorite girl."

Erica's face reddened, she grabbed Lionel up in a pre-run hug and kiss, she teased him by saying, "Good luck and I look forward to you paying for my lunch later."

Out of all the people ready to race, these two were the only ones smooching and hugging which brought attention to them, not to mention, the professional photographers, Lionel hired to snap pictures of them for the Houston Flyers.

Right before the Marshal fired off the gun, Marsha spotted the love birds and their crew, she wondered, "*Hey, wait a minute. That doesn't look like the woman I met the other day. Have I turned Lionel into a two-timing womanizer?"*

Posters, banners, signs and scores of people were at the finish line cheering and supporting those that made it beyond the threshold.

Erica finished at a personal best run time of 20:15, with her beau right behind her at 21:02, Joshua came in shortly after at 25:13, and Marsha followed up at 30:21.

Joshua searched and sought out Samantha at the finish line, he found her standing there waiting for him, looking angelic.

"Good job Joshua, I'm so proud of you."

"Thanks Samantha, it really means a lot having you here to cheer me on."

Testing the waters, Joshua posed a risky question, "You think you might want to show me later how proud of me you are?"

Samantha cleared her throat, "I guess my words of encouragement and me being here isn't enough, huh?"

"It isn't that Samantha, it's just...I mean, you and I have been seeing each other for a little while now and I'm really feeling you but it's time I actually start to feel you....if you know what I mean."

Samantha covered her mouth to keep the shock from spilling out of it, "I thought you were supposed to be a Christian?"

"I am but I'm also a man and I'm a man with needs. Plus, I try before I buy anything."

"Well Joshua, in that case, I think I need to tell you to go find someone else you can try out because it won't be me. Nice knowing you."

Samantha stormed off in haste, leaving Joshua standing speechless in the dust she left behind.

By all other accounts the run was a huge success, hundreds of thousands of dollars were raised for deserving students wanting to continue on their education at Historically Black Colleges and Universities.

Erica glistened in the sunlight and Lionel was enamored by her and likewise the beads of sweat that dripped from his perfectly sculpted body caused Erica to step back and admire her man.

Rubbing in her win, she joked around with Lionel, taunting him, "Man, I'm hungry after stealing the show from my honey bun over there. I wonder where he's taking me to eat."

Just as the two were playing around and enjoying the awards ceremony, Marsha stepped in front of them.

"Nice run, huh Lionel?"

"Marsha?"

"Why do you look so surprised to see me? We did sign up to do this run together, remember?"

Erica locked arms with Lionel thinking, *"So this is the infamous Marsha."*

The thought never entered into Lionel's mind that he would ever be in a situation where his past would meet his future but it just had.

"I'm not surprised to see you at all. I have no problems with you being here. This is a free country, you can be where ever you want to be. Plus, you know I how I feel, the more the merrier."

"Funny you say that Lionel because it seems like you are racking up more and more women these days."

Lionel stepped towards Marsha, "Excuse me? What are you talking about Marsha?"

Marsha stood back, "I just wonder if this young lady you've been hugging and kissing on when you should've been getting ready to run knows you're sending flowers to other women and telling them how much they mean to you?"

Both Lionel and Erica were confused.

"Nothing you're saying is making sense. I came to you yesterday asking you about my deliveries. There are no other women, I've been sending flowers to her."

Erica cocked her head to the side trying to keep her thoughts inside of her head, *"Hold up, did he just say he saw her yesterday? He's been sending flowers to me? I haven't gotten any flowers."*

"This isn't the woman we delivered flowers to the other day."

Erica interrupted Lionel and Marsha's heated exchange, "Did you say you've been sending me flowers? How long has this been going on?"

In their own world and ignoring Marsha, Lionel acknowledged, "For weeks now, ever since we got back from the conference. After you never said anything about getting them, I thought it would be awkward to ask you about it so I never did but I went to try and figure out what was going on."

Erica shook her head and folded her arms across her chest, "Oh, I'm pretty sure I know what's going on."

Waving her hand in the air, Marsha exclaimed, "Um, hello...I am still standing here. Lionel, we need to talk."

"Marsha, you and I have nothing to talk about. Well, let me take that back, I have one last thing to say to you."

Lionel took Erica by the hand and looked Marsha squarely in her face, "Marsha, I have someone I'd like you to meet. Please meet my stunning girlfriend, Erica Allen who I hope will one day do me the honor of becoming my wife. This is who I've been sending flowers to and oh yeah, that reminds me, I need to look for another florist."

Movement was happening all around them with the awards ceremony ending but in the tiny space they took up, everything seemed still.

Erica nearly lost it but she tried to keep her composure in the midst of the intense moment.

Walking past Marsha, Lionel stopped and whispered in Marsha's ear for extra emphasis, "She will be getting an upgrade on the ring I purchased for you. I was going to propose to you the night you left me for your 'perfect match,' do you remember that? Yeah, think on that for a while. Goodbye Marsha."

Lionel and Erica walked off leaving Marsha standing there to process all of what had just transpired. Her thoughts ran deep and wide, *"He was going to propose? What a joke that perfect match turned out to be, speaking of Dallas, why didn't he show up here today? He wants to marry her? Really though who was that woman we delivered those flowers to?"*

Marsha's body not only burned from the muscle strain sustained from the run but from the fiery words that seemed to ooze from Lionel's mouth to her ears.

She wanted to shrink, disappear, and melt away like lava back to her car. The decision to leave Lionel for Dallas turned out to have had a blistering effect upon her life.

Now that the festivities were coming to a close, Harold went around to say his last goodbyes before leaving.

Anna cornered him, "I hope you weren't going to leave without saying anything to me. You know, I think we should finally have that drink we've talked about for years now. What do you say?"

Harold smiled politely, "I think I have your number and I'll call you should I decide that's something I want to do."

Harold's new demeanor seemed to draw Anna in more and more, there was something about him she couldn't quite put her finger on. He was no longer cute and awkward but suave and debonair. Now when he talked, his words seemed to wine and dine you with a twirl of charisma. Anna liked the new Harold, licking her lips and stroking her elongated neck, she said, "Well in that case, I know it'll be something you want, so I look forward to your call."

CHAPTER 35

As an unintentional consequence, the meeting with Marsha casted a shadow over the couple's celebratory lunch.

Erica could not hold back any longer, "So are we going to just sit here and pretend like none of that just happened back there?"

The muscles in Lionel's face tightened, "What do you want me to say Erica, huh? How 'bout I start with this, Erica you just met Marsha, my ex-girlfriend who tried to insinuate that I'm cheating on my current girlfriend. And just so you know, I would never cheat on you."

Erica picked up her fork but put it right back down, "Well that's nice to know but you do realize you've never mentioned her to me before."

"Have you mentioned all of your ex-boyfriends to me?"

Erica hung her head low, "No, I haven't."

"To me, I could care less about them because you're with me now and I'm the last stop on this train. I have no intentions on letting you get away from me like those other clowns did. In fact, I should probably send them some flowers and a thank you card and have Marsha deliver them one last time."

Lionel wanted to bring some levity to the table and their conversation.

"Lionel, I love how you can find humor in any situation."

Sitting back in his seat he said, "When you're raised in the middle of as many brothers and sisters as I have, you learn how to find it real quick."

Thinking back on his exchange with Marsha, Erica couldn't help but ask, "Were you really serious about making me your wife or was that something you said to her to make her jealous."

"Serious as a heart attack." Lionel grabbed his chest and started bucking, pretending to be going into cardiac arrest.

"Boy, don't play around like that or else you'll give me one."

Lionel decided to take a more serious approach, "In full disclosure, you should know that I was going to propose to Marsha and on the night I was going to do it, she ended our relationship for someone else."

Erica reached out for Lionel's hand, "Oh babe, I'm so sorry to hear that."

"Don't cry any tears for me, it's all good. Well, it is now."

"Why now?"

"Because I've met you of course. In the beginning, I didn't handle the breakup all that well but later on I realized it was because my ego was bruised, not my heart. I was trying to force things with Marsha, we looked good together but truth be told, we just weren't a good match. I met you not too long after that and things quickly changed in my life as a result."

"Are you trying to tell me I'm the rebound girl?"

"On the contrary, no rebounds here, you are the right girl for me and all of Texas believes so too, they already have our photos from today and all of social media is buzzing about us. The team has been doing very well, I think we might actually be their lucky charms. They are probably going to make it to the playoffs this year."

Lionel reached over and he and Erica shared a deep and passionate kiss, if he didn't know it before, he knew it now, he was in love with Erica and she with him.

"I think you should know that I'm smitten by you Ms. Erica Allen, I'm pretty certain I've been bitten."

Batting her eyes, Erica said, "Bitten by what might I ask?"

"The love bug of course. You know the song don't you?"

Lionel started singing the lyrics and Erica could not believe how well he sounded, she joined in with him and their sounds blended well in perfect harmony.

Transitioning the conversation, Lionel asked, "Now do you want to talk about what might be going on at work with your flowers?"

Erica perked up, "This will be the easiest investigation ever, things are starting to make sense to me now. I'm pretty sure it's my partner. She's recently been getting flowers delivered to her which now I believe are probably mine. The thing I can't get over is, if she'll steal my flowers, what else has she been doing? I'll probably take Monday off to investigate a few things. The other thing is why didn't you ever ask me about the flowers? I mean she got like so many floral deliveries, you had to be thinking, why isn't this girl saying thank you or something."

Throwing his hands up to surrender, Lionel confessed, "You're exactly right. You thanked me for everything else but not the flowers and I have to admit I was a little weirded out by asking you about them. I knew something had to be up but I wasn't sure what so I guess I just..."

Erica announced, "Well you don't have to worry about it anymore because I will be handling this situation pronto and I can't wait."

Rubbing her shoulders, Lionel said, "I know you'll get to the bottom of it and boy when you do...I'm just glad you aren't investigating me."

"Who says I'm not? You just never know, do you Dr. Webber, you just never know?"

CHAPTER 36

Back inside of her car, Marsha reached for her phone from the leather glove box, she had ten missed calls from Dallas.

Dialing his number she began to wonder about all of the things she would say to him to make him feel badly for standing her up and subsequently leaving her alone to deal with Lionel.

The tremble in Dallas' voice caused Marsha's congested mind to bunch up.

"Why do you sound like that, what's wrong?"

"I'm calling you because Nicole is in the emergency room and I thought you would want to know."

"What's wrong with her and why are you calling me instead of her?"

Dallas began to share details, "She said she had a sudden onset of debilitating abdominal pain, she's undergoing testing right now but I'll explain everything when you get here."

Marsha rushed to the hospital, the highway seemed to have opened up for her to get by her best friend's bedside.

Nicole was back inside her triage room speaking with the emergency room doctor with Dallas standing by her side when Marsha showed up.

Right as she pulled the curtain back to enter, she heard the doctor say, "Based on what we were able to find, what you are more than likely experiencing is growing pains which can be exacerbated by stress. Have you been stressed out recently?"

Nicole blew out some of her stress in a long sigh, "Yes, yes I have but what do you mean about growing pains?"

Cutting to the chase the doctor announced, "Oh yeah, that's the fun part. Ms. Owens, you're pregnant."

Marsha pulled back the curtain, "Pregnant?"

In unison, both Dallas and Nicole also questioned, "Pregnant?"

"Hello there, Ms. Owens, are you okay with her being in here?"

"Yes doctor, she's okay."

"Well come on in and join the party, yes ma'am, you are pregnant. Newly pregnant but pregnant none the less. Often times what happens is that your body begins stretching and preparing for what's going to happen over the course of the pregnancy, unfortunately, it's not always the best feeling and it can be quite painful. I'd like for you to just take it easy and then follow up with your regular OBGYN. Other than that, you're free to go. Give me a minute and I'll go and get your discharge papers."

The doctor left the room.

Seeing Dallas comforting Nicole was different for Marsha considering the fact she was unaware they even knew each other. She'd been trying to get them all to go out to dinner so she could introduce her best friend to her new boyfriend but there was always a reason why they couldn't meet up.

Before she addressed that she wanted to take care of the matter at hand, seeing about Nicole.

"Are you alright?"

Nicole could barely look Marsha in the face, "Yes, I'm okay. I think I'm in shock but I guess I'd better get over that."

"Uh, ya think? I think I'm a little shocked too. I'm happy about being an auntie but I didn't even know you were seeing anybody."

Dallas had not moved from by Nicole's side.

Marsha realized that as the doctor reentered the room, "Here you are Ms. Owens, remember keep down the stress, congratulations, and take care."

Dallas started to gather Nicole's things, helping her to get ready to leave.

Marsha looked around the room, as if she was looking for answers, saying, "After the day I've had, I know that I might be tripping but can someone please tell me why Dallas is here and helping my best friend?"

Dallas stopped, he looked at Marsha, and then at Nicole.

Marsha experienced rapid upper lip movement as she tried to find the right things to say.

Marsha went for it, "Dallas, why are you here?"

Nicole started rocking back and forth in the hospital bed, talking to herself under her breath, the moment she'd been dreading was about to happen. Oh how she wanted to avoid having this conversation, especially now, she didn't need the added stress.

Without making any excuses, Dallas answered honestly, "I'm going to go ahead and tell you that you aren't going to like what I'm about to say. There was never going to be a good time to tell you this but I guess it's true when they say there's no time like the present."

Marsha noticed Nicole's protective body posture and Dallas' deliberate stance, he looked like he was ready to face the pending danger head on which made Marsha feel the need to sit down.

"I know this is going to sound crazy but it was never our intention to hurt you but unfortunately what I'm about to tell you is probably going to do just that."

Dallas sat down on the bed next to Nicole and pulled her close to him.

"To answer your question, I'm here because Nicole and I are a couple and based on what the doctor has shared, she's carrying my baby and the both of you need to know that I'm going to make an honest woman out of her so she and I will be getting married."

In elevated tones, the two friends questioned, "Married?"

Dallas turned and looked at Nicole, removing Marsha from their equation, "Yes, married. Nikki, baby, I was going to marry you without a baby but now this only confirms what I was already planning."

Marsha was experiencing de ja vue, here she was being the third wheel in the midst of another couple's conversation.

Marsha muttered, "This is incredible, can this day get any worse?"

In Marsha's presence, Dallas professed his love for Nicole and the baby.

Marsha got up abruptly, her chair slid across the tiny room, "I need to get out of here. I can't even begin to wrap my mind around what is going on right now so the best thing for me to do is leave before I catch a case from killing somebody."

Before leaving, Marsha walked up to Dallas, "Don't you ever contact me again, forget you ever knew me."

And of course, she couldn't leave without addressing Nicole now could she?

She made the quick turn to face her traitor of a friend and spoke in a chilling voice, "I want you to be real clear about this, you are dead to me, you and your bastard baby."

Marsha grabbed her things and bulldozed her way out of the room, running over anyone found on the path to her car.

The wellspring of tears Nicole had been holding were released upon hearing Marsha's words, she was overcome with extreme sadness.

Dallas comforted Nicole and whispered, "We knew she'd find out one day and that day is today. She now knows and it's all out in the open. You can let it all out now."

Nicole bawled as she rested her head on Dallas' chest. He held onto her for dear life as he repeatedly whispered in her ear, I love you Nikki."

CHAPTER 37

"Hey there Samantha, I'm just checking in on you, how was your day?"

"It was good mama, what did you get into?"

"So far so good....not too much. I thought about you off and on today. Your father and I had such a nice time with you and Harold yesterday."

"Yeah, I've always enjoyed Sunday brunch after church and it was nice to have Harold join us."

Ernestine affirmed, "He's such a wonderful man, I just love his spirit and I really love the way he looks at you honey."

Samantha laughed as her mother used her unrestrained ways of lobbying for Harold. Ernestine took one look at Harold the first night he came to bible study and proclaimed to Samantha that Harold was her husband. That night, he gave his life to the Lord.

"He sent me flowers today."

"Oh how nice, what kind?"

"Harold sent me one dozen white, long-stemmed roses, they were delivered at my school today."

"He's quite the guy, you know what those white flowers represent don't you? He really respects your decision to live virtuously."

Samantha took a chance in mentioning the other guy but then again, there wasn't much she didn't share with her mother.

Samantha spoke of the other delivery, "I actually received red roses from Joshua today as well; I guess he was trying to apologize."

Samantha filled her mother in on the details from her interaction with Joshua at the run.

Unmoved by the gesture, Ernestine said, "Trying to apologize and he sends red roses, hmmm, indicating passion. Well, I think you told him right. I told you last week to pray and ask God to show you their hearts before you got too involved with either one of them and He did just that. And it didn't take long either. I know God hears our prayers."

"I just can't believe Joshua switched out on me like that but I'm glad I found out now rather than later."

"Exactly. Now that he's out of the picture, I think you should really take the time to see what the Lord is saying to you about Harold and get to know him better."

"I'm already doing that mommy dearest. We are actually going out to dinner later with some friends he'd like to introduce me to."

"Introducing you to his friends, huh? I like the sounds of that."

"Mama, let's be real, you like the sounds of anything Harold does."

Ernestine laughed, "No I don't. I just happen to trust the still, small voice that speaks to me and I heard that Harold is your husband. So anytime you talk about the wonderful things he's doing, it serves as confirmation for me. Samantha, honey, Harold is the type of man your father and I have prayed for as it relates to a suitable spouse for you and I'm very excited at the possibility."

CHAPTER 38

Erica arrived to the precinct early after being off the day before. She wanted to be there before anyone else arrived. The first thing she noticed was the latest floral arrangement on her partner's desk that she was certain belonged to her.

She was so satisfied with herself, she baked cookies and brownies and brought them in for the entire department.

Morris was the first to arrive, "Oh my goodness, Allen brought in baked goods, should we be afraid? When did you start baking?"

Erica missed working with Morris but she felt confident they would be together again soon after she dealt with Det. Brown.

"I miss working in the field with you Allen but this paper pushing ain't half bad either. How's that case going that you and Brown have been working on?"

Erica walked over to Morris' desk and spoke quietly, "There have been some strange things going on around that case but I think the strangeness has been orchestrated. I believe someone has been trying to sabotage my investigation."

Morris looked around and whispered, "Do you have any proof?"

"No, not anything solid but I have a real strong theory and I'm going to throw it up against the wall this morning when everyone arrives and see if it sticks."

Morris cautioned Erica, "Now Allen you know the Lieutenant is not going to listen to any suppositions, you need rock solid proof when you start accusing people."

Pointing her finger towards Morris' face, Erica declared, "I'll have to make him listen because if I'm right, he'll have to launch a full investigation and I'm certain several things will be found out. You can trust me on that."

"And if you're wrong?"

"Then I'll be wrong and I'll have to admit that but I don't think I am."

The rest of the crew began to fill their seats and the day was about to begin.

Erica decided she would give everyone a chance to settle in and she'd wait to confront Det. Brown at the morning briefing.

Erica could barely pay attention, her heart was pounding like steel drums in her ears, a melody was being played up there as she counted down the minutes.

Wrapping up the morning meeting, the Lieutenant asked, "Does anyone else have anything they'd like to say before we adjourn?"

Erica raised her hand.

"What is it Allen?"

Erica walked up to the front of the room.

She didn't waste any time, she began to layout her speculative scenarios.

Clearing her throat she began, "What do you think would happen if your partner was involved in a random act of violence? You'd probably get reassigned to another partner until your partner healed, right? Well, what then would happen if your new partner started stealing things and trying to sabotage the investigation?"

Everyone looked at Erica trying to figure out what on earth she was talking about.

There was one who knew but pretended not to.

"Is there a point here Allen?"

"Yes, Lieutenant there is and I'll get to it in just a second."

Erica paced the floor and continued on, "If you will indulge me for a minute, I have a few questions I need answered."

Det. Brown shrugged her shoulders and heckled from her seat, "Some of us have cases to solve and not play these silly little pitty pat or make-believe games."

Erica lunged forward, "Oh I got your make-believe. Are you going to sit here in front of everyone and tell me that you didn't order the hit on Morris so you could get assigned to my case and then when you did you tampered with evidence and in the meantime tried to ruin my relationship?"

Lieutenant Conroy jumped up, "Det. Allen, those are some might strong accusations. Do you have any proof to what you are accusing your partner of?"

"No, I don't Lieutenant but ask, just ask her. If I'm wrong, I'm wrong but if I'm right, you need to launch an investigation and find out the truth."

The Lieutenant ordered Det. Brown to stand up, everyone in the room turned to look at her.

With Erica's allegations out in the open before everyone, the Lieutenant had to ask, "Is any of what Det. Allen saying true, what do you make of these claims against you?"

Det. Brown pulled her blazer in tighter, she thought about her words and decided to say the following, "This woman is crazy, I have no idea what she's talking about. I have not done any of those things, the only thing I've ever done was try to be a good partner to her."

Erica was fuming, the heads of their colleagues were like ping pong balls going back and forth between the two women and their finger pointing.

Raising her right hand, Det. Brown added a pivotal part to her performance, "And if I'm lying, may the good Lord strike me dead right where I stand."

Those words were Det. Brown's last.

She instantly began to convulse as she dropped to the floor. Her body shook uncontrollably for a period of two minutes and then by the time her body stopped, it had stopped for good.

Morris jumped into action when she started jerking and hit the floor trying to help her, he checked her pulse.

There was none.

Det. Brown was dead.

The other detectives in the room were in complete awe at what they'd witnessed. Gasps filled the room and then it was silent.

One of the detectives walked over to Erica and said, "I guess it's safe to say, she was lying. That was the wildest thing I've ever seen. Hey, remind me never to say those words ever in life."

Erica was well aware that life and death was found in the power of the tongue and she also knew from her undergraduate days that lying could lead to death. She just never thought she'd see it in action.

Erica grabbed her head, turning in circles, screaming, "Oh my God, I'm so sorry."

Morris went to comfort Erica, "Life is but a vapor. You can literally be here one minute and gone the next. This isn't your fault, okay? You are one of the finest detectives I know and you were only doing your job and there is no need to make any apologies for that. No one and I mean no one could have ever predicted that would happen."

Lieutenant Conroy walked over, "Allen, I want you to write up a full report and put in it, everything you said in here today. I want it by tomorrow morning." The Lieutenant rubbed his forehead, "Thank God there was a room full of witnesses because I don't think I would have believed it if I hadn't seen it with my own eyes."

Erica calmed down enough to reply, "Yes sir."

Shaking his head in disbelief, the Lieutenant said, "Allen, I want you to take the rest of the day. Go home and come back ready to start again tomorrow morning."

"I'm fine Lieutenant, I'll be alright to stay."

"Oh, in case you thought that was a request, it wasn't. Now go, get out of here."

Erica tried to bargain again, "But boss…"

Pointing to the door, he yelled, "Go. Get out of here now."

Erica looked around at her colleagues who were all pale in the face and slowly turned around to leave, "Yes Lieutenant."

Morris stopped her and asked, "Are you okay to drive home, do you want me to drive you, or shall I call Lionel?"

Erica snapped at Morris, "No, didn't you hear me when I said I'm fine. I can drive myself home; I'll call you later."

Erica's two-toned sling-backs helped her to charge out of the office and into the parking lot.

Chapter 39

In an attempt to cheer Nicole up, Dallas sang the words, "We're having a baby, we're having a baby."

It had been a few days and Nicole was still quite withdrawn, she and Dallas had not had any time to be happy about their pending bundle of joy.

Not that he was insensitive to Marsha's pain but he was more interested in the well-being of Nicole and their unborn child.

Pulling back the curtains in the room to expose her to sunlight, "I'm taking you out today. You will not stay in this bed another minute moping around." Dallas knelt down beside Nicole's bed, "I hate seeing you like this Nikki. I know this is bitter-sweet but I much rather us concentrate on the sweet, my sweet, darling Nikki."

From the night they met, Nicole loved it when Dallas called her, his darling Nikki, it was their little thing.

Protesting Dallas' idea, "I'm not going anywhere."

"How are you feeling in your body right now?"

"I feel fine Dallas."

"Well then, if you feel fine, we're going out. Listen to me baby, life moves on and what you haven't been able to enjoy yet is that life is growing inside of you, a life that you and I created."

Nicole sat up and propped the pillows up behind her, "Dallas, you only knew her for a few months, I've known for over twenty years and you just make it seem like I'm supposed to move on from the fact that I've betrayed my best friend. What makes it so bad is, she might've forgiven me for sleeping with you but now that we are having a baby, that'll be a constant reminder for her."

"You're choosing to look at it that way, I see this as a constant reminder of what our love was able to create. Through Marsha, I found you and I'm sorry but I will make no apologies for loving you."

"I've tried calling her but I think she's blocked my number."

"Listen, I know this is hard on you but you have to keep in mind your condition, you can't allow this situation to take you under baby."

Nicole rolled her eyes, "My condition? Dallas, I'm pregnant, last I checked it is not a condition."

Dallas laughed and tackled Nicole like a football linebacker, more gentle of course, he agreed by saying, "I know." He screamed as loud as he could, "We are pregnant."

Dallas was beyond thrilled at the changes taking place in his life, Nicole's scare at the hospital moved him into action. He wanted to wait until a better time but he felt like this was the best time.

Nicole tried to cover his mouth from screaming so loudly, "Boy you need to hush up, as loud as you are, the neighbors across the street probably heard you."

"Well let them hear. I'm a blessed man and I don't care who hears me."

Reaching into his pocket and going down on a bended knee, "I'll quiet down a little but not before you hear me say this. I know the way we wound up together was wrong but I knew deep down inside I would be able to make it right. I see how this situation has impacted you and that is because you genuinely care for people and I love that about you. Nikki, you inspire me to be a better man, to have compassion for people even in difficult situations. Before I met you, I was coasting through life, allowing my free-spirit to lead me wherever the wind blew but now, you've grounded me and given me purpose. You match up to me and point out the man I aspire to be. Baby, I'm ready to assume the greatest role of my life, I'm ready to create for you and our child a family. I don't know what life would be like without you in it and I hope I never have to find out so will you please do me the honor of becoming my wife?"

Hormones aside, Nicole was in a blubbering mess.

Through the tears and the other inaudible words, Dallas was able to hear the magic words, "Yes, I'll marry you."

Dallas got up and the newly engaged couple celebrated with a long and deep hug.

"You have made me the happiest man in the world. I could never replace your best friend but you are now mine and I love you very much."

The tears continued to flow from Nicole's swollen eyes. Overwhelmed by it all, she just nodded.

Dallas swayed her back and forth in a dancing motion, singing again, "We're having a baby and we're getting married."

CHAPTER 40

Erica drove around town without any real destination in mind. After several attempts to reach Lionel with no such luck, she called his office to speak with Michelle.

"Hi Michelle, this is Erica. How's it going girl?"

"I'm fine Erica, how are you today?"

Erica blew out the biggest breath imaginable, "Michelle, I'm not even sure how to answer that question right now but I guess I'm doing alright."

"Oh wow, is there something I can help you with?"

"Well that's why I'm calling, I've been trying to reach Lionel and I haven't been able to get him, has he made it into the office yet or do you know where he is?"

Feeling comfortable enough with Erica to disclose her boss' whereabouts, Michelle gladly shared, "He sent me a text saying he was running behind and would explain later."

"Oh okay, so he's at home. I'm not too far from his house, I'll just run over there real quick. Thanks Michelle. I'll talk with you soon."

"Alright Erica, you take care."

Erica drove the few miles left to make it to her beloved's sizeable residence.

Upon pulling up to the drive way like she normally did, she noticed another car resting in the spot where she now parked hers.

Slowing down to make an assessment of the situation, she thought, *"Hmmm, he has company. Is this why he's not at work? Is this why he's not answering me? Should I go in and see what's up?"*

She parked her car on the street and dialed Lionel once again.

He didn't pick up.

Lionel's unresponsiveness caused Erica to do what she did best, investigate. She decided to place another phone call.

"Hey there Delores, this is Erica. I'm out in the field right now in my car and I was wondering if you could do me a quick favor?"

"Sure Erica, you're always looking out for me, you know I'll do anything for you, what do you need?"

"Can you run a set of license plates for me?"

"Yeah, go ahead with the number."

Within seconds, Delores had a match.

"Hey Erica, that plate belongs to a, Marsha Miller."

"Uh-huh, Marsha Miller. Okay Delores, that's all I needed. I'll come down and see you soon. Thanks for the information."

"No problem Erica, I'll talk with you soon."

Looking at herself in the review mirror, she began a conversation with herself, "Why is she here and why is her being here stopping Lionel from answering me? Especially on a day like today. I need him and he's here with her. You know what, I don't have time for this. I have better things to be doing like solving my website case. Now more than ever, I need to find that hacker so I can prove myself."

Erica started up her car, in haste, her driving burned tread on Lionel's street, leaving behind tire tracks on the road.

She couldn't understand what business Lionel would have Marsha that would preclude him from answering her, she couldn't get over the nagging feeling she had inside. It felt all too familiar, her mind began producing thoughts centered around her ex, Patrick.

What she didn't know was that on the other side of the door, Lionel had been ambushed by Marsha.

In all of the hustle and bustle of life after Marsha, he didn't realize he hadn't changed the locks so she still had a key to his home and that morning, she used it.

Marsha walked inside as Lionel was about to leave for work and begged him to give her a few moments of his undivided attention.

"For all that we've been through Lionel, you owe me that."

Rolling his eyes, Lionel pronounced, "You must be out of your ever loving mind because I don't owe you a thing."

Marsha belted out, "Lionel, please."

She started to cry, "If I ever meant anything to you, please listen."

The twinge in his chest made him realize he didn't have to be a total monster to her. To him, choosing to be mean to her would signify he wasn't over her and that he hadn't truly forgiven her. He could see she was hurting, he decided to stop everything and show her some compassion in her time of need.

Leading her to the breakfast nook, he sat her down and began to make her favorite coffee, he still had some in his pantry.

"So what's going on with you girl? Why are you just walking all up in my house like you own the place? What's up with that? By the way, thanks for letting me know I need to replace all of the locks." Lionel laughed trying to bring up the mood in the room but Marsha wasn't amused.

She fiddled with her fingers, "I didn't know where else or who else to talk to. You were the only person I could think of that I would want to talk to about this."

Lionel sat down with the coffee mugs, "Talk about what?"

Marsha began to walk Lionel through the last several days since the race and the recent revelations about Dallas and Nicole.

Lionel offered his ear but nothing more. While he had compassion for her, he was quite unsympathetic. He didn't want to be that guy that kicked a man while he was down but he felt like it needed to be said, "You know what they say right, what goes around, comes around."

Marsha knew exactly what Lionel meant and that was partly why she felt like she could talk to him because she felt like he'd be able to understand her pain.

Sipping on the coffee, Marsha said, "Lionel, I know what I did was wrong but how was I to know you were going to propose?"

Lionel's patience was beginning to wane, his eyes were narrowed with an intense focus, "Marsha, you breaking up with me the night I was going to propose wasn't the issue, the problem was the reason you broke up with me...you were cheating on me with another guy, one you barely knew."

Marsha snapped back, "At one point I barely knew you too."

Lionel opened his mouth to say something rather sharply to Marsha but then he stopped and shook his head slowly, he realized Marsha hadn't learned a thing and this love triangle she was in had not taught her anything either.

Lionel made several attempts to end the conversation and get started with his day but each time, Marsha would become highly emotional and overly dramatic.

"Lionel, I'm so sorry. I never should have left you. We were so good together Lionel. Don't you remember?"

Marsha tried to test Lionel's limits when she stood to hug and kiss him, through her tears she said, "Don't you remember how well you and I were together Lionel?"

With a polite, yet powerful push, Lionel excused himself from Marsha's grasp.

"Marsha, I know you are going through a tough time right now and I really don't want to add to that but the truth of the matter is, this isn't my problem. You aren't my problem anymore. You did me the biggest favor when you called things off. By you closing the door on us, it led me to the door of a new relationship, a relationship I plan on making permanent."

"But Lionel."

"But Lionel nothing. I've about had enough of this. I really need to get to work, I'm sure my phone is blowing up. I've given you enough time and I'm no longer interested in being a guest at your little pity party."

Marsha slowly got up from the table and started to gather her things, including her keys.

"Leave my keys on the table. In fact, if you have anything else of mine on you, pull it out now and leave it too."

Marsha glared at Lionel as she walked by him and threw his keys in the trash.

As soon as Marsha left, Lionel picked up his phone and noticed all of Erica's attempts to reach him.

"Man, fooling round with that 'ole Marsha, I have missed my baby. Let me call her and find out what's going on."

Erica didn't answer.

CHAPTER 41

With Erica and Lionel's hectic schedules they had been unable to attend many of the basketball games but they were keeping up with their ever growing fan base through social media channels.

The campaign was turning out better than expected, everyone was falling in love with Lierica and they wanted to see more.

Alexis Bryne placed a call to Lionel.

"Hello Lionel, this is Alexis, how are you? Or should I be asking how is Lierica, Houston's favorite couple?"

Lionel blushed at their nickname, "We are doing great, thanks for asking."

"That's wonderful news, I can tell you that everything you guys have been sending in has been nothing short of fantastic. You guys look amazing together, some of these pictures are simply stunning."

"Thanks Alexis, we've been enjoying all of this, it's been fun. Definitely a different kind of way of getting to know a person, I can tell you that."

"Well Lionel, if I can offer any advice to you, do whatever you can to always keep that beautiful smile on her face. I promise if you can do that, you two will have a beautiful life together."

Lionel took in a deep breath, "I'm actually glad you called because I've been tossing around an idea and I'd like to get your opinion."

"Sure Lionel, what's up?"

"Despite only having dated for a few months now, without a shadow of a doubt, I know Erica is the woman for me. I already know I'm not interested in looking any further than her...she's it."

Alexis screamed through the phone, she was on the other end jumping up and down while she listened to Lionel's heartfelt words.

"I was thinking that since things have been going so well with the campaign and we did actually decide to date each other at the game that I would propose to her at a game. What do you think?"

Hoping from one foot to the next, "Lionel, I couldn't have asked for a better outcome from when I approached you two at that game. There was no "playbook" for this type of promotion in place, I just saw an opportunity and decided to run with it and to hear this news shows it has turned out to be more than I could have ever dreamed for."

Lionel expressed his intentions to Alexis, "You mentioned keeping her smiling and I want you to know I intend to do just that. I love her smile and I'm committed to doing whatever it takes to see it on her face. She's blessed my life in my so many ways and I couldn't imagine my life without her."

Alexis was now tearing up, "Lionel that is beautiful, oh my goodness, what can I do to help you pull this off, when are you thinking about doing this?"

Lionel tossed out an idea, "Well, the best case scenario would be that the team makes it to the playoffs and the championship games and I do it the night of the winning championship game but that is so risky, don't you think Alexis?"

"I agree with you Lionel, it's very risky but I haven't gotten this far in my life or career by not taking risks. I don't know who's credited with saying this but with great risks comes great rewards. I say let's take a chance and go for it."

"But what if the team loses Alexis, then I'll miss my chance and that's what I'm worried about."

"But what if they win? That's the part I'm looking forward to. I don't know Lionel, there is something uniquely special about you and Erica and I just choose to believe that everything is going to work out well here. You just need to have a little faith and believe. You do believe don't Lionel?"

Lionel paused for a moment, "I do have faith and I do believe."

Alexis was now doing her very own happy dance, "Awesome, I'm a believer too and this is going to be great. The playoffs start this weekend and the Flyers have clinched their playoff spot. If all goes well, realistically, we're looking at about four to six weeks before the championship game. My team and I will get to working out things on our end and I suggest you get things rolling on your end like a ring Mister or have you already picked out one?"

"I have not but I plan to pick out a ring befitting the gem Erica is to me. I'm going to call and set up a time to meet with my jeweler sometime this week."

"Lionel, I will need for you and Erica to coordinate your schedules to be here for the championship week. We can do several promotional things that week and that way, you guys can be here on which ever night the team actually wins the game. I'm speaking and declaring they will win."

"That sounds good, I'll speak with Erica and make sure she can get the time off and square everything up with her. I'd like to fly her mother and sister out there as a surprise to her so I need to get on that as soon as possible as well. Alexis, it sounds like I have my work cut out for me. I'm glad you called and I'll be in touch with you soon."

"Congratulations Lionel, call me if you need anything. You have truly made my day here today. I'm so happy for you two."

"Thanks Alexis, I'm going to call Erica now."

Lionel dialed Erica once again.

She didn't answer.

Lionel looked at his watch, talking aloud he said, "Half of the day is already gone. I think I'll just work from home the rest of the day. That way I can work on some of my proposal plans?"

Inside his home office, settling in to get to work, Lionel thought on Erica, he was so happy but he was getting concerned, *"Where are you baby and why aren't you answering me now?"*

Right in the middle of his thoughts, his assistant, Michelle called.

"Hey Lionel, I've been trying to reach you, Harold Johnson's office called, apparently, Erica has called a last minute meeting. She called here for you earlier, have you spoken to her?"

"No, I haven't. We've been playing phone tag, I'll head over to Johnson Enterprises; I guess I'll see her over there."

CHAPTER 42

"Well hello there beautiful."

Samantha gushed, nowadays you could find her doing that often. After she stopped seeing Joshua, Samantha and Harold started going out together more frequently and getting to know one another. Harold was attending the after church Sunday brunches with her family and he was fitting in like an old glove with the Richards.

"Hi Harold, how's your day going so far?"

"Much better now that I'm talking to you. I hope I'm not interrupting too much of your peace and quiet time during your planning period."

"It's always a pleasure to talk to you Harold and just so you know, I'm still smiling from last night."

"Mission accomplished then."

"Well if that was your mission, then yes, I'd have to say, you did that and you did it very well."

"You're still smiling huh? Send me a picture then. I think I need a Samantha selfie in my life right now."

"Okay, hold on a second."

Samantha did a quick once over in the mirror hanging on her door, she had to make sure she looked perfect for the picture she was about to send.

"Look at you. You are still smiling, I love it."

"I'm glad you like it Harold. Now, for as long as I have lived in Texas, I have never experienced it the way I did last night with you. Oh my goodness, cruising down the river walk by way of the horse drawn carriage was amazing. I was already feeling like a princess but when you pulled out those glass slippers and placed them on my feet and then oh my goodness, the shoes actually fit, I could have screamed. I'm still trying to figure out how you knew the right size to get?"

"Hopefully by now you've learned that I'm a pretty resourceful guy."

"Indeed you are. Well, I just want to thank you again for a beautiful evening and this princess is happy to call you her prince."

All throughout Harold's life, he'd made decisions by trusting his gut, his instinct, whatever felt right to him. However, while he still relied on his ability to do such, he was now choosing to make decisions in a different way. Although he was new to seeking God for direction, he wasn't going to let that stop him. Each moment that he spent with Samantha, it solidified his initial thoughts about her. With such a life changing decision, he would not take it lightly. He sought counsel and he prayed for wisdom and understanding as to how to proceed with his relationship with Samantha. He was thrilled with his new life and he didn't want anything to mess it up so he was careful about everything.

Samantha was still unaware of what Harold actually did for a living and his net worth. If they were to move forward in the way he wanted them to, he needed to know she was in it for him and not the money. He didn't want to be dishonest but he was trying to determine the best time to reveal his assets to her.

"I like the sounds of that, Princess Samantha. I've looked at your picture like one hundred times already. That smile inspires me. When I see that smile, it makes me want to be a better man."

Placing her hand over her chest and closing her eyes, she said, "Ahh, what a sweet thing to say."

Harold took a glance at his clock.

"Hey, I'm going to have to get ready to go, I have a meeting in a few minutes but I wanted to call and see how your day was going."

Just when Samantha's smile couldn't get any bigger, it did, "Well, I'm glad you called me. It was nice to hear your voice during the middle of the day and I look forward to seeing you soon, my sweet prince."

Samantha hung up the phone smiling and thinking, "*What an amazing man. What did I do to get so lucky? Lord, whatever you are doing in this season, please don't do it without me or him.*"

Opening up her notes to begin planning again, Samantha closed the notes, "*Did I just really have those thoughts? Lord, am I falling for Harold? Is he the one for me?*"

Excited and overwhelmed all at the same time Samantha stood up and smoothed out her dress, saying a quick prayer under her breath, "Okay, so I'm going to trust in the Lord with all my heart and lean not to my own understanding but I'm going to acknowledge Him in all my ways that He might direct my paths and Lord I acknowledge you in this situation with Harold, I pray that You lead, guide, and direct me and for Your will to be done in our lives. Amen."

Samantha jumped up and down as she looked at herself in the mirror saying, "Oh my goodness, this is so exciting...I can't wait to see how all of this plays out."

CHAPTER 43

Harold walked into his spacious conference room with an extra pep in his step. Leonard was already seated and noticed his new stride.

"She must be one special lady."

Harold landed back on earth from cloud nine, "What are you talking about Leonard?"

"You know exactly what I'm talking about man. It has be a woman, only a woman could bring forth this kind of transformation in you Harold. Hey, c'mon...am I right about it?"

Leonard was convinced of the source of Harold's new outlook on life.

Harold took his rightful place at the head of his long, cherry wood boardroom table.

"You're partly right...a man and a woman."

Leonard scratched his head, "Say it isn't so Harold. I've never pictured you to be one of those freaky-deaky types."

Harold shook his head and laughed, "Calm down man, I don't even know why your mind took you there but through the woman, I met 'The Man,' the one upstairs, you know, the big guy. I met a young lady that took me to church and as a result, I gave my life to Christ."

Harold loved telling his story of transformation, he was not ashamed because it was the best thing to have happened in his life.

"What? You're a Christian now? The one who didn't believe in much of anything now believes in Jesus Christ? I don't know what to say....congratulations?"

Harold smiled brightly, "I'm sure it's hard to believe but as you can see, I'm a brand new man and if I can believe, I'm a living witness anyone can. Leonard, you've been around me long enough to know who I am and what I'm about but now even if I didn't have money I'd still feel like the richest man around."

"Wow, Harold that's incredible; I think I may need to meet somebody like that. Lord knows I need a change in my life."

Harold tuned into what his employee was really saying.

"And you can Leonard. You don't need a woman to lead you, that was my way but I can introduce you to Him right now."

A hush fell over the room. It was decision time. Leonard paused for a moment, "Well, we don't have much time, Lionel and Det. Allen should be here any minute. I mean, she called this meeting, I thought she would have been here by now."

Harold was relentless with his witness, "The good thing is, we don't need a lot of time. You only need to do two things, believe and confess."

Harold was now adorned with the handprint of grace and it showed and he was now in a position where he was ready to share it with anyone who would listen.

In the next few minutes, Harold shared with Leonard the same message of reconciliation he heard the night at Samantha's church and he led Leonard to and through the sinner's prayer. Leonard accepted Jesus as his Lord and Personal Savior and invited Him to come and live in his heart right there in the boardroom.

Over the years, an innumerable amount of powerful decisions had been made in that room however one of the most powerful decisions had just been made by Leonard.

"Okay, now that was interesting. How come I don't feel different, I was expecting fireworks or lightning and thunder or something."

Harold acknowledged, "You may not feel anything right now but something is going on, you should know that all of heaven is rejoicing for you at this very moment. The fireworks are going off up there. Take each day one by one and begin to develop your relationship with Christ, I promise, you and everyone around you will start to see a change. Take it from me."

Leonard believed in what Harold said because he had witnessed firsthand a dramatic change in his boss. Leonard was a trusted member of Harold's team, he'd been around for about seven years, allowing him the opportunity to see Harold through various facets of life.

"Alright Harold, I'm going to do what you said. You think I can go to church with you as I start this new journey?"

"Absolutely, I'd love for you to join us?"

"Us?"

"Oh yes, now that's the woman part. I've been attending church with my girlfriend, Samantha and her family."

"Girlfriend huh? Things have definitely changed for you my man."

Harold couldn't help but smile, "Yeah man, life is good. Samantha is my little princess and one day, sooner rather than later, I hope to make her my queen. Yeah Leonard, right now, it's really good to be Harold."

Leonard grabbed his chest and pretended to faint, "Whoa, in all the time I've known you, I've never heard you talk like this. I just figured you'd be the perpetual bachelor. But, I have to say, it sounds good to hear that you're happy."

"I am happy Leonard and I'd be even happier if Det. Allen and Lionel would get here."

Leonard laughed, "I hear you on that one, they both are usually on time; I wonder what's keeping them?"

CHAPTER 44

Lionel parked his car in the parking garage at Johnson Enterprises and on his way to the elevator, he saw Erica whiz by, nearly clipping him. He stopped and said aloud, "Jesus girl, what's up with you?"

More than half of the day had passed and they hadn't been able to connect so Lionel decided to wait at the elevator for Erica.

Pushing the down button ten times in about five seconds, Erica stood with her arms folded accompanied by an iced expression upon her face to match, not paying any attention to Lionel.

Waving his index finger, "Um, hello there. It's only your boyfriend over here waiting to greet you. What's up with you today?"

Erica lashed out at Lionel, "What's up with me, what's up with you Lionel?"

Trying to figure out what in the world was going on with Erica, Lionel calmly replied, "Well, I've had a very interesting day so far. It started out quite awkward but baby it got much better with two very special phone calls. I saw where you called me a couple of times and I'm so sorry I couldn't answer but I called you as soon as I could, how's your day been?"

"You say yours has been interesting well I bet your interesting doesn't top my interesting."

Lionel touched Erica at her elbow, "What happened sweetheart, do you want to talk about it?"

Pulling her elbow away, Erica snapped back, "When I wanted to talk about it, you didn't answer, you weren't there for me when I needed you so no, I don't want to talk about it. All I want to do is go inside and have this meeting to discuss my recent findings with Harold and Leonard."

Lionel stepped back, "Hey, hold on a minute. I'm not sure what's going on with you but I'm sorry I couldn't answer the phone when you called but as I just stated, I called you as soon as I could and then you didn't answer. So guess what, it happens, sometimes people can't answer the phone right when you call."

Erica wanted to see if Lionel would tell her the truth or if he would try to hide he spent the morning with Marsha, so she asked, "Okay, so what were you so tied up in that you couldn't answer me this morning?"

Lionel placed his messenger bag on the ground so he could speak freely and with expression.

"Well, I was going to tell you when I called but you'll never believe this. Marsha showed up at my house this morning. Apparently, she still had a key to my place and never in a million years did I think she'd ever use it so I never changed the locks. But she did. Home girl walked right up in my house as I was getting ready to leave."

Erica interrupted, "What did she come there for?"

"Get this, she claims she came by because she felt like I'd understand what she's going through because how about, her best friend and her boyfriend are now together and are expecting a baby."

Erica seemed to be loosening up, Lionel appeared to be telling the truth but she didn't like the feeling she had surrounding his relationship with Marsha.

Her activities earlier that day, swam around in her head, *"I wonder how he would feel if he knew I was stalking him earlier and went by his house? I'm glad he told me the truth though, I can deal a whole lot better with the truth over a lie."*

Erica responded, "You know what they say about that thing called karma and the bible says, you reap what you sow, whichever way you believe, it's best to treat people right."

"Exactly, that's the same thing I told her. But Erica, I really don't want to talk about Marsha anymore, she's part of my past and I'm only interested in the present and our future."

"So did you tell her that?"

"Oh most definitely, Marsha knows she and I are done and that you, my friend, are the one for me."

Lionel reached in to try and give Erica a kiss. The warmth of his lips thawed her cold, trembling ones.

"Now tell me what happened with you? What did I miss this morning where I wasn't there for you?"

Erica broke away and placed her hand on her forehand and the other on her hip, "Boy, I don't have time to go into all of the details but let's just say, everything I thought about my partner turned out to be true. I confronted her this morning in front of everyone, she denied everything and tried to get all self-righteous and said something like, if I'm lying, may God strike me down now."

Lionel covered his mouth, "No way, say it isn't so."

"Man, as soon as she said those words, that heifer straight up passed out and died."

"You have got to be kidding me?"

"I wish I was but I'm not. That whole scene freaked me out, I've never seen anything like that in my life. My lieutenant sent me home for the day and since I was still tripping, I called you to try and calm me down....but."

Lionel reached for Erica, to console and comfort her, "Man, she took that whole life and death lying in the tongue thing to another level didn't she? I'm so sorry you had to go through that alone."

"Yes, she did and she thought she tried to sabotage our relationship and my investigation but she wasn't able to. Speaking of investigations, you have made me late for a meeting that I called. Sometimes being alone has its perks because I have some new information I want to share."

The elevator button was pushed once again, only this time, Erica pressed once.

"New information huh?"

Still trying to rub it in, Erica acknowledged, "Yeah, when you didn't answer me, I decided to look into a couple of things and I'm glad I did which is why I called this meeting today."

The two boarded the elevator and proceeded to meet up with Leonard and Harold but not before Lionel dipped Erica and kissed her with profound passion as his mind wondered, *"This should be interesting; she seems quite confident in her findings. I wonder what she knows."*

CHAPTER 45

"Come, sit down with me. I have the calendar here, are you ready to choose our wedding date?"

Nicole sat down next to Dallas, "Yes and no."

"Why the hesitation Nikki?"

Nicole began to tear up, "I just, you know, I always imagined that when I chose my wedding date I'd be doing it with my best friend."

Dallas grabbed Nicole's face by her chin and turned it towards him, "And you are...with me."

Nicole wiped her tears, "Yeah but you know what I mean. It's just that choosing this date is very bitter-sweet for me, I didn't think it would be this hard. I really miss her."

Dallas pulled Nicole closer, "I understand love and hopefully in time things will get better. She probably misses you just as much. I'm sure it was a tough blow but not one that she can't recover from. When she sees how happy you are she might realize that while unfortunate, things do happen for a reason."

Nicole shrugged her shoulders, "I didn't tell you this but her cousin called me and gave me the tongue lashing of a lifetime, she cursed me out from downtown to uptown."

"What? You give me her number, I have a few words I'd like to give her for calling you. She didn't upset you did she?"

Nicole laughed a little, "At first, I was a little upset but I realized had it been my cousin I probably would have done the same thing. This situation isn't the easiest and you can't fault people for feeling how they feel about it. Those are their feelings, the only thing is; we can only control what we do in life and how our actions count against us, not the other person. Now, I'll have to wear what I did to Marsha but how she and other people respond will go against them, not me."

Dallas lovingly rubbed Nicole across her shoulder blade, "See there, you're so smart, just one of the many reasons I fell in love with you. I know it's hard right now baby but as with anything time brings about a change, you'll see. If Marsha is anything like I think she is, you two will find your way back together again."

"I can't be so sure about that. As much as I'd like for that to happen, I think it's probably best that in order for you and I to make it, I need to make a clean break from her. Seeing us together and also with a baby will not give her the time she needs to heal because it will be like the constant stab in the back and the baby will be like a constant twist of the knife. I don't want to keep hurting her like that."

Dallas kissed her hand, "I hear you Nikki and I'm here for you however you decide to handle this situation. I love you my sweet, darling Nikki."

Fanning himself with the calendar in an effort to remind Nicole of the matter at hand, she playfully grabbed it from him, "Give me this thing boy. Okay, now let's see."

The swell from Dallas' heart matched the smile on his face, he was elated to be choosing a wedding date with Nicole. He'd already let it be known he wasn't interested in a long engagement and that he desired for them to be married before their baby made its grand entrance into the world.

"How long do you think it will take for us to plan a wedding?"

Nicole put the calendar down, "Wait a minute, you want to help plan a wedding?"

Dallas replied, "Why not? I am getting married too, right?"

"Yeah but most men just say tell them where to be and what to wear and forget them when it comes to the details."

"Well there you have it, I'm not most men. Now am I?"

Nicole responded to Dallas with a kiss, "No you are not."

Sitting close to one another, side-by-side, their legs touched and Dallas pulled up Nicole's feet to rub them.

"So what kind of wedding would you want to have Dallas?"

"No, let me ask you first. I know how you women are, you've dreamed of that day your whole life so before I say anything; I want to hear from you first."

Nicole's cheeks were flushed as she knew Dallas was telling the truth. She had dreamed of the day she would get married and in her mind, it had been planned many years ago, the only thing needed...insert groom. Despite the way things happened, she was over the moon in love with Dallas and tickled pink to be marrying him and having his baby, two for the price of one.

Nicole grabbed a sheet of paper and tore them into little slips, "I have an idea, let's write down elements of our idea of a perfect wedding such as location, colors, food, anything you can think of and let's put them in the bowl and we'll let fate decide the details of our wedding day."

"What a great idea. I love it and I love you, let's get started."

Just as the plans for the wedding were about to begin, the doorbell rang.

"Are you expecting someone Nikki?"

"No, I'm not...are you?"

"No, you sit tight, let me see who it is."

Dallas opened the door but no one was there. What was there was a long white box from Miller's Floral.

"See there honey, Marsha is starting to come around, it looks like she's sent you some flowers. I told you to give her some time and she'd come around."

Dallas handed Nicole the box and walked into the kitchen.

Before opening the box, Nicole said, "If that's the case, why isn't there a delivery person at the door? This seems strange to me, she never sends out a delivery without a driver."

Walking back to the sofa, Dallas replied, "I told you to give her some time, I knew she'd come around. It probably just hit her to send the flowers over, no fuss; no muss right?"

Nicole muttered under her breath, "I guess," as she opened the box.

The bone chilling shriek caused Dallas to drop their refreshments, the plate smashed and the glasses shattered as they both hit the floor. His heart pounded out of his chest as he rushed to Nicole's side, "What? What is it, what's wrong sweetheart?"

The box was now lying on the floor with its contents scattered abroad, contents that included twelve long-stemmed black, velvety roses.

Dallas walked over to see Nicole wrapping her arms around her knees that were pinned up to her chest, rocking back and forth.

Down on his knees he frantically searched for a card but there was none, however, he knew who they were from, he didn't need a card. He felt like Marsha had spoken loud and clear with her actions.

Dallas quickly grabbed a trash bag to clean up the mess and remove the symbolic gesture out of the house and on his way out of the door, he grabbed his keys.

Nicole yelled out, "Where are you going?"

"I'm going to pay that low down dirty dog a visit. How dare she send you these flowers? I mean, are these to represent some sort of threat, is she wishing gloom and doom on you by sending you black roses? I know that she's hurting but I'm not going to stand by and watch her threaten us like this. I'll be back."

Nicole screamed through her tears, "No, don't go Dallas. Don't do it. That's what she wants, she wants to get a rise out of us and if you go to her, you'll be playing right into her hands. Plus, you are way too upset to be confronting anyone, I don't even want to think of what might happen if you see her right now."

"I want these out of here, hold on." Dallas tossed the bag into the garbage outside and ran back in, "Listen to me, I don't play around about the people I care about. She is dead wrong for this and she needs to know it. She's out of control, Nikki...after a stunt like this, I don't trust her."

Nicole was beginning to calm herself down, she tried to put a positive spin on the situation. "You know, over the years, I've spent many days at the floral shop with her and I've picked up a thing or two there. Now, I don't know what her intentions were by sending these but black roses don't always mean death, or black magic, they can also mean rebirth, regeneration, or a new beginning. I choose to look at this through that perspective. You and I are getting married and having a baby, to me, that is the best new beginning I could ever hope for."

Dallas' rigid posture slumped, "I love how you always look for the silver lining in everything. If you are okay then I'm okay but I have to say, I'm not happy about this Nikki. If

Marsha will do something like this, who knows what she might do next which is why I need to go check her."

Nicole grabbed Dallas' hand, "Nope, there will be no checking, promise me you won't play into her hands and go see her. I will admit, seeing those roses did shake me up a little at first but I'm fine, we're fine...let's leave it alone."

"I don't trust her Nikki but for your sake, I'll leave it alone but we are no longer staying here. If you are ready to move on from here and with our lives, we are going to make a clean break, don't you worry about a thing, I'll take care of everything."

Dallas had been afforded the opportunity to live carefree for most of his life because he grew up as a child of privilege. His father was the owner of a bottler company that started small but grew steadily into massive millions over time.

Being the only child out of the McCants' union, he was spoiled rotten. Although highly educated, he never found his place so he lived his life without any boundaries and expectations. However, now that he'd met Nicole, he was ready to finally put down some roots and be the man she deserved. She made him want to be that man.

Dallas placed Nicole back in the bed to allow her some time to rest and he left the room to make a few phone calls to confirm their new living arrangements.

They would be moving by the end of the week, moving into a new life together, leaving Marsha and everything else behind.

CHAPTER 46

"Well look who decided to join us Leonard. It's none other than the lovely, Det. Allen and Lionel who I see is closely following behind the detective."

"I see that too Harold, just like a little puppy dog."

Harold's light-hearted humor allowed for the couple's tardiness to not be an obvious issue. Normally, Harold would have not waited for a late meeting but he was beginning to see how everything happens for a reason. Had they not been late, he might have missed an opportunity to present the Good News to Leonard.

Erica placed her bag on the table, "I'm sorry we're late, please accept my apology, especially considering I called the meeting. All I can say is, today has been a different kind of day."

Leonard looked around, "Are we still waiting on one more? Where's your partner, Det. Brown?"

Erica hung her head down, "Hey listen, it's not my place to judge, I'm not quite sure where she might've ended up."

Both Harold and Leonard prepped up to speak and Lionel, shaking his head, stopped them before they could, "Don't ask."

Harold took Lionel's advice and decided to move on, "So, I'm guessing you have some updates you'd like to share about our case which is why you called this meeting?"

Thinking on how she'd answered about her partner's whereabouts, Erica quickly got lost in her own thoughts about where she might spend eternity; *"If it had been me that died today, am I certain that I'd make it to heaven? I think I am but I need to make sure, this is serious business."*

Harold called out to Erica again, "Det. Allen...are you okay?"

Snapping back to the conference room, Erica replied, "Yes...yes Harold, I'm fine."

Lionel sat back and watched Erica mimicking her as a way of appearing to be normal. All the while curious as to what she'd discovered.

Erica got herself together and began to present her most recent findings, "So we all know the dating website was hacked and for the last few months we've been working together as a task force to one, close out the known vulnerabilities which Lionel has done a fine job and two, to ultimately catch the perpetrator that did it."

Harold chimed in, "Yes, Lionel has done an amazing job and we are grateful to have the two of you on board. It's almost like he knew how to find every hole we had and he was able to patch it right up for us. Thanks Lionel."

Lionel nodded, "No sweat man, that's what I'm here for."

Erica continued on, "Based on today's events I took it upon myself to look into some of the data files, server logs, and other evidence we collected from you all. I looked over the coding from the corrupted files and I went over every line by line searching for anything that might pop out at me."

Lionel asked, "And what did you find, if anything?"

Eager to respond, Erica said, "Oh I found something alright. Whoever did this, left a signature. I compared the code from the source files to the corrupted files and I found the following line: **th3 lov3 b*g m@kes bl33d1ng h3@rts**. Your site went haywire as a result of what I now know is because of the love bug virus. They put in all types of traps where if someone typed in the perfect combination of keys, they'd get something crazy to show up on their screen or their computers might lock up. It also appears that two sets of databases were created in an effort to be able to randomize the profiles, there was the actual database that was a part of your site and then there was an additional database created by the hacker to mirror the actual one but it was for the sake of mismatching people. So instead of sending seemingly perfect matches like the site is designed to do, your members were now getting mismatches."

Harold placed his hand on his neck, "This is all too much for me to take in right now, this person is very sophisticated in their thinking but what I don't understand is why the site would be targeted in the first place?"

Erica's news was more than Harold could comprehend at the moment but he couldn't help but think if Samantha was from an organic match or was she indeed a mismatch. Either way, it didn't matter to him but he needed to know for sure, although he believed she was indeed the match God had created for him.

"Sometimes people hack sites just to see if they can, some like to expose vulnerabilities to computer networks but in this instance, I believe this is either the job of a jilted lover or someone who didn't like who you matched them up with."

Everyone around the table laughed at Erica's last guess.

"The more I look into this case, I'm starting to see a pattern here, it's not hard to figure out what happened, the problem is figuring how who did it, nothing I've tried has led me anywhere. The culprit was smart to use hidden proxies and IP addresses, they were prepared for the battlefield of computer networks. I keep feeling like whoever is responsible for this is slipping beyond my reach. I did however, track down a small piece of code that indicated the perp might be located here in Texas. But I tell you what, I won't stop until I find out who did it."

Lionel shifted in the squeaky, leather chair, *"Man, she's very good at her job; I love seeing her work though, she's so cute trying to figure this out."*

"Well Det. Allen, you have our full support and cooperation, this experience has actually forced us to take a good look at how our site is run. We've added disclaimers and changed some of the wording in our marketing efforts. So while I wasn't happy about this happening to my site and my business, in a way, I'm glad it did. It has shown us various areas of improvement."

Lionel jumped in, "Well, that's good news Harold, glad you can see the positive side in all of this."

"Yeah man, you have to and I appreciate all of the hard work you and Det. Allen have put in for this case."

Erica set the stage for what to expect next, "So, I have a few other leads that I'm working on but I'll continue to keep you all posted through email but if I find out anything super-duper important, I'll schedule another meeting."

Harold stood from the table, "Sounds good guys, well I have a date tonight and I want to do a couple of things to prepare so I hate to run out on you guys, well, no I don't but you understand where I'm coming from. I'll talk with you all soon."

Leonard followed behind Harold, "Hey man, wait up. I'll walk out with you. I want to get the service times for the next church service."

Erica overheard Leonard and Harold as they walked out and thought after the day's events, she might need to make a visit to church herself.

"You are one fine detective, Det. Allen."

"Do you mean in deed or in looks?"

"Why both of course, but you already knew that didn't you? What you should know is that I'm very impressed by you Erica Allen."

Erica's desire to hunt down the person who hacked into Harold's site had become a fascination to Lionel, he was intrigued by the chase and her pursuit.

Left alone in the conference room, Erica remembered parts of her previous conversation with Lionel, "Hey, before we came up, you mentioned you had two very special phone calls that turned your day around, what were they about? I could use some good news right about now."

Lionel perked up, his phone calls were indeed good news, "Well, the first one was from Alexis, you know, with the basketball team. The playoffs are coming up and they'd like us to be there for the week of the playoffs as part of the promotion we signed up for and I guess to bring the team good luck. So, I know you have a lot going on at work but can you look into taking that time off?"

Erica sighed deeply, "I'm not sure about taking time off right now Lionel."

"Erica, I understand but we signed up with this team to do this and I promise you won't regret taking the time off, it's going to be great; I can feel it."

Packing her bag up to leave, "Alright, I'll look into it but what was the other call about?"

Lionel sat on the edge of the table, "So listen, I've been waiting to tell you this because I didn't want to get my hopes up but after I got back from the conference, I received a phone call from a governmental official telling me that I'd been selected to be a part of an initiative for creating a next generation cyber innovation and technology center of excellence."

Erica joked around a bit, "Try saying that three times fast."

"I know right, anyway since the conference, I've gone through an extensive background check and interview process to determine if my company would be one of the partner organizations with this initiative and I'm pleased to announce that I've made it to the final round."

Erica snatched Lionel up for a hug, "Oh Lionel, that's awesome news, I'm so proud of you."

"Hey, I haven't gotten the final word yet."

"Yeah, I know but you and I both know you're probably going to get it. You are a mastermind in this industry, a true thought leader and the world is starting to recognize what I already know to be true. You're going to get it."

Lionel took Erica by the hand, "Not that I'm hurting for anything now but baby, if I get this, we will be set for life."

"We?"

"Yes Erica, we will be set for life; I plan to share my life with you and I hope you feel the same way too."

In being with Lionel, Erica wasn't as guarded as she'd been in the past but she was still trying to work out her trust issues so she wasn't so quick to answer Lionel but she did respond to him with a kiss and a smile as they walked out of the conference room together.

CHAPTER 47

"Good evening, I'm Harold Johnson and I'm here to pick up a package, it should be gift wrapped."

"Oh yes, Mr. Johnson the store is pretty busy right now and I'm the only one here but if you give me a moment, I'll grab that for you."

Harold tried to calm his nerves as he waited patiently for his gift. He was scheduled for a date with a special someone and he didn't want to be late and with the gift he was hoping to score some extra points in his favor.

The store clerk honored his patience and paused for a minute to grab his package.

Harold thanked her graciously and left.

Driving across town, he couldn't help but think about the dinner he was about to have. He was nervous but he was doing his best to conceal his anxiety.

Inside of the restaurant, his guest was already seated.

Harold walked up to the table and made his presence known, "Sorry I'm a little late, I hope I didn't keep you waiting long. I hope this will help make up for my tardiness."

Conrad Richards, Samantha's father stood to greet Harold and accept his gift. "Oh Harold, you're fine, I just got here myself. Now what do we have here?"

"It's a gift for you sir. Samantha told me about how you are aspiring to become a weekend warrior angler and so I thought you could use one of the best rod and reel combos on the market."

Conrad opened up his gift from Harold and looked it over, "Will you look at that. I'll be bringing in a catch in no time with this beauty. That was very nice of you. When I start catching some fish, I'll have to have you over for dinner."

The two men shared a laugh, Harold replied, "I'd love that."

Once the pleasantries were out of the way, Conrad got right down to business, "So Harold, the reason I invited you to dinner tonight was so that you and I could talk man-to-man, if you will."

Harold took a sip of his lemon infused water from the crystal glass before him, "Okay, well what do you want to talk about?"

"You."

Harold gave off a nervous laugh, "Me? There's not much to me sir, what do you want to know?"

"Well it's clear you've been spending time with my daughter and therefore I see you as a potential suitor. We've been around each other a few times but I wanted to have a little one on one time with you. You need to know that from the time my daughter was a young girl, I asked her to trust her heart to me until she found a suitable mate to give it to. Samantha made a vow to us that she'd allow her mother and I to be a part of her mate selection process so as her dad, I screen all potential suitors, whether they like it or not. Now, I asked you not to mention our meeting to her and I haven't said anything to her about it either, she doesn't know we are here but I want to know what your intentions are towards my daughter?"

Harold pulled his collar away from his neck, the glaring gaze from Conrad made him a little hot underneath but he handled it well.

Harold emptied out his glass, there wasn't enough lemony water available to quench the dryness he was feeling in his mouth.

"Well sir, I think your daughter is amazing and I'm actually glad to hear you see me as a potential suitor for her. In fact, I was glad you called this meeting because I'd been praying for the right time to approach you about presenting my case for your daughter's hand in marriage."

"Oh really now? Presenting your case, huh? I've never heard it put that like that before."

"Yes sir, she doesn't know this but the day I met her, I said in front of everyone that she would be my wife one day. I never dreamed she and I would connect in the way we have. She and I have yet to even discuss marriage but I believe in my heart that she is who God designed for me."

Conrad looked Harold squarely in his face, "Harold, I'm from the old school, right now, I'm the man in my daughter's life, she's a grown woman but I hold the position of protection over her until I transfer that over to her husband. When she gets married and the preacher asks, who gives this woman away? I want to be able to do so with confidence to the man she's chosen."

For the next two hours over dinner, Conrad grilled Harold on subjects like his goals, family life, philosophies, finances, children, and everything in between.

Conrad got serious for a minute, "Harold, I don't want you thinking I'm putting any pressure on you but I just needed to know where your head is and make sure you aren't being guided by the wrong head."

Harold took a pause before he answered and because of the delay, Conrad couldn't hold it any longer. He erupted with laughter, "Boy, I wish you could see the look on your face right now."

Conrad's laughter put Harold back at ease but he wanted to assure his potential future father-in-law, "Sir, Samantha is precious to me, I will in no way shape or form disrespect her in that way, I believe that if and when that time comes, I will be the benefactor of all the passion she's stored up for that special person. She's told me of how she's made the conscious decision to wait until marriage and I highly respect that sir. She's truly a gift. I'm in a business where you don't see too many woman like her."

"Yeah, Samantha has been a great daughter to us, we've had our ups and downs, she's not perfect, but overall she's active in ministry, she's diligent and trustworthy and like her mother, she's quite virtuous."

Harold couldn't agree more with the head of the Richard's family, he was quite taken by Samantha.

"So then Harold, what's your next move?"

"Well sir, I've stated my intentions with you here tonight, you know where I stand but I need to know your daughter feels the same way."

Sipping his after dinner coffee, Conrad explained, "Harold, I've met a lot of people in my life and I have to say, there is something very special about you. Please know that no matter what happens between you and Samantha, you and I will have some sort of kinship. You are a good man Harold, you have my blessing, and full support."

Harold smiled at the affirmation, he looked upon Conrad as a father figure, he hoped he could be the kind of father and husband he portrayed to be.

"Thank you sir, that means a lot to hear you say that. Now, let's hope Samantha feels the same way."

CHAPTER 48

"C'mon in Allen."

Erica walked into Lieutenant Conroy's office and sat down slowly. She had not been to work since the untimely passing of Detective Brown. Each morning as she got up to come in, Lieutenant Conroy would call to say, "Not today, take the day off."

Erica had been going stir crazy being at home for the last few days so she was grateful when she got the call to come into work.

"Good morning sir, even though it was only a few days, I feel like I've been gone forever and it feels good to be back at work."

Never having been at a loss for words, the Lieutenant shifted in his seat as he struggled with increased difficulty in finding the best way to deliver the news to one of his most talented detectives. He glanced around one last time as if he was looking for answers. There were none, he'd have to come out and just say it.

"Um, Allen I've checked with Human Resources and you've built up quite an impressive amount of paid time off."

"Yeah, you're right, since I've been here I've hardly taken any time off. Why were you checking into that for me sir? With all due respect, with everything going on, this isn't exactly the best time for me to be going on vacation."

The Lieutenant's eyebrows squished together, "Actually Allen, as of today, you are on vacation...indefinitely."

Erica's mouth opened but nothing came out. She rubbed her forehead in a way to gather her thoughts together before speaking.

"Come again. I'm not sure I understood what you just said."

"Starting today, you are on an extended vacation. You will use up your time and once that is over, you will be on paid administrative leave."

Erica tried to keep herself together, she reigned in her emotions before damaging the relationship she had with her boss. Through restrained lips she asked, "But why? What is this all about?"

Lieutenant Conroy pulled out a stack of papers from his desk drawer and plopped them down in front of Erica, "This is why?"

Erica looked over the documents, the official paperwork that would certify the family of the late Detective Brown was suing the department for the wrongful death with Erica Allen being the cause of death.

Erica's stomach tightened and went hard, she felt her body instantly grow hot. Throwing her hands in the air, she asked, "Are you serious? You have got to be kidding me. This is unbelievable."

The Lieutenant cautioned, "You need to calm down."

Erica went on the offensive, citing examples of her partner's shortcomings, "You mean to tell me, they are blaming me for her death when she was the conniving little minx no one knew about. I can't even believe this. They have no case, you know this right?"

Lieutenant Conroy flipped through the mountainous stack of papers, "That's just it Allen, whether they have one or not, they've filed a lawsuit against my department and the city doesn't want the bad publicity so they are probably going to settle this out of court. All they have to prove in wrongful death is negligence, whether the death occurred here whether in whole or in part, and some other stuff our attorneys have pointed out. It doesn't matter, none of it matters. The city is going to try and make this go away but in the meantime, I have to make you go away too. You can't be associated with the department during this time. It's all politics and this is the way it has to be played."

Erica rubbed at her eyes, trying to hide her tears.

It didn't work.

Lieutenant Conroy admonished, "Allen, the best thing for you to do now is take this mandatory time off and figure out what is next for you. Depending upon the outcome of this case, you may or may not be able to come back here. You've been a little slow closing cases but you are one of my best detectives so I'm going to fight for you but you just never know how these things might play out."

Erica gave a toneless response, her eyes were vacant as she slumped into her seat.

The Lieutenant said, "Her family was requesting for your termination from the force but we worked that out with them. I'm sorry it has come down to this but in a way this is the best thing, I can protect you like this, you know what I mean?"

In a way, Erica understood what her commander was saying but really everything going in her ears sounded scrambled, nothing was making any sense. She thought, *"Even from the grave, she's still trying to ruin my life...darn you Brown."*

Lieutenant Conroy walked over and placed his hand on her shoulder, "To spare you any embarrassment, come in early tomorrow morning or come back tonight and get anything you'd like to have. That way, you won't run into anyone and feel like you have to explain anything. I'll do all of that. I know it's easier said than done but don't worry, one way or another, everything is going to work out."

Erica sneered by saying, "I'm practically getting fired, getting pushed out of my job and you tell me not to worry?"

Lieutenant Conroy challenged Erica, "What is worrying going to do Allen? You can't live in the past and you can't predict the future so what I mean is that worrying can't and won't change a thing."

Still trying to hold on to her work, she asked, "Now what about my cases, am I not supposed to worry about those? I can feel it Lieutenant, I'm so close to solving the website case and now I'm being taken off of it?"

"Detective Morris is back on track with work and up to speed, he'll take over all of your cases. I know you two are friends so you can consult with him on the case files."

CHAPTER 49

"Will you look at who's here...nice to see you Lionel, I was hoping I'd get to see you again."

"Maria, with such wonderful service you provide, you should've known you'd see me again."

Lionel returned to Boites a Bijoux with a renewed sense of determination. While it could have seemed like de ja vue to him, it didn't because he knew without reservation Erica was indeed the woman for him.

He'd chosen a bold and beautiful cut diamond for Marsha that would've covered a nice portion of her ring finger but this time, Erica would be the recipient of an exquisitely stunning halo wedding set fit for an angel that featured superior pave' set diamonds boasting multiple carets with exceptional clarity. This was the design he had in mind as he greeted his familiar celebration specialist, Maria.

"It's been a while Lionel but I can tell you are a man in love."

Lionel licked his lips and smiled, "Now how is it you didn't mention that the first time I came in here, how can you tell now?"

"Lionel, when you've been in this business for as long as I have, you learn how to pick up on these things. I can tell you this, she must be one lucky lady to have taken you down after what happened before."

Maria meant it as a compliment but it reminded Lionel of the low place he was in after Marsha's infidelity. Despite his misdeeds surrounding the break up, he was grateful for having had met Erica and the future they were building, he was happy to be moving beyond his past.

"So Lionel, I'm not going to jinx you this time asking you a whole bunch of questions, plus, not only that, you already know what you want which makes my job a lot easier. I will ask you this though, when are you planning to propose?"

Lionel searched for the calendar on Maria's desk, he pointed to championship week with a smile and said, "Somewhere during this week."

"Huh, I'm confused Lionel."

Lionel took Maria down memory lane, explaining to her how his relationship with Erica blossomed from the night at the basketball game and their journey through social media, becoming the team's good luck charms.

"So before each game, you and Erica send in a message to the team and the fans to keep their momentum going on?"

"Yes, and apparently it's been working because the team has been on fire, they're in the playoffs now and are poised to make it to the championships which is where I'm planning to propose to my number one fan in front of all of our fans."

Maria clasped her hands together across her chest, "Oh Lionel, that sounds wonderful, I'm not into basketball but now I'll have to tune in every night so I can catch your proposal. In fact, I think I'm going to tell the owners of the store and see if they'd like to sponsor your proposal since you're getting the ring from here."

"Maria, you don't have to do that."

"I know I don't have to but I want to, it'll be great. They love doing stuff like this plus it's advertising for them. Is there someone with the basketball team you can put me in touch with?"

Lionel looked through his phone, "Yes, you can contact Alexis Byrne, here is her contact information."

Lionel sat back into the chair, "Wow, I'm so excited, this is going to be great. Now that I've selected the ring, I need to call her mother and make arrangements with her and Erica's sister; I'd like to have them there the night I propose."

"Will any of your family be there?"

"Probably not, I've been pretty quiet with my family about our relationship because I didn't want to get their hopes up again, after you know..."

"Yeah well they'll know soon enough with a proposal on national television, don't you think?"

"You're right, which is why I'm planning to tell them before we leave for the games."

Maria wrapped up all of the final details for Erica's engagement ring, "I'll call you when you can pick it up. I'm so happy for you Lionel, I can feel it, this time, she's going to say yes."

CHAPTER 50

"I know we have bible study tonight and we were supposed to go out afterwards but I got a call from a colleague who'd like to join us for service tonight. Do you mind if they came along to dinner with us after church?"

"But of course not Harold, that sounds great, it has been so nice to see how your witness has brought people to know more about Christ."

After the conversation Harold had with Samantha's father earlier that week, he was anxious to find out if Samantha felt the same way he did. He'd plan to test the waters with her after church but now with plans to entertain friends, he thought he might try it out over the phone.

In a joking manner, he asked, "And what has my witness done for you?"

Samantha gushed, "What do you mean Harold?"

Harold felt a spike in his pulse, his breath hitched up and stopped briefly, he didn't know how far to take the flirtation, "Uh, I mean, I guess...I guess I'm just wondering what do you think of me? You know, we've been I guess you could say, getting to know one another and going out and stuff but what does any of that mean to you?"

Samantha clutched her belly, she gently bit her lip, she'd been thinking and praying a lot about the question Harold had just confronted her with. Harold was unlike any guy she'd ever seen before, from each interaction she'd had with him, he seemed to be respectful and caring. She didn't know if it was all an act, she had come across a few sheep in wolves clothing and she didn't want to be deceived. She didn't want to be vulnerable to intimacy with the wrong man, she needed a sign from the One on high to help her know what was right, despite her recent feelings of attraction towards him. She'd waited thirty-five years already, she needed to be sure.

"Samantha, are you still there?"

"Yes, Harold...I'm here. You know what, before I answer your question, I have one for you. Thinking to herself before she asked, *"Here goes nothing, I don't want shattered fairy-tale dreams by choosing the wrong guy; I want the real deal."*

The cat and mouse game they both were playing was electrifying to the both of them.

Samantha took in a deep breath and went for it, "What if I told you that I'm barren, that I can't have children...would that make you change your mind about wanting to continue to see me?"

Harold took a thoughtful pause, would the thought of not being able to have children with the woman he named as his wife on the first day they met pose a problem for him or could he live through it?

Despite the question, Harold held a willingness to believe that everything would be all right. He felt a flutter in his stomach, he was excited she was thinking in those terms, considering him for such a position.

Samantha spoke up, "Now, I have to wonder, are you still on the phone Harold."

"Yes, I'm here. Well Samantha, I'm honored you felt comfortable enough to ask me such a personal question and I want you to know that your ability to have children doesn't change my mind one bit about seeing you. You are an amazing woman with or without children. There were many women in the bible who were actually barren but the Lord still blessed them with children. Samantha, no matter what, the fruit of your womb is blessed and you have been a blessing to me."

Harold paused briefly and then he went for it, "Listen, I don't date just to date, I've been looking for love for a long time and when I find it, I want to keep it and cherish it and I have to say, I think I've found it in you."

It was out, how would she respond, would she now run away as so many others had?

Samantha beamed on the other end of the phone, "Harold, you sure know how to make a girl feel good. I'm not dating just to date either and your words of encouragement have blessed me tremendously."

"Well, I meant every word."

"Um Harold, guess what?"

"What's that?"

Samantha chuckled a bit, "By the way, as far as I know, I'm perfectly capable of having children. You don't have to worry; I was only testing you. I only asked you that to see how you might respond and boy did you pass the test."

"Why you little stinker, well it doesn't matter to me either way but I'm glad I passed your little test."

Samantha took the lead, "I'm glad we've had this talk Harold and I can't wait to see you tonight."

Harold's heart swelled, he was beginning to see that Samantha did indeed feel the same way towards him, he told her, "I can't wait to see you either princess. I need to do a couple of things before church, I'll see you there okay."

CHAPTER 51

"Hello, Mrs. Allen?"

"Yes, this is Mrs. Allen, who's calling?"

"It's me, Lionel...Lionel Webber, Erica's boyfriend."

"Oh hi Lionel, yes sir, how can I help you? Is everything alright with my daughter? I know she's been going through with her job lately but has something else happened?"

"Erica is fine and I'm calling you because yes, something has happened."

Helen Allen sat up straight in her seat, "Oh lord what's wrong?"

Lionel laughed nervously, "Oh no ma'am, nothing is wrong, what I meant is that something has happened and that is I've fallen in love with your daughter. I know we haven't met but I'm calling because I'd like to change that and to also ask your permission to marry Erica."

Lionel took some time to fill Erica's mother in on his feelings and his intentions towards her daughter and the plans for the proposal.

"I'd love for you and Erica's sister to fly out to meet us during championship week, you'll have to plan for the entire week because we don't know how the games will play out."

"Oh my goodness this is wonderful news. Every time I talk to Erica, she's always talking about you and I've asked her several times when we were going to get a chance to meet you?"

"Yeah, I know...our schedules have been pretty busy so the time just hasn't been there and I know we haven't been together long but you know what, when you know...you just know."

Helen nodded in agreement, "I wholeheartedly believe that Lionel, I taught my girls to trust their guts when it came to love and I know for a fact that Erica's gut confirmed you."

Lionel laughed out loud, "Are you serious, I'm not sure what that really means but I'll take it."

Helen was confident in her beliefs about the lightning bolts of love, "Trust me son, you can take that to the bank and cash it."

"Okay, Mrs. Allen, I'll trust you on that. I know it's not a lot of time but do you think you and Leah will be able to fly out and join us?"

"Yes, Lionel I don't see this as being a problem. I wouldn't miss this moment for the world. She hasn't said any of this to me so I'm assuming my daughter doesn't know what you're planning?"

"No, she doesn't and I'd like to keep it that way if you don't mind."

Helen cleared her throat, "You have my solemn vow Lionel, I'll keep the surprise and I look forward to meeting you."

"Wonderful, I'll have my assistant, Michelle coordinate all of the travel details and everything else with you later in the week. Will that be okay?"

Helen was beyond thrilled for her daughter and future son-in-law, "That'll be just fine....son."

CHAPTER 52

"I'm surprised you wanted to attend bible study on the same day you were put on leave but I guess it makes sense."

Erica and Lionel stood outside of Harold and Samantha's church as they waited for them to arrive.

Lionel grabbed Erica's hand and tried to offer her words of comfort, "See how God works, you didn't think you'd have time to take off for championship week but He's opened the door for you to go. Now we can go and have a great time. Plus, who wouldn't like not having to go to work and still getting paid? You got it made it girl."

Erica knew he meant well but her response was quite lackluster in comparison to his demeanor. He took her hand and kissed it while visiting his private thoughts, "*If she only knew what I have planned for her. I do hate she's so upset about her job though.*"

Within minutes, Harold and Samantha greeted the couple, "Hi guys, so glad you could join us. Detective Allen, I have to say, I was a bit surprised but happy to get your call about coming to church tonight. I'd like to introduce you two to my friend, Samantha. Samantha, these are two of my business associates, Detective Allen and Dr. Lionel Webber."

Samantha, Erica, and Lionel all shook hands and traded friendly gestures with each other. While Harold stood back and watched, he loved introducing Samantha to his friends, he was hoping for more of that.

Before going inside, Samantha looked at Lionel and Erica and said, I pray you two hear a word from the Lord this evening."

Erica responded, "Yeah, I hope so, I need to hear something positive after all I've heard today."

Inside the church, the service had already begun, the foursome made their way to their seats and got comfortable.

Midweek service at Holy Road Christian Church was a time of refreshing and refilling from Sunday's worship. Often times, midweek services are not well attended like Sunday services but not at Holy Road, their members were dedicated and responded in kind with their attendance.

Pastor Curt Shaw got up to begin his teaching, "Tonight I want to talk about something we don't really bring up in the church anymore. Something that we shouldn't do but it's done on a daily basis. I want us to have an interactive time of study and so with that, tonight I want to discuss the truth about lying."

Everyone in the church nodded their heads and made hmmming noises.

"The Wharton School at the University of Pennsylvania released a study recently about the ethics of lying and how when not telling the truth is a good thing. May the Lord have mercy upon us. Is there anyone in here tonight who believes lying is sometimes a good thing?"

Interestingly enough, a few people raised their hands.

Pastor Shaw scanned the crowd, taking note to the ones with their hands raised. He called on one lady who raised her hand, "Sister Reece, you had your hand raised, can you share when you think there are times lying can be good?"

Sister Reece felt her cheeks fill as she was embarrassed to be called upon but she pushed past and responded,

"Sometimes, you might need to tell a lie in order to spare someone's feelings, you may not want to hurt a person and the best way to avoid that is by lying to them."

Pastor Shaw called on another, "Brother Samuel, you too had your hand raised, in what instance do you believe telling a lie might be a good thing?"

Brother Samuel stood to give his answer, "Even though I know it's not the right thing to do, I think in cases where you're faced with trying to help someone and you have to lie to protect them from further harm, to me, I don't consider that to be a bad thing."

Pastor Shaw asked the gathered body of believers, "Could it be the father of all lies is perpetuating these lies for us to believe that lying can be good when lying goes completely against what God wants[6]? One of the biggest lies out today is that just because you're Christian that somehow stops you from lying. Hey guess what, it should but it doesn't. The truth of the matter is, people in the church lie just like people in the world. That's something isn't it? Thou shalt not lie is one of the Ten Commandments but baby some of us Christians have a hard time taming that tongue. I mean David admitted to speaking in haste in Psalms 116:11 but he said, all men are liars. Do y'all believe this is true? Look at the person next to you and ask them, are you a liar, are you lying to me?"

The congregation laughed but they knew what the pastor was saying was true.

He continued on, "From Genesis to Revelations there are scriptures highlighting admonishments against lying. Here's

---

[6] **John 8:44**: "For you are the children of your father the devil, and you love to do the evil things he does. He was a murderer from the beginning. He has always hated the truth, because there is no truth in him. When he lies, it is consistent with his character; for he is a liar and the father of lies."

the thing, we all are born into a world of sin and therefore shaped by it and as a result, sins like lying have the potential to become commonplace because of the propensity we have from our sinful natures. However, the beauty comes in the form of grace, the grace that God gives for us. He grants us grace to become new creatures in Him and to cast off the works of our flesh and the old ways of doing things when we invite Him to live in our hearts. It is then that our nature should change. The sad part is that while it should change, sometimes it doesn't change or sometimes we simply forget. Which is why for the next few weeks we are going to spend some time on this topic. Listen folks, in Proverbs 6:16-19, we're told, God hates a lying tongue and a false witness who speaks lies, this is serious business. Therefore, over the course of the next month, I want to remind you about the truth about lying, we need God to help us be truthful and honest in every situation. As it has been written, then you will know the truth and the truth shall set you free...Amen?"

The students of the word all acknowledged, "Amen."

"Webster's dictionary defines lying as, marked by or containing falsehoods. I spoke about it earlier but I want to go back a little bit, in John 8:43-45, the heading is tagged, children of the devil, and it reads:

"Why do you not understand what I am saying? It is because you cannot hear My word. "You are of your father the devil, and you want to do the desires of your father. He was a murderer from the beginning, and does not stand in the truth because there is no truth in him. Whenever he speaks a lie, he speaks from his own nature, for he is a liar and the father of lies. But because I speak the truth, you do not believe Me."

"Wow, the devil is the father of all falsehoods, the bible says, there is no truth in him, it says he was a murderer from the beginning, do you know what that means? The devil can be called the father of lies because he's on record as being the one to tell the first lie and what lie was that? You guys guessed it, and the serpent said to the woman, you shall not surely die. With his lie, he murdered the life God planned for Adam and Eve, a plan for mankind with a supposition that they might not die. And you know why? The bible says, he didn't hold the truth, he wanted to fulfill his own desires and act out of his nature which got him kicked out heaven; he lost his place of dominion so why not get the ones God created to lose theirs? The word shows how it can be easy to believe a lie over the truth but that's how the devil wants it. Revelation 12:9 tells us that he's the deceiver of the whole world. Are you guys starting to see a pattern here with him?"

Lionel began to chew at his lips, he felt like a weight had come down in his chest. In reality, it was the words spoken by the pastor that was weighing him down.

Erica stroked the embossed cross on her leather bible case, she listened to the words spoken by the pastor with thoughts bouncing around in her head, "*Should I tell Lionel about what Lana and I did in college, is this something he should know about me? Do I need to be honest about it? I'm looking to have a future with this man, I don't want anything from my past, messing that up. What he doesn't know won't hurt him, right?*"

Lionel tried to maintain and keep his internal conflict under subjection, he reached for Erica's hand and held onto it.

The pastor broke both of their wandering thoughts as he asked, "Are you interested in being about your father's business or your father's desires? Do you speak lies or do you speak truth, are you a child of God or a child of satan? Whose nature are your nurturing...the truth about lying. This is just the beginning folks, we are going to get into a lot more of this in the upcoming weeks."

The pastor closed out the service with a prayer and admonished the group to be watchful until the following week for how easily lies can come up in our daily lives and to take notice of the response to those lies.

Within the closing prayer, everyone on that row, Lionel, Harold, Samantha, and Erica each included the same prayer, "*Lord, I need you to lead, guide, and direct.*"

After the service was over, Erica was the first to respond, "Harold, I'm so glad I decided to call you, this bible study has really got my mind going in a lot of different directions. It's like, based on what happened with my partner and now hearing this message, if I didn't know it before, I know now that just telling the truth is the way to go, no matter what."

Lionel stood listening, there wasn't much he felt he could add to the conversation, other than, "Hey guys, how about we continue this conversation over a dinner table, let's get something to eat, my treat."

Harold joked around, "I hope you aren't lying to us all Lionel, you sure you treating us man?"

Lionel laughed it off, "Yeah man, I'm treating...now where are we going?" Lionel looked at Erica and thought quickly, "*I've got to tell her, but how do I do that without losing her? How do I fix this?*"

CHAPTER 53

"Who is this calling me from Virginia?"

"May I speak with Detective Allen please?"

"This is she, who's calling?"

"Oh now tell me it hasn't been that long, have you really forgotten the voice of your favorite captain?"

"Oh my goodness, Captain Martinez, how are you?"

"I'm doing well Erica, I'm calling to check on you? I spoke with my buddy, Conroy and he filled me in on all of what's been going on with you. How are you holding up?"

Captain Joseph Martinez and Lieutenant Marcus Conroy were fraternity brothers. Martinez was Erica's first boss out of college and he realized early on the raw talent she possessed, he took her under his proverbial wing, mentoring her, and helping her move up through the ranks to detective. In a way, he was like a father figure to her. While he was sad to see her leave, he knew she needed a clean start after her breakup with Patrick so he called his good friend, Conroy to see if she could join his force. Martinez, however, made it clear to Conroy not to show her any favoritism, to be hard on her to see if she could withstand the pressure.

Erica took in a deep breath and slowly let it out, "I guess I'm doing the best I can which right now, to be honest, doesn't feel like much. What am I supposed to do if I can't work?"

"Listen Erica, who says you can't work? You're on leave right now, enjoy it. If you are waiting to see if you can go back there then chill out and enjoy your time off, if not start looking for another job."

"Another job? I hadn't even thought about that."

Testing the waters, Martinez offered, "Yeah, another job...like back here. If I told you your old desk is missing you and would like for you to come back, what would you say?"

Erica jerked her head back quickly, "Come back there? Really? You have an opening?"

"Yes, I never filled your position, it's been open since you left."

"Are you serious?"

"If I'm lying, I'm dying."

Erica screamed, "No, no, no...please don't say things like that."

Martinez joked around, "I only said that for you but no, I never filled your job. I guess I always hoped you'd come back to us."

"You really thought that even after I said, "I'm never coming back here?"

Martinez smiled, "I figured you were speaking out of your pain, you know how you women are."

Erica tipped her head back for a moment and closed her eyes pondering her former boss' words, *"There is a possible chance I might not get my job back but do I want to go back to Virginia? What about Lionel? I feel like I have a life here now, like I'm moving forward in life, do I really want to go backwards?"*

With Erica's silence, Martinez decided to alleviate some of the pressure, "So listen, the job has been open for over two years now, it's not going anywhere. Take some time and think about it, will you? I'd love to have you back here kid."

Erica was grateful, happy to know someone appreciated her work and abilities, "I will captain, I promise."

Changing the subject, he asked, "So, are there any new knuckleheads I need to know about? Conroy was telling me about some guy that has you all wide open but I need to hear it from you. What's going on with your love life?"

Perking up on her cushy love seat, Erica beamed with pride as she spoke about Lionel, "Well, his name is Dr. Lionel Webber and he's amazing and you should know that I'm madly in love with him and secretly I hope to marry him and have plenty of babies."

Martinez remarked, "Well you can't be in this industry and not know who he is and you've somehow fallen in love with this cat, huh? Now, you have looked into his background and made sure he isn't hiding a wife and kids somewhere haven't you?"

Erica rolled her eyes, "You just had to bring that up didn't you? To answer your question, "Yes, I have done a thorough investigation on him and he's squeaky clean."

"Haven't I taught you anything, those are the ones you need to be wary of?"

"Oh lord, are you trying to make me feel bad about all of my dating decisions?"

"Nah, I'm just giving you a hard time. I miss you and I just want the best for you. I'm glad to hear you've found someone who makes you happy and I guess it doesn't hurt that he's a rock star in the world in which we fight to preserve and protect. Just make sure I get an invitation to the wedding, I'll be sure and do one of my famous dances."

Erica teared up a little, "I miss you too and please know that I'm very happy with Lionel. If you are already talking about dancing at my wedding, don't be surprised if your invitation gets lost in the mail."

The two laughed because it wasn't clear if what Martinez did on the dance floor could be considered dancing.

Erica made a pronouncement, "I'm just joking around with you. In fact, if I ever get that proposal, I would love it if you'd walk me down the aisle. I hope that isn't asking too much?"

Martinez nodded with glowing eyes and a sentimental voice to match, "I would be honored to walk you down the aisle. Now given you've asked me to do this, I'm going to need to meet this guy and look him eye to eye. I know you and I know in the past, you had a clear vision of your ideal mate, you had your career all mapped out and you refused to settle for anything less than that. So until I can judge for myself, I need to know from you, does he make you laugh, do you feel like he loves you for who you are, Erica, is this your best friend?"

Erica found herself a little tongue-tied, "Uhhh, Martinez...Lionel is all of that to me and more. He's shown me through his actions how much he cares for me. You know, while I thought I was in love with Patrick, I had to realize that love doesn't hurt and he hurt me. He lied to me repeatedly and as a result, I lost all respect for love and relationships but Lionel changed all of that for me. I feel like he and I can make it through anything, I love him Martinez."

"Well alright then but I want you to know that us guys, we can do stupid things sometimes. What Patrick did was wrong but you never know what a person is going through or how situations are going to impact them. Have you ever considered what he must've felt knowing he was married but in love with you?"

The room instantly felt cold, she reached for the blanket draped across her sofa, "No, I don't think I've ever given that any thought."

"I'm not condoning him at all, I've just lived long enough to know that people make mistakes and they sometimes make bad decisions. I just want you to consider that a lot of times, things people do to us have nothing to do with us but everything to do with that person's inability to deal."

Erica listened carefully to the wisdom Martinez shared, "You know, I think you might be right, what you're saying makes sense. I'm just glad I'm not dealing with that type of deception with Lionel, things are different now."

CHAPTER 54

"This isn't what I envisioned when you called me but I was happy to receive your call nonetheless Harold, how've you been?"

Harold and Anna stood on the edge of an embankment overlooking approximately fifty acres of untreated land.

Harold gladly reported, "I couldn't be better Anna and how about you? How are things going in the world of real estate?"

"Professionally, things are going great, business is booming, but I wish I could say the same about my personal life."

Harold was carefully surveying the landscape, taking pictures with his cellphone when he casually asked, "What's going on in your personal life?"

Harold continued to walk through the grassy knolls pulling his slacks up to his knees as Anna tried to follow him in an attempt to remain close, "Well, I mean, you know, I have everything in my life that I could ever want, except someone to share it all with."

Harold calmly answered, "I know what you mean."

Fiddling with her low cut blouse, Anna was trying to draw Harold's attention to her ample bosom, "You do, see there, I knew it. I figured you felt the connection we shared at the race the other day and I was so happy that you called me so we could link up to discuss our relationship."

Swatting at the gargantuan mosquitos from around his now bald head, Harold stopped dead in his tracks, "Wait. What? Our relationship? What are you talking about woman?"

"C'mon Harold, you and I have been playing this hard to get game for far too long now, I think it's time we stop playing and turn this flirtation into something more formal. That is why you set up this meeting, pretending to be looking for property, right?"

Harold's eye crossed from hearing the mixed up commentary from a very serious Anna, "Anna, I think you have misread my reason for calling you. I am not pretending to be looking for land, I'm here for a specific reason. You are the best in the business and I need the best person on the job in helping me find a substantial amount of land."

The setting sun couldn't hide the apparent disappointment shown in Anna's face, Harold interjected to lift her spirits, while he wanted to point out she was only interested because of the new changes in him, he spared her feelings. Placing his hand on her shoulder, "Listen, you're a beautiful woman and when the time comes, the right guy will come along and scoop you up, he'd be a fool not to. Anna you're a prize, you don't have to do the chasing, learn how to be chased. You are worthy of the pursuit."

Anna was speechless.

In hopes of changing the subject and getting back to the matter at hand, Harold mentioned, "Hey, um I like this location but I think I'd like to see the other two properties you have for me to see before I make a decision. Do you have time to do that this evening?"

Anna looked down, now unable to meet Harold's eyes, she muttered under her breath, "Yeah that's fine, the sooner we get going, the sooner we'll be done."

Despite all of the years he'd flirted with Anna, none of it mattered to Harold as he was now totally and completely smitten by Samantha Richards, he was in love...finally.

CHAPTER 55

"Hey, who's not on the call yet, who are we still waiting on?"

There was so much chatter and background noise on the conference call as all of the members of the Webber family gathered for Lionel's call to begin.

Laureen answered, "Lionel, honey, I think we're still waiting on Dale Jr. and Leontyne to join us."

Lionel was speaking in bubbly, loud tones, "Alright, alright I'll give them a few more minutes but after that I'll go ahead and get started."

There were several conversations going on while the majority of the Webber clan waited for the remaining two.

Trying to expend some of his nervous energy, Lionel asked, "So how's the anniversary party planning going?"

His parents chimed in, "Things are going well with the planning, everything is coming together nicely Lionel." Laureen added, "Things would be even better if by that time you brought home someone for us to meet."

Everyone on the call jumped on the bandwagon with Laureen and started teasing Lionel. As the teasing was going on, the last two to bring up the rear were joining the call, Dale Jr. announced, "Hey everybody, sorry I'm late to the call." Leontyne replied as well, "Yeah, me too...sorry Lionel"

Lionel assured his siblings, "It's all good y'all. Well, I asked everyone to get on the call because I have some news I'd like to share and I only wanted to tell this story one time. First of all, my company has gone through rounds of rigorous interviews for an opportunity to partner up for creating a next generation cyber innovation and technology center of excellence."

Dale Jr. interrupted, "I have no idea what you just said."

Donald snapped back, "Well maybe you should just shut your block head up and listen."

Everyone on the call laughed aloud.

Lionel continued, "Long story short, I wanted my family to be the first to know that I made it, my company has been selected to participate in this initiative."

Congratulatory responses were heard from all over the phone.

Donald jumped in and said, "Man, Lionel this is a real game changer for you, huh?"

Lionel kept going, "Yeah it is, there's more I need to tell you guys because that's not the only thing I'm changing."

Lynda blurted out, "This is fantastic news little brother, what else do you have for us tonight?"

"Well remember how you guys were just on me about bringing someone home for you all to meet? Well that's the other reason I wanted to get you all together. I've met someone and I'm head over heels in love with her and I'm planning to propose to her next week. I'm proud to say I'm getting ready to change my status and her last name."

The questions and the comments started pouring in from all over the phone.

"Next week?"

"How are you getting ready to propose and we know nothing about this girl?"

"Who is she?"

"What does she do?"

"How did you meet her?"

"She's not another Marsha is she?"

"How are you planning to propose?"

Lionel's family grilled him, he was bombarded with questions, so much so, he couldn't keep up with all of them.

"Hold up, wait a minute. Let me fill you guys in on how everything has gone down and how I've found the woman I plan to spend the rest of my life with, will that work?"

For the next hour, Lionel told his family about his romance with Erica and fielded their questions.

Lynda spoke up, "So Lionel, is this the same young lady you were going out to meet when we called you that night?"

Lionel thought back to that night, "Yeah that's right, you and Laura called me right before I was about to go and meet her. Yep, it's the same woman."

"See there Laura, I told you there was something different in his voice. Lionel, you can ask Laura, I told her that night you were going to end up with whoever that woman was...I could hear it in your voice."

Laureen asked, "Laura, is Lynda telling the truth and is this the same girl Lydia called me about?"

Lionel gushed, "Oh lord, what did Lydia say?"

"Nothing for you to worry about Liney, Lydia was actually quite impressed by her. I'm now a little jealous that she got to meet her and I haven't had the pleasure."

"No need to be mother, you'll get to meet her soon enough. In the meantime, all of you need to make plans to watch the basketball championship games next week because that's when I'm going to propose."

Dale Jr. scoffed, "On national television, you're going to propose?"

Lionel explained to his family the basketball promotion and the significance of why he was choosing to propose in that way.

All of the female Webbers swooned, "That sounds so romantic Lionel. We love you and we'll be watching and rooting for you."

"Thanks guys, I heard someone mention Marsha and just so you know, she's nothing like her. I know I was planning to propose to Marsha but I was forcing her to be the one when nothing with Erica is forced, she's just it and I'm ready to make her mine...forever."

Dale Sr. popped in, "Son, all of this is wonderful news. I'm so happy for you and I know you'll make a great husband. Learn these two words and you'll be just fine."

"Which two are those dad?"

Dale Sr. remarked, "Yes dear. Can the husbands on the call testify to what I'm saying?"

Everyone cracked up on the call. Not only did the husbands agree with the eldest Webber but the wives chimed in as well.

Even on a phone call you could feel the love and support within the family, distance was not an issue for the connection they all shared.

Everyone was feeling lighthearted and upbeat from Lionel good news, this was a happy time for the Webber family.

CHAPTER 56

Media trucks and vans along with thousands of fans descended upon the basketball arena where the Houston Flyers would square off in a head to head match up against the Boston Bullets.

Each team had fought tirelessly to get to the coveted championship showdown, however, the Flyers believed they had an unfair advantage, Erica and Lionel.

Having Lierica as their good luck charms had provided them with their best season ever.

"Are you nervous?"

"Why would I be nervous?"

"Oh, I don't know, maybe because it is media day and you and I are getting ready to be interviewed like crazy by all of these reporters along with the basketball teams?"

Lionel took Erica's hand in his, "I could never be nervous about telling the world how much I love and appreciate you."

Erica melted in the arms of her beau, Lionel. She reached in to give him a kiss when Alexis walked up to greet them, "There are my two favorite love birds. Lionel and Erica, you two have surpassed all of my wildest dreams for what I imagined this promotion would bring. We are all in love with your story that you guys have shared with us along the way. The team has made it to the championships, ticket sales and merchandising is at an all-time high, and right now the media can't wait to meet you two. I may not get to see you guys again until later at the game tonight so have fun and enjoy the moment. Are you guys ready?"

The line of interviewers waiting to interview Lionel and Erica along with the players stretched for what seemed to be miles. The bright flashes from camera bulbs blinded the couple but they reveled in every moment. They hung together closely, being loving and playful for the cameras, they played it up and showcased their love well for the world to see. When you looked at them it was hard not to fall in love with this beautiful couple.

"Oh my goodness Lionel that was amazing."

"I know it Erica, this entire experience has been nothing short of amazing and guess what baby, it's only going to get better from here on out."

Standing face to face, Erica smiled as she noticed for the first time, the small, hidden dimples Lionel had on both sides of his face, he smiled because he could not believe he'd finally met the woman of his dreams and how she had no idea he was planning to make her his forever.

The warm and endearing moment demanded they kiss amongst the crowds around them, they submitted to the moment and felt the earth move beneath them.

Only it wasn't the earth, it was Lionel's vibrating phone. His buddy, Corey was calling.

"Hey man, I know you are in town for the games this week and was planning to stop by and see us but we are about to have our own championship, Rosalyn and I are headed to the hospital, the baby is coming today."

"You're kidding, the baby is coming today?"

"Yeah man, I just said that...get your head out of the clouds over there and open up your ears. Yeah, I saw you and

Erica being interviewed, my boy at work sent me some clips of y'all."

Lionel laughed off his friend's comments, he was happy because with Erica, he now lived on cloud nine.

Lionel checked his watch, "We have to be at the game tonight but Erica and I will meet you at the hospital, we'll stay for as long as we can, hopefully, he'll come before we have to leave."

Corey replied, "Bet, we'll see you soon."

Lionel turned to Erica, "Hey, I included you in coming but if you don't want to go, I completely understand. My godson is about to be born and I'd like to be a part of that for as much as I can."

Erica pulled Lionel close, "Why wouldn't I want to go? I'm going wherever my man is going, plus our godson is being born, I wouldn't miss it this for the world."

Erica's words confirmed for Lionel that she was his one, his only, for now, and forever.

CHAPTER 57

"Why won't you tell me where you're taking me? Do I really have to ride blindfolded?"

"It's a surprise Samantha and yes, you must keep your eyes covered. The good news is, we are almost to our destination."

"Oh Harold, what is a girl to do, you and all of your surprises, I used to hate surprises until I met you, you just make them so fun."

Harold smirked for only he knew what this surprise would reveal, "Well, I hope you will feel that way about this one."

The mild, springtime Texas weather was perfect for the romantic plan Harold had dreamed together in his mind.

Pulling up to their destination, Harold's chest swelled, his smile followed, he was beyond pleased with the sight his eyes held.

Careful to remove a blindfolded Samantha from the car, Harold guided her to the marked spot. She fussed the entire time, "I can't see. Where are you taking me? I'm so nervous, what is going on?"

Standing behind Samantha, Harold positioned her. Her salmon colored chiffon dress flapped in the evening breeze, coordinating in the palette of a setting sun on its horizon. Her lady bug bracelet dangled by her side as Harold whispered in her ear, "Uncover your eyes."

Samantha's heart pounded quickly, she had no idea as to what she was about to see, with great anticipation and excitement, she removed the silky scarf from her face.

She looked to her left and then to her right, trying to adjust her eyes but nothing was there, no matter where she looked it was all green, grass, and trees. Samantha titled her head to the side and pursed her lips. Trying to gather her thoughts before speaking, she turned around to see Harold down on one knee.

Samantha's mouth flew wide open, her words fluttered out, "Oh my God, Harold -."

Harold stopped her, "Samantha, William Shakespeare said something once that I believed happened to us, he said, when I saw you, I fell in love and you smiled because you knew. From the first day I met you, I knew that you were the one for me. Since that day, you've proven to me over and over again that I was right. Every time I see you smile it makes me want to keep you smiling because I haven't stopped smiling since you came into my life. I'm a changed man because of you. I've lived my life trying to find out the meaning of it, searching all over and never really finding it until I met you. Thank you for being the woman you are. My life is better because you are in it and I need you in it. Forget that a website sent you to me as a potential match. You are the woman God created for me and for that reason, I'm down on bended knee, wanting to know one thing, Samantha Grace Richards, will you do me the honors by saying yes and become my wife?"

Samantha's skin tingled, her breath was short, she was overwhelmed to the point where words were trying to form but she couldn't get them out as she stared at a gorgeously fine diamond ring that sparkled in the glimmers of the evening dusk.

Shaking her head yes, Harold stood up and grabbed her up in a twirl as they celebrated with a long and passionate kiss.

Harold placed Samantha back down on the ground and lovingly placed her engagement ring on her perfectly manicured hand.

Still confused as to where they were and why Harold had chosen what looked like the forest to propose she asked, "Um Harold, why are we here? I mean, why did you chose this location to propose to me?"

Harold pulled out an envelope from his pocket and handed it to his new fiancé. Samantha opened the envelope and read its contents.

Lifting her head, she said, "I don't get it, this says, I now own this land...how is that even possible? I've never been to this place in my life."

The smile on Harold's face spanned for days, he could barely contain himself, he took out a sign from the trunk and put it in the ground as he announced, "This is your engagement present."

The sign read, **Future Home of Grace Academy**.

The papers fell to the ground because her hands could no longer hold them as her hands now covered her mouth. Under her hands, she voiced her amazement, "I can't believe this....my school, you did this for me?"

Harold stepped in closer, "Yes love, you deserve it. Having your own school is all you talk about and now that I'm your future hubby, I'm here to make that happen for you."

Samantha did a twirl in the grass with outstretched arms, "This is all for me, I'm standing on the grounds of my new school. Well, will you look at God?"

In all of her twirling, Samantha realized that out of all of the premarital conversations they'd shared, they had not really talked about their finances.

During the time of their courtship, Harold had downplayed his lifestyle to ensure Samantha was the real deal. He was now going to disclose the true size of his assets.

"How are you now able to make this happen for me Harold? I can't even begin to think about how much this land must've cost you. Do websites make that kind of money?"

Harold checked his watch, "It's getting really dark out here and I still have more surprises for you but I do need to tell you something before we leave. You'd be surprised at how much money websites can bring in but that's not the source of my money."

Harold went on to clue Samantha in on his wealth, money she'd now have access to.

Shaking her head, "Is there no end to you Harold Johnson?" Samantha paused for a moment, in all of the excitement, she needed a serious moment, "I'm so incredibly blessed to have you in my life. You are the man that I've prayed and waited for my whole life. You've shown me tonight that not only do dreams come true but that God does still answer prayer. I want you to know that I love you for who you are and not for what you have."

Harold hung his head, Samantha's words obliterated his deep rooted concerns about women only wanting him for what he could do for them.

With a tear in his eye, he said, "I believe you and because of that, I'll be here to make all of your dreams come true and give you whatever your heart desires. For now, I have one last surprise."

"I don't know if I can handle any more surprises tonight."

Wrapping his arms around Samantha's waist, he said, "You're going to love this one. Your family and friends are all waiting for us at our...engagement party. Everyone is there waiting on us, including those evil teacher colleagues of yours."

As Harold opened Samantha's car door, she joked around, "Nice, they'll get to see firsthand how waiting does have its rewards. But wait a minute, you did a lot of planning for all of this, how did you know I'd say yes?"

Harold joked back, "C'mon now...I'm Harold, who wouldn't say yes to me?"

The newly engaged couple laughed and shared a kiss as they drove off to their engagement party.

CHAPTER 58

"Hey Liney, we've been enjoying seeing you and Erica on television, she's even more beautiful than you described. How's everything going out there?"

"Everything has been going great mother, I've met her mother and her sister, they are out here as a surprise to Erica, she won't see them until tonight probably, you know the series is now at 3-2 with the Flyers projected to win tonight with home court advantage. It has been crazy keeping them away from her but they've been enjoying themselves and we have too. Rosalyn and Corey had the baby the other day and Erica and I were there with them for the birth so we've been having a ball. Tonight could be the night though, I've been put on standby."

"Liney, all that sounds wonderful but I have another reason for calling you."

Lionel cleared his throat, "Okay mother, this sounds serious, what's going on?"

In a loving yet stern tone, Laureen inquired of her son, "Lionel, is there anything you need to tell me or better yet, tell that girl before you decide to propose?"

Lionel forced a calming demeanor, "What are you talking about mother? I'm not sure what you're getting at. What is this about?"

Laureen began to explain, "Liney, after my prayer time last night, I fell asleep and I had a dream where I saw you in a big, black, deep hole. The thing is, Erica was looking down over you but she walked off from you, not even offering to try and help. I didn't understand it so I asked the Lord why He would show me such a thing. Lionel, honey I feel like the Lord was showing me a warning and it has something to do with you and Erica."

"You got all of this from praying last night?"

"Well honey, I know this is a big week for y'all so yes, I was praying for you two and then I dreamt about y'all. What do you think it means? Does she know about Marsha? Are you having second thoughts, are you feeling stuck? Is there something, anything that would put you at odds with Erica honey?"

Lionel's chest tightened, a pain in the back of his throat sprang up, his palms began to sweat, he thought by confessing back at his mother's church, he could disassociate himself with his duplicitous actions. Even in developing a romantic relationship with Erica and a friendship with Harold, he never thought he'd have to confess to them.

"By your silence, there is something, isn't there honey?"

Lionel began to weep, "I can't lose her mother, she's the best thing that has ever happened to me. If I tell her this, she could leave. She may never forgive me....oh God, what have I done?"

"And if she ever found out later on, she could still leave you. Liney, it's better you tell her now so there isn't anything that could come back on you. Son, what's meant to be will be, if you lose her, she wasn't yours to begin with. Now if you love her how you say you do, you can get through whatever this is but you need to tell her. See because in essence, omission can be considered the same as lying and you don't want to start a marriage out based on deception."

Lionel knew his mother was right but he was on standby to propose on what could be one of the biggest nights in sports history.

"Liney, the best thing I know how to do is pray and I'd like to do that before I let you go. Father, in Jesus' name, we come before you right now with humbled hearts and minds. Lord, I pray that you send comfort and peace to my son in his time of need, I pray that Your spirit would lead him in the right direction towards the right decision. Lord, right now, we accept Your will over our own. Be with my son Lord and Erica in Jesus' name I pray. Amen."

"Amen. I love you mother. Thank you for helping me to realize how much I do indeed love Erica, there are some things I need to tell her. I don't know how I'm going to be able to do it, this is going to hurt her but it has to be done. I guess you'll see how she takes the news by watching the game tonight."

"I love you too honey, it may be tough right now but one way or another, trust and believe, all will be well."

CHAPTER 59

Preparations were underway for potential victory celebrations for both Lionel and Erica's engagement and the team's win.

Lionel was sick to his stomach, not that he had much pigment in his skin to begin with but he'd lost the little he did have.

Holding his hand to knock on Erica's door, he snapped his hand back, second guessing his decision, he turned away from the door thinking, *"There is no way Erica would ever find out anything; I'm proposing tonight and that's that."*

Just as he made it halfway back down the hallway, his mother sent him a text: **"Praying for you son, all will be well**."

Laureen's text stopped Lionel midstride, he slowly made a U-turn and headed back to Erica's room.

Surprised to see him, she welcomed him in, "Hey you, I thought I wasn't going to see you until it was time to go to the game. What's going on, you were missing me weren't you?"

Inside the palatial penthouse suite, Lionel was not his usual playful self, Erica quickly picked up on his glum disposition as they sat in the sitting area of the room, "What's wrong babe, you don't look so good, is everything okay?"

Lionel's eyes were bloodshot from speaking with his mother, he sat down and closed them to keep from having to face the inevitable.

Erica felt a chill creep up her spine, "Lionel, you're making me nervous, what's going on? Tell me...and tell me now. Whatever it is, I can handle it."

Lionel stood up and rubbed the back of his corded neck, with audible shakiness in his voice, he started talking, "Erica, there is no easy way to tell you this. Please know that I love you very much and I never meant to hurt you."

Erica's mind began to race, she speculated one hundred different scenarios within minutes but she was truly stumped at what Lionel might have to tell her.

Lionel's pending confession weighed on him, not because of what might happen to him but he hated what his admission might do to his relationship with Erica. He stood by a wall with a pounded fist and slightly beat the wall.

Erica jumped in and pleaded, "Please tell me you aren't married with kids. I'm telling you, if it ain't that I can handle it, you and I are strong enough to handle anything Lionel."

"You say that now."

Erica bargained with Lionel to spill the beans.

Lionel sat back down on an expensive leather chaise lounger and dropped his hands between his legs, he began to explain, "Before I met you, as you know, I was in a relationship with Marsha...I was going to propose to her."

"Okay, her loss, my gain...so what?"

"So, she had no idea I was planning to propose so on that night she informed me that she was and had been seeing another guy and owed it to herself to see where the relationship was going to take her."

Erica laughed, "And we all know what happened with that....keep going."

Releasing a sigh, Lionel asked, "Do you remember I told you I didn't handle the break up well?"

"Yeah but I mean, who would? I went through a really bad break up that nearly destroyed me so I can understand how you must've felt."

Lionel knew that when he uttered these next few words Erica might figure it out, "The guy Marsha was seeing, she met him online...through the Match Up America site."

Not quite sure how to process what Lionel said, Erica's face went blank with a slack expression, "You mean the site you and I have been working on together? The case I've been trying to bust my butt to solve?"

Lionel's hand swept across his forehead to get rid of the sweat building up there. He knew the hammer was about to drop. He turned his back to Erica with his hands on his waist and said, "I did it, it was me."

Erica stood up, "It was you that did what exactly?"

Lionel stood silently, he couldn't speak any more; he wanted to let his words sink in with Erica.

Erica's mind began to wander again, *"He can't be telling me that he's the person who hacked into Harold's website. The day in his office, the energy drinks, hackers drink a lot of them. We talked about the dark side of hacking. He did specifically say that he'd been bitten by the love bug and he didn't seem moved by any of the findings from my investigation."*

Lionel started up again, "That night she told me she never closed out her profile even after she and I started dating and when she got the match for Dallas she checked him out despite being in a relationship with me. She said he was her perfect match. I was cool until she called me to help her with a problem for him. I lost it for a minute and in a moment of weakness, I hacked into the site. The thing is, you would have never found it was me. If you had found a suspect, it would have been Marsha's boyfriend or now ex-boyfriend, Dallas."

Erica walked up to Lionel and with all the strength she could muster, she slapped his face, "All this time, you've watched me nearly kill myself trying to catch the person who did this because my freaking job was on the line and it was you the entire time and then you were going to pin it on someone else? Who are you, what kind of man does that?"

Lionel turned towards Erica.

Erica screamed aloud, "What kind of detective am I? How does this happen to me...twice? The men I claim to love are perpetrators right up under my nose. I thought you were different. The moment I decide to let my guard down and trust again, I get smacked in the gut again by a shiesty-behind dude like you. You must have gotten plenty of laughs off of me, huh? And you supposedly love me? Did you ever think about me or even Harold for that matter Lionel? I hate to say it but what about Marsha, were you just going to ruin Dallas' life like you've just ruined mine?"

Lionel rushed in and grabbed Erica by her arms and yelled, "I do love you woman, more than you'll ever know. What you are seeing is the true cost of me as a human being. I felt betrayed by the system that sent her that match. Being backed into a corner I lashed out in an attempt to exact revenge on that same system. I wasn't thinking about Harold, I was only thinking of myself. I did a bad thing, it was a terrible lapse in judgment. I felt horrible after I did it but it was done and then I met you and then somehow we both got put on the same case....everything moved so fast. It was crazy I know but you have to understand that I tried to separate what I'd done with my feelings for you. None of what I did before was about you but everything I've done since then has been. As far as Harold goes, his site was vulnerable to all kinds of breeches, if I hadn't hacked it, someone could have. Luckily, I've fixed all of that for him. Nevertheless, I've decided to go and confess to him and turn myself in when I get back."

Erica broke free from Lionel's grip, "Get your dirty hands off of me, you better let me go."

The hotel phone rang.

"Ms. Allen, this is the front desk confirming your transportation to the game this evening."

Cutting her eyes deeply into Lionel's soul she said, "I won't be needing it tonight." Erica slammed the phone down.

"What was that about?"

"I cancelled our transportation to the game tonight."

"Why did you do that? We have an obligation to be at that game tonight Erica."

"Just like you had an obligation to be honest with me and tell me the truth?"

"What do you think I'm doing now, huh? Based on where we are headed, I didn't want to have any secrets between us."

Erica scoffed, "Where we are headed? You're headed to jail and I don't see being a prison bride in my future."

Lionel gathered his things and turned to leave the room, "I'm going to that game tonight, you should really think about coming, tonight could be the night the team wins. You said we could get through anything, I guess I'll see if you really meant that, if you show up."

Erica screamed out at Lionel, "Get out Lionel, get out of here now...just get out."

On the other side of the door, Lionel stood with his back up against Erica's door shaking his head, he felt like a piece of his heart had been ripped out. At least now, it was all out. Looking at his phone, he noticed a missed call and a message from Harold, he thought, *"I'm not ready to talk to him yet...I'll deal with that later."*

Inside, Erica soaked her pillows with clear, salty tears. She picked up her phone, she too had a missed call and message from Harold but she dismissed it in an attempt to call her mother and sister.

CHAPTER 60

"It's almost time for us to leave for the game, this is Erica calling, it has been torture keeping this secret from her."

"Hey baby, what's going on, how's my girl doing?"

A heartbroken Erica answered, "Mommy."

Helen jumped up, "What's wrong honey? What's happened, where's Lionel?"

Through her tears, Erica said, "Hmmph, Lionel...where is he you ask, too good to be true, that's where."

Helen could tell her daughter was in bad shape, while she hated to give up the surprise she asked, "Erica, what room are you in?"

"Why do you want to know that mommy?"

Motioning for her other daughter, Leah to grab their things and come on, Helen demanded, "You don't answer a question by asking a question, what room are you in?"

"I'm in room 503, now tell me why you are asking?"

Within minutes there was a knock at Erica's door.

Upon sight of her family, Erica screamed and dropped her cell to the floor, "What are y'all doing here? What in the world is going on?"

They all stood in the foyer and hugged one another.

They walked into Erica's bedroom where she had been drowning her sorrows.

Helen sat on the bed and said, "Now what was that you were trying to tell me about Lionel?"

Erica relayed to her mother what had just transpired, Helen and Leah sat unmoved by Erica's tears and her situation.

Helen leaned into her oldest daughter, "I have one question for you. Do you love him?"

Erica fell backwards on her bed, "Yeah but it doesn't matter. I don't understand how he could knowingly let me investigate a case where he was the person I was searching for. He was supposedly all supportive in helping me solve this case, how funny is it the hunter became the hunted. How could I be so blind, so stupid?"

Helen let Erica rant but she brought it right back around to the same question, "But do you love him?"

Sitting straight up in the bed, Erica yelled, "Mommy...why do you keep asking me that? It doesn't matter whether I love him or not because he's about to be going to jail, he said, he's going to turn himself in."

Leah pleaded with her sister, "You're going to let him do that? I mean, for all that you've told me about him, before a little while ago, you were madly in love with him and because of a little dumb mistake you're going to let all of that go? According to you, Lionel is the type of guy, one can only hope and pray for. I mean, only the two of you know about this, right? You said he fixed the system so he more than made up for what he did. Girl, you wanted to do bodily harm to Patrick like kill him when you broke up with him. All I'm saying is, you don't ever know how people are going to react to certain situations."

Erica stood with her hands on her forehead, "Um, I'm still trying to figure out, why are you guys here and how did you happen to get here so fast?"

Without giving the surprise away, Helen revealed, "Lionel wanted to surprise you, this was supposed to be such a great week for the two of you that he flew us out here so we could be a part of it. He was going to surprise you at the game tonight."

In a way, Erica's heart betrayed her, she wanted to feel hurt by Lionel but she was warmed by his generosity for bringing her mother and sister to Houston to visit.

Leah turned on the television, "The game is about to start, shouldn't you be getting dressed to go?"

Erica looked at the television, "I'm not going to that mess."

Helen put her hands on her hip and said, "I've asked you repeatedly how you feel about this man. Now, you're a grown woman and I can't tell you what to do but listen here, if you love him, that should be a done deal, see because love covers a multitude of faults. What Lionel showed you here tonight is that he's not perfect, he's flawed...but who isn't? To me, he knew the risks involved with telling you this information tonight but he did it anyway and that speaks volumes to me. It's your life and you can live it how you want, but here me when I say, I just hope you never find yourself in a situation where you need forgiveness or mercy shown towards you Miss Erica."

CHAPTER 61

"Lionel, where is Erica? When is she getting here? The series is 3-2, the Flyers could win tonight. They are losing right now but tonight could be the night."

"I know, everything is all set but she might not show up. We had a fight and I don't know where things stand between us right now. If she doesn't show up tonight, I'll guess I'll have my answer."

Alexis gasped for breath, "Please tell me you're kidding, this can't be happening right now. After all I've put into you two, we have all kinds of sponsors here because of you guys, we have a sold out arena, you and I talked about this, you are supposed to be proposing not causing fights."

"Alexis, I'm sorry. I never meant for it to go down like this."

Alexis jacked Lionel up by his sports coat, "You're sorry, that's all you have to say is you're sorry. Not going to cut it Lionel, not going to cut it. If the team loses tonight, the series will be tied 3-3 and the only other chance on home court will be tomorrow night. You'd better find a way to get Erica here and preferably tonight."

Alexis stormed off, punching buttons on her phone, feverishly thinking of a backup plan.

Harold was calling back.

For a minute, Lionel considered not answering but he decided he would deal with whatever fallout there was, he was no longer hiding behind what he'd done, Harold would learn soon enough.

"Lionel, Harold here. I called you earlier and left you a message to call me when you could and I called Det. Allen and left her the same message but I hadn't heard from either of you and decided to try you again."

Lionel wanted to flee but he stood strong, "How can I help you Harold? What's the emergency?"

"There is no emergency, I do however, have some news that could be perceived as urgent."

"Okay, what's going on?"

In a jubilant tone, Harold proceeded, "Lionel, my friend, Samantha and I are engaged. I proposed and she said yes."

"Harold, that's wonderful news...congratulations. How is that urgent news though?"

"Well, this is where Det. Allen comes in, I wanted you two to know that I've called and spoken to Lieutenant Conroy and called off the investigation to my website breech."

"Huh? Why would you do that?"

"Lionel, my man this breech has turned out to be the best thing that could have happened to my business. You helped us to locate all of our vulnerabilities, we've changed some of the ways we do business, and most importantly, I found my wife during this process. Instead of prosecuting whoever did this, I'd like to actually shake their hand and tell them thank you. I tell you what, God sure does work in wonderfully mysterious ways don't you agree?"

Lionel did a double take at his phone, he couldn't believe what he was hearing, he replied, "Yes, this is truly mysterious."

Harold confirmed, "The hack to the site was a complete blessing in disguise, had this never happened, I may not have met Samantha. I don't know if she was a mismatch or a perfect match, either way, she's the woman for me and to me, that's perfect. We put our story up on the site and the memberships have increased by over 400% in the last forty-eight hours. I'm beyond thrilled at how all of this worked out."

Lionel asked for two things, "This is incredible news Harold, do me a favor though. Will you try and call Erica again. I think she should hear this from you, it's an amazing testimony. Also, take it from me, make sure you and Samantha now close out your match up profiles, based on your news, you guys don't have a need for them anymore. Congratulations again to the two of you, I'll be looking forward to receiving my invitation, I'll be sure to come and do a dance at your wedding."

Harold laughed, "No man, I don't need that profile anymore, I'm officially off the market and I'll make sure Samantha closes her profile as well. A dance, huh? That'll be awesome Lionel, I'll call Detective Allen and I'll talk with you soon."

CHAPTER 62

"So do you think you'll leave before the championship games are over Liney?"

Lionel was nibbling on the continental breakfast that had been delivered to his suite. He didn't have much of an appetite.

Moving over to his bed, he sat down, "I don't know what I'm going to do mother. I've made a huge mess of things with Erica, she's not returning any of my phone calls. I've tried calling her mother and her sister and they just keep telling me to give her some time. The organizers for the team are all on my back about this promotion. Sponsors are here, including my jeweler...everything is such a mess."

Laureen spoke up, "My heart sank for you sweetheart when the team lost and she didn't show up last night which is why I had to call you this morning to see how you are holding up?"

"Yeah, the series is tied now, whoever wins tonight, wins the series. To be honest with you, it may look like we brought that team luck but they've just been playing good basketball, they just happened to pick up their game after we were introduced. It has been a fun ride though."

"Your father and I plus your brothers and sisters are all worried about you, no matter what you're thinking, you're going to get a chance to propose one of these good old days."

Lionel laughed, "Yeah, how about that, maybe I should stop trying to plan surprise proposals. They aren't really working out that well for me."

"Liney, everything is going to work out how it's supposed to work out son."

Sitting on the edge of his king sized bed, Lionel's pensive expression caused him to confide in his mother, the first love in his life. "You know mother, I allowed Marsha to take me to a place completely outside of my character and now I've possibly lost the love of my life. Do you have any idea what that feels like?"

On the other end of the call, Laureen offered a sad smile, her heart bled for Lionel, she offered a bright side to lift his spirits, "Honey, I have no idea what you did or how you must be feeling as a result of what's going on but maybe, just maybe all of this happened to teach you an important lesson."

Intrigued by what possible lesson life could be teaching, he asked, "What lesson might that be Mother?"

"Liney, as hard as it might be, we should never give another person that much power over us to change who we are. That transference is powerful because nine times out of ten, when that happens, situations come up that we aren't proud of. When we can learn to take ownership of our feelings and acknowledge them, we then maintain our control. We are then held accountable for our own actions and not driven by the actions of others. Every one of us is accountable to God for our conduct and in that we should be accountable to ourselves as well. Don't look at this like, I did this because of Marsha, take ownership of what you did and make it right."

With a hanging head, Lionel rubbed his forehead in slow motion, purposely closing his eyes, as if to process his mother's words.

"Keep your head up honey and know that I'm praying for you and for her too."

Lionel acknowledged, "Nothing like having a praying mother."

"Well Liney, what I know to be true if I don't know anything else is that, the prayers of the righteous are powerful and effective...prayer works so I'm going to keep on working my prayers."

Lionel replied, "I believe that, you made sure of that. You and dad instilled that in us from children. I just pray Erica can come around and forgive me. Mother, I wholeheartedly believe that if we can get through this, I know we can make it through anything."

Laureen encouraged her son, "If you believe that then always remember, we believe we receive when we pray. Keep the faith son, you go to that game tonight, you show up even if no one else does. We'll be watching and looking out for you, we're all pulling for you Lionel."

"Thanks mother, I'll talk with you soon."

CHAPTER 63

"So what's your plan girl? Are you leaving or are you staying? Do you ever plan to talk with Lionel again, I mean you've been quiet all night and I really need to know what's going on with you."

Erica's mother and sister ended up staying in Erica's room as a source of support and comfort. As the game played in the background, the women realized the team lost. Erica took it personally, she worried she'd let people down for not showing up.

Leah, not one to be tolerant of things that seemingly made sense, lived in a world where there were no gray areas, only black and white, right or wrong, just plain straight up and down. In that line of thinking, she often times sought to bring others around to her viewpoint.

The early morning sun was rising high above the clouds and shining into Erica's room, she got up to close the privacy curtain and block the light.

Getting back into bed where she and her mother and sister all slept, she requested, "Leah, please leave me alone. I'm not really interested in being interrogated by you right now."

"You see Erica, that's always been the difference between you and me, if I believe in something, I don't let setbacks or failure knock me off track, I keep going for what I believe in. You on the other hand, stuff happens to you and you are out for the count, you just sign off from reality and that's not…reality."

Erica sat up in the bed, "You want to talk about reality, huh? My reality is that for me, anything less than my best is failure, everything I've done in my life, I've always had to prove that I was better so when I fall short of that, my reality kicks in that maybe I'm just not good enough."

Helen had been listening but had chosen to remain quiet but she turned over and weighed in. Tears began to fill her eyes before she spoke, "Erica, I have watched you grow up trying to compete when there was no competition. You have always had this compulsion to be the best. You grew up placing unnecessary pressure on yourself and as a result placed unrealistic expectations on other people. I've tried to get you to understand in so many ways throughout your life that you didn't need to compete to be number one because you were already number one. You need to resolve this within yourself that you are good enough. Pretending to be perfect is too much work Erica, I'm not going to love you any less, your family isn't going to love you any less, and I certainly don't think Lionel is going to love you any less because you show us that you are human and not superwoman. Listen to me, we all have issues, stop trying to hide yours."

By now, both Erica and even the tough warrior princess, Leah were both crying and emotional.

It had been many years long overdue but Helen knew the time was now, she sensed the moment for having to get up close and dig in with her daughters.

She pulled the covers back and got out of the bed, turning to Erica and Leah, she said, "The truth is, both of you, have put on these facades, Leah, you made up one and Erica you did too. When Harrison died, y'all were too young to grieve, too young to know how to process what you were feeling in those hard to reach places in your little hearts. I know you didn't know how to because as an adult, I didn't know how to. If we are honest, you girls grew up disappointed, you had thoughts and questions you never voiced, why did daddy die, why did he leave me, was I not good enough for him to stay alive?"

Helen's soothing voice could not compensate for the piercing taking place within her daughters but she couldn't stop, she had to go in and get the root.

Helen paced the room, "Despite my pain and grief, I did the best I could with what I had in raising y'all. I realize now that no matter what I said, y'all were always trying to one up each other or other people because you were looking for your identity and validation that your father wasn't there to give you. Everybody processes things differently, we often times find ways to fill the voids or compensate for what we don't understand. Erica, you tried to be Miss Patty Perfect and Leah, you just turned into Betty Bad-behind with a wardrobe made of Teflon."

Leah asked sharply, "Why are you bringing all of this up now?" Leah was overwhelmed by the emotions raging through her, they were ripping into places she was unfamiliar with.

Helen knelt down beside Leah, "Sometimes you have to pull back the scabs in order for the proper healing to take place. I didn't know when this time would come but I always knew it would where we'd have to deal with this and that's exactly what we are going to do...deal. Now Erica, I don't know what you are planning to do where Lionel is concerned but before you enter into any other relationships, we need to address this. While you girls no longer have an earthly father, your heavenly Father loves you with an everlasting love[7]. The beauty is that because He's perfect, we don't have to be. We can just be who He's called us to be, flaws and all."

For the next several hours, the women laughed, cried, hugged, shared, and cried some more. Helen was able to minister wholeness and much needed inner-healing to her girls. She knew the time together had been effective because both Leah and Erica's countenance were brighter, they looked different, they looked free.

Leah looked over at the night stand beside the bed, her phone was vibrating...again. Making a joke, she said, "Let me take a guess at who this is. If a person isn't answering their phone, why do people call other people to talk to them, there must be a reason they don't want to talk to you. Erica please check your phone, text that man or something so he can stop blowing up me and mommy's phone."

The women all shared a laugh, the mood in the room was clearly lighter from the previous moments.

Erica walked to grab her phone, looking through it, she shouted, "Oh-my-goodness, I have so many missed calls and messages here, let me see what's going on."

---

[7] **Jeremiah 31:3**: The LORD hath appeared of old unto me, *saying*, Yea, I have loved thee with an everlasting love: therefore with loving kindness have I drawn thee.

CHAPTER 64

"Where is Erica? Lionel, are you seriously trying to tell me she's not going to show again tonight? I made a lot of excuses for her no show last night but I don't know what to say about tonight. Do you two not realize tonight is the last game?"

Lionel tried his best to keep calm, Alexis was working his already stressed out nerves, "Alexis, please, stop...I'm here, Erica isn't. Why don't you call her and ask her all of these questions?"

Alexis stormed off.

Lionel fumbled around with the ring box in his pocket, he was beginning to accept things the way they were, he believed in the love he had with Erica and he was hopeful she'd eventually come around. If she showed up, he'd know for sure. It was a big if though, she hadn't returned any of his calls and her family had stopped communicating with him as well.

Lionel placed a call to Corey, he knew he was on baby duty but he needed his best friend's support, his positive reinforcement, he would serve as a buffer from the media and of course, Alexis.

Corey made sure his wife and newborn son were taken care of and he rushed off to the arena.

Finding Lionel in the suite, he sat next to him and asked, "How you holding up man? It's already half-time? Is there still no sign of Erica? And the Flyers are losing...man, this is crazy."

Lionel took a sip of his drink, "Way to point out the obvious Einstein. There's still time though. Hopefully, no let me rephrase, prayerfully, the Flyers are in the locker room now making all of the necessary adjustments for the second half of the game. I mean these guys are missing everything."

Corey jumped in, "I was watching the game at home. How about all of those easy layups they've been missing? Both their offense and defense plays are weak tonight. You can tell they are tired but they need to tighten up, they can rest in the off-season."

The Flyers came back from half-time with noticeable improvements, they were making drives to the basket, staying in the paint, and they made several back to back, short-range jumpers to move the score up in their favor.

Time was drawing nigh and Erica was still nowhere in sight. Lionel started looking for escape routes, he was trying to figure out the quickest way to leave the arena if the Flyers lost the game without anyone seeing him.

Constantly checking the time, against his earlier optimistic attitude, he was beginning to consider the notion that things were over with Erica.

On the other side of the arena in another suite box, Erica, Helen, and Leah were standing and talking with Alexis who was popping antacids like candy, "Well, it's about time. Do you know I've been going crazy over you not being here? Poor Lionel, he's been handling this situation like a true gentleman...you've got you a real winner with him Erica. Trust me on this, true love is hard to find and when you find it, you shouldn't ever want to let it go."

Helen raised her hands in the air, "Hallelujah, praise the Lord...you better preach on Ms. Alexis."

The women shook their heads and giggled at Helen doing a quick praise dance.

Alexis looked over at the score board, "This game is so close, it's really anyone's game. We have about two minutes left before it's over, I have an idea, c'mon lets go."

Lionel and Corey watched with intensity, even with the clock winding down, it was still uncertain who might pull out the win. Both teams were fighting to the bitter end. Their concentration on the game was broken when they all of sudden heard, "Alright you Flyers and Flyer fans, it's your girl, Erica and I'm here to say, leave it all on the floor. I'm doing it and I hope you will too. Go Flyers."

Corey nudged Lionel, "Hey man, did you hear that...that was Erica man. She's here, let's go find your woman."

The best friends rushed out of the suite with nearly no time left on the clock.

In the final seconds of the game, the Flyers took Erica's advice by leaving nothing on the floor and a player made one last final attempt and with all of his might fired off a cross court shot that landed in the hoop at the buzzer.

Alexis' plan worked. The arena went wild in an uproar, pure pandemonium ensued, the Flyers left it all on the floor and won the game.

Those in the crowd stood by Erica alongside her mother, sister, and Alexis. Within minutes Lionel found his needle in the humongous haystack, in pure dramatic fashion, before any words were spoken, they kissed.

Alexis broke up their happy reunion and pulled them to the stage that had been set up for the awards ceremony. She signaled the team owners that both Lionel and Erica were present and that it was time.

The owner of the Flyers, Craig Houghton made a special announcement, "We have seen some phenomenal basketball played here during this championship but we have a slam dunk in our midst tonight, Lionel."

Lionel stepped up to the stage and shook hands with the owner and the league's commissioner.

Erica stood with a glassy stare, unsure as to what was about to happen.

With a slight tremble in his voice, Lionel spoke up, "From the first game I attended here months ago to the final game here tonight, I have been on the most amazing journey of my life. That first game turned my whole life upside down, due largely in part to you guys, you fell in love with Lierica. Well, I want you all to know from me that while you fell in love with us, I fell head over heels in love with this beautiful young lady over here."

Lionel walked to the edge of the stage and motioned for Erica to join him, nervously, she did.

Blocking out everything around him, Lionel focused squarely on Erica and spoke directly to her, "You showed up and because of that I promise to forever and always show up for you. I've never loved nor will I ever love another woman as much as I love you. I've waited my whole life for this moment and Miss Erica Renee Allen, far beyond my imagination, I've been bitten by the love bug. Erica, my love, in front of everyone here and those watching, I want to know, will you marry me and become my wife?"

Lionel dropped to one knee in front of Erica and everyone surrounding him, the crowd was cheering them on like crazy.

Helen and Leah were crying and jumping up and down celebrating with everyone else.

Erica's hands covered her face, her chest heaved in and out and she looked down at the dazzling, custom designed, Boites ring.

She pulled Lionel up and squealed the words, "Yes, I'll marry you."

Lionel finally got his chance to propose. Overhead, the announcer gladly pronounced, "She said yes. Congratulations Lierica."

Coming down from the stage, Lionel and Erica were greeted with all sorts of well-wishers, congratulating them and giving them high-fives.

The Flyer's organization hosted a celebratory reception for the team's victory and the engagement, they had high hopes for both and neither one let me them down.

Inside the reception, Alexis hugged and congratulated the couple, "Now, the real fun begins, planning the wedding and I think I should be your wedding planner. What do you guys think? C'mon, you guys know it will be great."

Lionel and Erica looked at each other and shook their heads laughing, kissing in the process, and enjoying their moment, Erica offered her a little hope, "Lierica will think about and let you know."

CHAPTER 65

The Houston Flyers were the National Champions and the patrons at the local sports bar, Instant Replay were celebrating both the win and Lionel and Erica's engagement.

Everyone except Marsha.

The sports bar was next to the floral shop and not having had any dinner, she decided to grab a bite to eat from her neighbors. In all of the years they'd run their businesses side by side, not one time had she stepped inside. Clueless as to what they might be showing on their large flat screens that surrounded the establishment, she sat down and watched.

After witnessing Lionel's proposal and Erica's acceptance, Marsha's dinner turned into a liquid one.

She drank herself unrecognizable, she was left admitting to herself, "I've lost Lionel, I've lost Dallas, and I've lost Nicole."

The conversation with herself turned into deep thoughts, *"What has happened to me? I've lost everyone who ever meant anything to me, I've driven them all away. Everyone is all happy and in love now, except me."*

With a party of one, Marsha hosted another one of her pity parties. She embraced the excess of the constant refills of libations from the bar. She settled into and believed the lie that alcohol helped her to numb the pain.

Getting agitated because her latest drink order was taking too long to arrive, Marsha was about to make a scene until

Boris Larson, the owner of Instant Replay sat down at her table.

In a drunken stupor, she asked, "What are you doing here and where is my drink?"

Boris looked at Marsha and said, "Your instant replays have been cut off. You're done for the night Ms. Miller."

Despite her hazy disposition, Marsha demanded her drink from the enchanting entrepreneur, "I'm a paying customer just like everyone else in here. So you saying my money ain't no good here? If that's the case, I'll just get up and take my business elsewhere."

Marsha abruptly grabbed her bag, stood up to leave and fell down to the floor. Marsha was knocked out, she'd passed out under the weight from all of her worries, her body was all lumped up into an inebriated mess.

Boris picked her up and tried to preserve her dignity as he walked through the crowded bar by exclaiming, "Nothing to see here folks, mind your own business."

Left behind on the floor, the flower from her hair.

Offering tenderness in her torment, he carefully laid her on the sofa in his office and covered her up with a chenille blanket.

Boris stood back and watched Marsha sleep before he turned to leave, he looked at her and felt like he was staring at a radiant reality of choice.

EPILOGUE

"Yes, finally, I'm engaged y'all. I'm the last of the Webber clan to get married and it's about to go down. Erica and I are getting married, she has snagged and bagged one of San Antonio's most eligible bachelors. I have to say, I'm thrilled to be giving up that title, I've found the love of my life. Yes, let's be clear, I have found my good thing."

"Can you believe what happened with Harold? My man, Harold went from wanting to prosecute his offender, that being me, to wanting to shake the offender's hand, again, me. I think it was Harold who actually spoke about God's mysterious ways and boy are they. Harold says Samantha is his perfect match and I couldn't agree with him more, they are made for one another. Erica told me when she heard Harold's message about dropping the investigation, she couldn't believe it. Throughout this investigation, Harold came to be a good friend. I may never tell him what happened but I'm truly sorrowful for what I did."

"I know it was wrong of me to try and pin it on Dallas but I was mad at him and Marsha. The whole situation was messed up, I wasn't thinking of how I was ruining an innocent man's company with my hurt and anger. But listen, can you blame me for being upset, tell me, how would you have handled that situation?"

"I should have never allowed my anger to take me there. Trust me, I know I haven't gotten away; I'll have to live with this for the rest of my life and make this up to Erica. However, throughout this process I've learned so much about myself, other people, and the redemptive power of God. I know now how vitally important it is to be honest and truthful and to deal with my feelings as they come up, not to let them fester and boil over."

"My parent's anniversary party is coming up soon and they can't wait to meet Erica. Oh and in case you're wondering about her job, Erica will not be returning to the force. She's decided to come and work at the cyber technology center with me. And by the way, the wrongful death case hasn't been resolved, it is still ongoing."

"Since the game, Alexis has been harassing us about planning our wedding. As you saw during the campaign, she can be something to deal with. So what do you think, should we let her plan it? We can't really decide so Erica and I would like to hear from you, email us at shakirabelieves@gmail.com and give us your vote."

"Last but certainly not least, I have one more thing. Now, Leonard, Harold's head tech guy made an important decision, the best decision of his life. If you want to make a change in your life and make the best decision like we all have, I'd like to invite you to try Jesus. It doesn't have to be anything hard or complicated. If you feel a tugging at your heart to make a change, I invite you to invite Jesus to come live in your heart. You can do so by repeating these words:

Heavenly Father, I acknowledge that I'm a sinner. I believe that Jesus Christ is the Son of the living God and that He died on the cross so that I may now have forgiveness for my sins and eternal life. I believe in my heart that You, Lord

God, raised Him from the dead. Jesus, I ask You now to forgive me, for every sin I have ever committed or done in my heart. I ask You Lord Jesus to come into my heart as my personal Lord and Savior today. I need You to be my Father and my friend. I know that if I confess with my mouth, Jesus is Lord and believe in my heart that God raised You from the dead, I will be saved. I believe and I confess You to be my Lord and personal Savior and I pray this in the name of Jesus. Amen.

"If you followed through, congratulations, all of heaven is rejoicing on your behalf right now. Just like Leonard did, you should first tell someone of your decision and then connect with a church where you can develop your relationship with Christ. May God bless you and until next time."

ABOUT THE AUTHOR

Shakira R. Thompson, a natural born storyteller who submitted to her God-given talents and in doing so, God showed up and made her a **BELIEVER.** He's transformed her into an author, publisher, and entrepreneur.

She is the founder of **Believer's Choice Media**, an inspirational content company dedicated to encouraging believers to live the life they were created to live on earth and beyond.   She's penned five, well-received inspirational fiction novels with a sixth on the way.

With a renewed sense of purpose, Shakira is not only writing and speaking, she's living...living her life according to Ephesians 2:10:

"For we are his workmanship, created in Christ Jesus unto good works, which God hath before ordained that we should walk in them." (KJV)

Shakira is a proud Alumni of Florida A&M University in Tallahassee, Florida where she holds a B.S in Business Administration as well as an M.B.A. with a concentration in Supply Chain Management.

Shakira has always delved in the world of real estate, but most recently made it official. She is a Realtor®, licensed in the State of Florida, where she's the listing agent for EquityPro. Naturally, she' s expanding the Believer's

Choice brand and is in the process of developing Believer's Choice Realty, LLC.

Living her life with purpose has pushed her into her latest venture, co-hosting *The Dee Lee Show,* where she has the opportunity to encourage **BELIEVERS** over the airwaves.

Although Shakira may wear many hats these days, the most important role to her, is that of wife and mother.

Born and raised in Fernandina Beach, Florida, she now resides in Orlando, Florida with her family.

For more information you can visit her at
www.shakirabelieves.com

You can also get connected with Shakira at the following:

/shakira-r-thompson   /ShakiraBelieves

/ShakiraRThompson   /shakirabelieves

A SNEAK PEEK
The Big Bonanza, A Psalms 37 Novel

"Regina, why won't you stop packing? I don't understand what has gotten into you lately."

Each garment she packed, Bishop Montgomery unpacked it.

Without saying a word, Regina continued taking steps from her closet back to her bed, packing for her next speaking engagement.

"So are you just going to ignore me and pretend like you can't hear what I'm saying to you?"

Regina walked past her husband, she could hold her silence any longer, "Stop unpacking my bag Eugene. When you say something worth my time, I'll respond."

Bishop Montgomery got up and blocked the entrance to Regina's closet, "How many times do I need to tell you, now is not the time for you to be leaving. Too much is going on for you to be going away. Ever since your little luncheon you've been going here and there with no consideration to me or what is going on with our church or our family."

Regina snapped back, "Now you take that back Eugene. I'm more than involved with what's going on at Wondrous Works. I've stood beside you for years, decades....why can't you support me a little huh? It's always about you Eugene, you, you, you, isn't that right?"

Bishop Montgomery huffed, "This is nonsense woman, I'm asking you not to go and that should be enough. It used to be enough, now nothing I say seems to matter to you anymore."

Regina pushed past her husband's barricade, she stepped back into her closet to grab more items.

Reentering the bedroom she said, "Now why would you say something like that Eugene? You think because I've decided to expand my role of ministry beyond being your wife that nothing you say matters to me anymore? What does me leaving to go to a women's retreat to speak have to do with me not listening to you?"

Bishop Montgomery collapsed in the chevron chair tucked in the corner, "Women's retreat this weekend, prayer breakfast, the next weekend, ministry luncheon last weekend, I mean, when is it going to stop? We have some real issues going on right here and you're trapesing off to hither and yonder."

Regina stopped packing, narrowing her focus with her husband as the target, she laid it on heavy, "If I didn't know any better, I'd think you were jealous of me getting to go out and evangelize."

In a dismissive tone, Bishop Montgomery said, "Jealous...that's crazy talk woman. I'm trying to get you to understand that with our son's recent admission, we need to present a united front with every available opportunity we have. Not to mention the boy is sick...real sick. If you are always gone, how is that going to look to the congregation? We need to be strong and together during this time. I'm now faced with having to put off my retirement, there is no way Carson is fit or ready to lead this church. Let's not even begin talking about Courtney and Christian. Those two have only been married a month and they are already at each other's throats. You know Cayden-James' appeal is coming up in a couple of weeks and how important that is. Honey, why can't you see you need to be here?"

Regina slammed her suitcase shut, "Eugene, no matter where I've been or what engagement I have coming up; I always make it back to Sunday morning service. Despite our sons being grown men, I'm here and will be here for them."

Bishop Montgomery held his hand to his chest and asked, "But what about me Regina? Who is going to be here for me? You certainly haven't been."

Sitting on top of the full luggage trying to zip it, Regina mocked her husband, "Who's going to be here for me? This is so typical. I've given you the best years of my life and the one time I get to be more than First Lady Regina, you now have a problem with that. You know what Eugene, let's just call these trips I've been taking what they are, breaks...breaks from each other. For the amount of time we've been in ministry, we've been able to move and grow together and here recently it feels we are growing in different directions."

Bishop Montgomery threw his hands up and exclaimed, "Yeah because you are going off on your own without me Regina."

First Lady Regina stomped off into the bathroom to grab her toiletry bag, walking back in, she began stuffing things into her shoulder bag. She looked over at her pouty mouth husband and asked, "How is going to preach the Gospel going off without you Eugene? You know, that's the part I can't seem to understand."

With dull eyes and a monotone voice, Bishop Montgomery's half-hearted shrug, indicated he was tired of arguing with his wife. He leaned forward with his elbows on his knees and said, "I promise to God, I don't think you need to go on this trip. Regina, I'm asking you, no, I'm begging you to stay but knowing you, you'll probably just ignore me and go anyway."

Regina lugged her bags next to the door, she turned to Bishop and said, "Honey...you just aren't being fair. Yes, I'm going but I'll be back before Sunday morning service."

Unwilling to offer any additional pleas, Bishop Montgomery issued parting words to his wife by saying, "Well then Regina you've made your choice so go ye therefore and teach all nations...go."

Bishop grabbed his keys from the nightstand, not only did he leave the room but he also left the house.

Regina breathed out a deep sigh, she calmed herself by picking up her bible and going over her notes for the upcoming message she would share.

The Big Bonanza

Note from the Author

The Love Bug is the book I was writing that High Noon Justice hijacked. I'm so overjoyed you've chosen to read it and hang out with me up through to this point. All I can say is **THANK YOU**!

With each story I'm involved in, it is my intention to give the very best of myself. I've embraced the notion God has blessed me with an ability to tell stories. Therefore, for as many as He gives me, I'll continue to write them and I'm grateful to have you on this ride with me.

Even though these are fictitious stories, I pray you are blessed and encouraged by them. If this story has blessed you in any way, I'd love to hear your thoughts and feedback. Therefore, feel free to email me at shakirabelieves@gmail.com

One Last Thing...

If you enjoyed this book and believe your friends and family would enjoy it as well, I'd be honored if you decided to spread the word, tell them about it, and also posted an online review. Sharing your experience online would be greatly appreciated.

If I leave you with nothing else, please remember to aim all of your duties and services to the Glory of the Lord and to love one another deeply because love does indeed cover a multitude of faults.

Shakira ♥

.

www.ingramcontent.com/pod-product-compliance
Lightning Source LLC
Chambersburg PA
CBHW020408260626
47156CB00007B/2287